QUANTOS CHRONICLES

The Scents of Memory

Alan Parkin

Firelight Press LLC

"The life of the dead is placed in the memory of the living."
Marcus Tullius Cicero

"There is no pain so great as the memory of joy in present grief."
Aeschylus

"You never know when you're making a memory."
Rickie Lee Jones

"Forgiving does not erase the bitter past. A healed memory is not a deleted memory. Instead, forgiving what we cannot forget creates a new way to remember. We change the memory of our past into a hope for our future."
Lewis B. Smedes

"Memory is a complicated thing, a relative to truth, but not its twin."
Barbara Kingsolver

"Drugs are a waste of time. They destroy your memory and your self-respect and everything that goes along with with your self-esteem. They're no good at all."
Kurt Cobain

INTRODUCTION

"The Scents of Memory" emerges as a captivating novel that delves into the profound power of memory and its ability to shape our emotions. The protagonist, Jenna Floyd, embarks on a fateful journey where her memory drives the narrative.

Memory plays a pivotal role in our lives, acting as a bridge between the past and the present. It allows us to relive cherished moments, learn from our mistakes, and navigate the intricate web of human relationships. "The Scents of Memory" explores this concept through the lens of Jenna's experiences, highlighting how memory can transport us through time and influence our emotional landscape.

The novel delves into the intricate connection between scents and memories, revealing how certain aromas can trigger vivid recollections and evoke powerful emotions. Through Jenna's journey, readers gain a deeper understanding of memory's profound impact on our lives and its profound role in shaping our identities.

"The Scents of Memory" is a poignant and evocative exploration of the human experience, offering readers a thought-provoking reflection on the intricate interplay between memory and emotion.

1

After what seemed like an eternity of being confined in the windowless van, a sudden stop signaled our arrival at a strange and desolate place. We stepped out into the empty garage, the echo of our footsteps reverberating around me in an unsettling symphony. My heaviness was making it difficult to walk.

The woman I had just met led me down the long hallway with her brown hair drifting back and forth like a ghostly specter, taunting me further as we descended deeper into the unknown. As I followed her blindly, my sense of dread only intensified. A chill ran down my spine as we entered the cold elevator, the doors sliding shut with an ominous sound.

We made our stop at an unknown floor, its disquieting silence broken only by the sound of steel doors opening to a long hallway. With each step I took through this foreboding dreamscape, I could feel a darkness growing within me, my fear intensifying with each moment. At last, we arrived at three elevators where the middle one seemed to call us inside. I hesitantly stepped in, feeling an impending dread that something sinister awaited ahead.

The elevator made a short descent and then stopped. A speaker announced *treatment* as the doors opened to the bright passage. As we walked I noticed the doors were all painted in soft hues that seemed almost mocking, as if this was an elaborate deception.

Despite her assurance that she knew the way, I was lost in this unfamiliar place. No matter how free I was supposed to be, I was like a caged animal in an uncharted forest. After what seemed like forever, we stopped in front of a door painted baby blue—an attempt at kindness that only made me feel more anxious.

My heart pounded as I stepped into the office, a vast expanse compared to our tiny living room. The sun illuminated the space from the ceiling-height windows, creating an eerie atmosphere with nothing but stark walls and scattered chairs to break up the emptiness.

"This is your office?" I heard myself ask, my words coated with anxiety.

Jessica smiled, her hair cascading down her back as she sat at her desk. Even dressed in her informal button-up shirt and shorts, she exuded power and control that made me feel even more intimidated.

"I've gone from an eight by ten to this," she said, still smiling despite the overwhelming experience she must have had. "Please have a seat, Jenna."

She gestured for me to sit on the forest green loveseat, and I obliged, trying not to let my nerves take over as I sank into the cushion.

"Just call me Jen."

My heart raced as she eyed me. "Jen." Her voice was firm, as if my soul was made of porcelain. "I want you to feel safe here. So let's start with a few questions. If at any point you are uncomfortable, don't hesitate to tell me."

I nodded in agreement, my stomach flipping into knots.

"First question." She had a very soothing sound. "Do you provide consent for our audio conversation to be recorded?"

I remained still, my chest heaving from the memories that stormed through me. She repeated, this time more slowly.

"Yes, I do." I forced myself to stay present in the moment, despite the feeling of dread coursing through my veins.

She grabbed her tape recorder and pushed the red button. "Today is Monday, July 15th, 2030. And the time is 3:43 pm. My name is Jessica Albers; I am a clinician at Olympic View Treatment Center. I'm about to interview Jennifer Floyd, who is visiting." She smiled my way. "We'll begin with some basic questions, then gradually move deeper."

My stomach twisted into the knot as my mind raced, trying to predict where this was leading.

"What's your full name?" she asked.

"Jennifer Sarah Atkins Floyd," I replied in a monotone voice.

"Can you please tell me your birthday?"

"August 17th, 1993."

"Where were you born?"

"Aberdeen, Washington—my birthplace and home forevermore."

For a moment we sat in silence, until she asked, "Have you ever been in a committed relationship?"

My chest tightened, and my palms sweated. I knew this question would come up, but I still felt blindsided. "Yes. I was married to Jackson Floyd," I replied with a lump in my throat. "We were together for over twenty years." The words seemed to echo through the room.

"Twenty years is a long time. Were you high school sweethearts?" she inquired.

"Jackson was a junior when I started tutoring him in math as a freshman. Next year he asked me out on a date, and from then on we were inseparable." I explained, trying not to show how uncomfortable I was feeling.

She nodded and leaned forward. "Had you experienced any other romantic relationships before meeting him?" Her voice was direct.

"I had no interest in dating. When Ty came around, I never thought about him like that."

"Do you have children?"

The question shredded through me like a razor blade. I struggled to keep my voice steady. "Yes, two beautiful kids. Donnie was 10 and Mandy was 8 when they were taken to a higher place."

Jessica's eyes widened, but she didn't push further. She approached with a box of tissues and placed them gently on the table beside me. "I'm so sorry, Jen," she murmured. "We can talk about something else if you'd like."

"I'm fine," I lied. My voice shook as I remembered the day that changed my life forever. "July 5th, last year. Ty took them to the beach, and they had a great day. On their drive home, a drunk driver took their lives."

Jessica extended her arms in an offering of a hug, and I couldn't refuse. I let her embrace me, feeling nothing but emptiness inside.

"It must be so hard, Jen," she spoke in my ear before pulling away. "Do you feel comfortable continuing?"

I sighed. "Yes, please go on." It has been months since I talked about that day.

"Were you in the car?"

"No." I shook my head, unable to utter more than a one-word answer. "I was out with my friend Barb at a local bar."

Her eyes understood what I left unspoken. "So Ty had the kids, and you were with Barb." Silence filled the room as she chose her following words. "Why didn't you go with Ty and the kids that day?"

I took a long pause. "The day before the accident, we celebrated the Fourth of July at the beach." My eyes filled with tears, the memory still all too painful. "Ty and I argued. It was nothing more than a heated exchange over Donnie. We had neglected him all afternoon. Mandy had consumed our attention with her new kite." I paused for a moment, taking deep breaths to control my emotions. "Donnie was calling for our attention, and I asked Ty to come with me. He blew everything out of proportion, saying he didn't need to see another sand castle."

"How did you react? Was this normal for him to respond that way?"

I shook my head. "It was never an issue until this day. I called him an ass, I think. He got so angry that he strutted off to our car. I had to grab the kids, hoping he would not take off. It seemed like my heart was about to jump out of me.

"I trudged to the car with my children clinging to my sides, unaware of the impending doom. As we reached the car, I ushered them to wait outside. As I entered, the silence was deafening as he nonchalantly announced that he was leaving us. I couldn't move, couldn't even muster a response. This was not how it was supposed to be."

"Has anything like this ever happened before?"

"No, never," I whispered, tears streaming down my face. "Our arguments had always ended with a mere retreat to separate corners of our home. Two years ago, when Ty visited his dad, our children were left broken-hearted without him."

"Did Donnie and Mandy understand what was happening this time?" she asked.

"I tried my best to explain things to them that night. Donnie reacted flippantly—throwing around the word 'divorce' like it was just another household chore."

"Unfortunately, children encounter these situations through peers or family members," she paused. "When did Ty invite them to the beach?"

My reply came out as a whisper that only I could hear. "He invited them within minutes after our argument—it almost felt like he was trying to escape."

"I can't imagine. It must have been difficult. Did Ty plan the trip before or after your disagreement?"

"Do you mind if we talk about something else?" I asked.

She gave a slight smile and winked. "How much do you know about Remsen and the study we are conducting?"

"Not much. After the phone interview, I didn't want to rely on the internet for info."

"That's good since there are many misleading stories or clickbait." She clasped her hands together. "First, let me welcome you to the Olympic View Treatment Center. If you participate, this will be your home for thirty days. After that, you may decide to continue in the home program we offer. It can be indefinite."

"If I were to become a resident here, what would a normal day be like? How would I start my day?"

She smiled. "I'm confident over the next day you will have an excellent idea of what a normal day is like here. Of course, today and tomorrow are just a tiny picture of what you may expect. There are over a dozen classes that are offered seven days a week. We even have a few clubs run by participants."

"So, what can I expect with this drug?" I was desperate for relief.

"We have had an eighty percent success rate with participants in our thirty-day study. However, fifteen percent have not been amenable to treatment."

I sighed, becoming increasingly impatient with the lack of information. "What can I expect from Remsen? Please give me an example!"

Jessica tightened her lips before beginning her story. "I have a client who had a negligent driver kill his wife. Just moments after she dropped him off at work, he heard a tremendous bang and turned to see his spouse's car in flames. He ran to the intersection to find his wife had already succumbed to her injuries. He passed out before the emergency crews arrived." Her gaze pierced me as my chest tightened. I could scarcely breathe. "Would you like me to continue?"

"Yes, please go on."

"The trauma the client suffered tormented him. He had become homebound. Any loud bangs would cause him to have panic attacks. All aspects of his life became formidable. After he arrived at OVTC, we crafted a new narrative for him based on his traumatic memory. Gradually, we rewrote the negative memory into a positive one."

My confused expression deepened. "You're saying I can... replace it? What will happen to the memory of what happened?"

"Your memory will always exist. We are just storing it away in a closet. The idea is to create a permanent detour that directs away from the traumatic memory. The new memory will be similar until it's not."

"How much time should this process take?"

She nodded, understanding flooding across her face. "It all depends on the client. On average, it takes around 13 days until there's a breakthrough. After the breakthrough, it's all about rewriting the narrative."

"What are my chances of success?"

"Once we have a baseline for your trips with Remsen, we will create a timeline."

I nodded.

"Are you ready to go into more detail with your memory?"

"What do I need to do?"

"You will need to recount your memory as much as possible. Sights, sounds, and smells. Our team will help build an alternate script. Once you achieve the breakthrough, we will help you construct your new pathway.

"Am I going to have some fake memory overtake my memory?"

"Pretty much, yes."

I was feeling no way out. "I'm ready to start."

2

"Please focus on your memory. The sights, sounds, and smells. Try to find a trigger point. Somewhere in that memory, you can latch onto it as a start. Remember, we will only have fifteen minutes to work with for your dry session, so you will need to base it on just before your argument."

I closed my eyes. "It was just before 3 p.m. Ty had to be at work 4, and we had a thirty-minute drive home. I had just realized how late it was when I mentioned going over to check on our son, Donnie."

She nodded. "Do you remember any specific smells that day?"

I closed my eyes. "The smell of burning charcoal and Mandy's overbearing banana sunscreen."

"What were the conditions like?"

"It was a breathtaking day with the sun shining through the clouds. There were so many people on the beach that it made Ty and me feel claustrophobic. But I couldn't help but admire the beauty."

Jessica nodded with understanding. "The thought of not needing a special occasion to visit the beach must have been liberating for you."

I opened my eyes, feeling the safety of this place. "Yes," I whispered, "it was."

"Do you remember what you were discussing before the argument?" Jessica asked, her voice gentle.

I nodded, feeling my temples tighten. "Mandy, Mandy, Mandy, lunch, and then Mandy," I whispered with a bitter undertone.

"Was this a point of contention between you and Ty?" Jessica asked.

My heart raced as images of his glaring eyes seared through my mind. I took a deep breath to steady my nerves. "Yes, it was. Ty was all about praising Mandy and how athletic and smart she was. Rarely did he ever give Donnie any attention—we'd talked about this so many times."

I wiped away the tears that had fallen on my cheeks as a sharp pain twisted inside me. "We had only fifteen minutes left until we had to leave for the day." My voice quivered as I recalled Donnie's small body jumping up and down, begging for attention from his father. "Ty just rolled his eyes, telling me it was nothing but 'just another sand castle'. How could he be so cold? All I wanted was for us to go admire Donnie's creation."

Jessica placed her hand on mine. "How did you respond?"

"I smirked at him and walked away, praying that our kids wouldn't have to witness this. I felt my insides twist in laughter as I thought of how quickly he had blown up the situation. Only a minute was all Donnie needed, and it became something else entirely."

"So you walked over to Donnie?" Jessica asked.

"Donnie's resilience astounded me. He had crafted a magnificent sand fort with no help. Yet, on this day, his loneliness showed through. It was the moment he finally accepted his father's apathy that caused my inner wrath to ignite. I yelled at Ty with such ferocity that everyone around us gawked and snapped pictures. It was the first time I'd ever spoken to him in such a way, and it seemed to push him away more than anything else."

"So now you have onlookers. How did Ty react?" Jessica asked.

I swallowed hard. "He scrunched up his face in rage and said something like 'screw it' before storming to our car. I wasn't sure if he was going to drive away or not. I kept my eyes on him until he reached the car, but it never moved."

"What were you doing meanwhile?"

"My heart was beating a million miles an hour as I helped Donnie pick up his toys while making my way over to Mandy, who was still happily flying her kite. She had no idea what was happening."

Jessica's gaze softened. "Were the kids aware there had been an argument?"

"Donnie witnessed it." I sighed. "It wasn't until he saw Mandy that the tears stopped streaming and a smile lit up his face as he watched her with the kite."

"Did you guys ever argue in front of the kids?" she questioned.

"Besides some minor disagreements, we never allowed them to see us raise our voices at each other. I'm not confrontational, and Ty can be—I mean—he was. Ty was so relaxed about things." I shook my head. "But those days seemed so long ago now."

"Did you ever attempt marriage counseling?"

"He never took the idea seriously. He would always bring up his parents and how great they were together and never needed counseling."

"I think this will be enough to get us started."

I swallowed hard and asked her, "What happens tomorrow? During the dry run?"

"Tomorrow morning, we will meet here with my assistant, Doreen. We will take some brief readings and then begin the test. I will give you three five-microgram doses of Remsen to begin your trip," Jessica answered.

My eyes widened. "What is it like?" I asked, desperate for answers.

"It's like reliving your memory again, in vivid detail in real-time," she said. "All of your senses will come alive—you'll feel every moment as though it were happening right now."

I closed my eyes, not wanting to relieve my worst memory. "Why can't I change the memory tomorrow? Why do I need to relive this?"

"Yes, you can try to change your memory, but that doesn't mean you won't keep experiencing your original memory. Trying to alter your memory at the start of Remsen is like paving over a road using sand. It may work a little, but it won't cause any long-term effects. Remsen works to create new pathways in your memory. New pathways that can hopefully lead you to an improved memory."

"I'm a little tired. Can we take a break?"

"Yes, we can. I will walk you to your room, and later I would like to take you to dinner and to come observe a class."

"A class? What kind of class?"

"It's an art class that can get lively."

"I'm not sure about that, Jessica."

"That is fine. You can decide later."

3

We departed Jessica's office going straight for the elevator. We ascended to the fourth floor, and the door opened to a long, carpeted hallway that looked similar to the hotel I stayed at in Vegas except this one seemed spooky with no one in sight.

"Are there others staying on this floor?"

"Yes, normally we have three to eight guests staying. For tonight, I am only showing you and one other."

We continued down the hall until we reached a door marked 13.

"I guess it's your lucky number," she said.

I chuckled. "I hope it is. I can use a little."

The door swooshed open, and I cringed. Lavender invaded my nostrils, giving me a false sense of security. The room opened up to a large living area with couches and recliners. I swallowed hard, trying to contain the dread and curiosity that bubbled within me. I surveyed the area—five chairs clustered around the dining table—all empty. Even with their presence, they meant this place for people who weren't here... and never would be. "Do clients have guests?"

"Not on a day visit." Jessica walked to the dining table. "This room will be identical to the room you will have if you take part. When you take part, you can have up to four guests at a time for a weekend visit."

A glass partition faced the grove of trees. Dusky light glowed through the windowpanes. Jessica approached the glass wall, and it slid open. "All rooms have a balcony. With this view, it's required. This stays locked until you have reached your breakthrough."

That seems odd to have in a place where people could be suicidal. "Impressive. So I would gain perks?" I asked.

"Yes, normally once you clear your breakthrough, you earn extra privileges," Jessica said as she walked past me and into a hall, turning towards me. "Follow me. There's more."

I followed her down the hall into the bathroom.

She guided her hand across the stunning bathroom. "How does this suit you?"

I looked at the sauna tub. "It suits me very well," I said. I was so ready for the time from my prison.

"Does everything meet your expectations?"

"More than ever," I said, noticing with surprise how big it was: two sinks, a jacuzzi tub, and even a shower. Why would we need all that?

Her face seemed more at ease. "Great. I am going to leave you to relax a little." She walked towards the front door, and it slid open. "Can I pick you up in about an hour for dinner?"

"Sounds like a date. Where are we going?"

"Great. I will take you to my favorite place here," Jessica said.

"I will be ready." I looked at my travel bag.

Jessica pointed next to the door. "This display."

I nodded.

"This is your key to anything. You can make calls or even order food or drinks." She touched it, and it lit up. "Touch the green button, and it will connect you with our staff. You can ask them almost anything. You also have identical displays in the bathroom and in your room."

"Thank you, Jessica, for everything,"

She returned the smile. "You are so welcome, Jen. See you in an hour."

Jessica exited, and the door slid closed.

I approached the display and pushed the green button.

"This is the front desk, Miss Floyd. How can I help you?" the stranger asked.

"Is it possible for me to make a call out?"

"Yes, of course." She paused. "Do you have the number?"

"I don't remember her number. It's my emergency contact, Barbara Stein."

"Oh yes, I have her number. Connecting." The line paused.

It seemed like they had their eyes and ears on everything.

"This is Barb."

"It's me. I have a few minutes before dinner," I said.

"Give me a second, Jen. It's too loud in here." She put me on hold for a few seconds. "This should be better. Are you okay?"

"Oh, I'm fine. Jessica gave me a room that looks very similar to the one in Vegas."

Barb laughed. "You're kidding. Really, at the place I dropped you off?"

"Oh no. Jessica took me in a blacked-out van to the treatment center. It's called the Olympic View Treatment Center. It's about fifteen minutes from that place."

"Are you safe?" she asked.

Barb was my guardian angel, and she flew with a pack.

"I'm fine, Barb. They keep everything top secret with this drug."

Barb let out a sigh. "Okay, thank God. You scared me. So, how do you feel about this whole thing?"

"I'm nervous. Jessica seems confident that it will help," I said.

"You will get through this. You're one of the strongest people I know," she said.

A lump formed in my throat. "Thank you, Barb. That means a lot."

"Of course. You know I'll always be here for you," she said.

"I do. And I appreciate it."

There was a moment of silence before Barb spoke up again. "So, what's the room like?"

"It's like a fancy hotel suite. It's crazy," I said, looking around.

"Really? Well, at least they're treating you well," she said, chuckling.

"I guess so. How are things going for you?" I asked.

"This little antique shop had this beautiful chair I picked up. It's not a sitting chair; it's for decor. Now I'm having a drink at the Rusty Spoon."

"It's been a day or two since we hung out there."

"It's just like I remember. A dive bar with the right amount of filth," she said.

She never had an issue with making friends in those places.

"Just how you like it," I said.

Barb laughed. "Exactly. Did they give you a schedule?"

"Not yet. Jessica and I will meet for dinner in less than an hour."

"Sure they didn't whisk you away to Vegas?" Barb chuckled.

I laughed. "Pretty sure. I have a balcony, and the view is nothing like that. I guess after dinner, Jessica will give me the grand tour. This place is massive. I'm on the fourth floor."

"That sounds impressive. How does it feel to be away?"

"I feel good. Everything seems very comfy, like I'm at a nice resort."

"That's great. I hope this is what you need. It beats any alternative."

"I hope so." I sighed. "Tomorrow is the dry run. Jessica said I may not react to Remsen."

"What does that mean?"

"I guess it means back to square one."

"You will be fine. If anyone can pinpoint a memory, it would be you," she said.

Her voice assured me.

"I love you, Barb," I said. "See you tomorrow."

"I love you," she said with a low laugh. The line went silent.

4

From my room, we went to the second floor and entered a space that looked empty.

I pointed to the covered window, a sense of unease rising within me. "What are they putting in there?"

She shook her head, her lips pursed. "They'll be adding more restaurants and some retail shops."

"A treatment center with restaurants and shops?" I was taken aback, unsure if this was really what they were doing—turning this place into some sort of resort?

"When the study is complete, this facility will be open to the public. They will have around 500 participants at a time. Right now, there are just under 60 in the study at Olympic View and over 100 at home continuing the study."

I noticed the plainness of the doorway to this restaurant. It had no label or name; just a number. "No sign?" I asked, puzzled.

"For participants, we try to make things as simple as possible and not loud."

This almost felt too quiet. The door slid, and a man approached.

"Hello, Jessica. It's so nice to have you. And you must be Jenna. It's so nice to meet you." The man had a slight accent that I couldn't decipher. "Jessica is wonderful. Every one of her clients loves her."

She was blushing.

"You're too much, Grecco." Jessica laughed. "And if you want to have the best cheesesteak around, this is it."

He's from Philly.

"The director of the center wanted a Philly touch," Jessica said.

"He came to my restaurant." Grecco paused for emphasis, his voice dropping to a movie mobster's growl. "And said I have an offer you can't refuse." The words dripped like honey from his lips. "And lo-and-behold," he continued, his tone shifting back to normal, "I'm chained to this place now. But let me tell you something"—he leaned forward, excitement glinting in his eyes—"this is my best job ever. I get to create the dishes I love for the people I see every day." Grecco's smile grew wide, infectious even as I forced one back. He led us down a spacious hall that had doors every several feet.

"Jessica, what is beyond the doors?"

"Just tables," she answered.

Made sense in a place like this.

Grecco stopped in front of the last door.

"Thank you so much for remembering my table." Jessica gave him a pat on the shoulder.

"Of course, Jess. You will always be a VIP here," he said.

The door opened with a swoosh, and we stepped inside. We took our places at the circular table with three chairs. I occupied the seat opposite Jessica.

"Here are the menus. I'm making a Philly cheese dog today for the special."

Jessica shook her head. "I brought our guest to try one of your Philly favorites." She turned her head towards him. "We should be ready in a few minutes."

"Sounds good." Grecco turned and exited our room as the door closed. Soft music was playing in the background.

I stared at her. "Where are you from?"

"I grew up on the outskirts of Syracuse in Upstate New York. We were near enough to a few attractions but far enough away from anything noteworthy. I made it out of high school, and upon graduating, I went straight off to Temple University. The rest is history," she said.

"What do you think of the Pacific Northwest?"

"It's my new home. I can easily see myself living here for a while."

"With or without Quantos?" I asked.

"It doesn't matter all that much. If Quantos can provide me with a job, then I'm happy," she said, her voice tinged with agitation. "What catches your eye?"

I turned my focus to the menu. "I already know what I want."

Jessica looked at me. "What's that?"

I muttered, "I need to have a healthy mind."

Jessica winced at my statement, but continued, "May I order for you?"

"Yes, looking at this menu is overwhelming."

She pulled out her phone and opened an app. "Besides Remsen and this food, we have over a dozen different classes we offer. We have Yoga, Dance, and Art classes."

The thought of social activities made me feel ill.

"This will be your choice. You aren't obligated to attend anything outside of the sessions. We have found that clients have higher success rates when they attend classes daily."

I inhaled deeply, gathering the courage to speak again. "I understand that. I just don't feel comfortable talking with others. I'm always bombarded with questions like 'Do you have family?' or 'Are you married?' There's no way around it."

Jessica turned her head slightly. "I'm sorry, Jen. I can't imagine how painful it must be."

"Please don't be. It's part of my life now."

"How about we change the conversation?" Her eyes had a sparkle I hadn't seen in a therapist before. "Tell me more about your friend, Barb. She is in law enforcement?"

"Barb is amazing. She is family." I laughed. "She is a detective in our sheriff's department. She is a badass, and I think she would even tear me up if I broke the law."

Jessica chuckled. "How long have you been friends?"

"We met in fifth grade. She was playing kickball with the boys, and they said they needed another girl, so I remember her yelling at me. 'Hey, you, blondie! Come play with us.' I think she was even meaner back then. I guess she liked how I played, and we became best friends."

Jessica was nodding. "Has Barb been closer to you over the last year?"

I teared up. "Barb has been everything for me. My other 'friends' just stopped calling. I wasn't much help. I wasn't really trying."

"Losing your family is incomprehensible. Losing friends is part of life. If those we have aren't strong enough to be with us during our worst moments, then why keep them along?"

I nodded, and she handed me a tissue.

"Reading your case file shows Barb has been a real advocate for you," Jessica said. "She gave up her job offer in Seattle last year to stay close to you."

I wiped my eyes with the tissue. "She didn't even tell me she turned it down until I asked her months later. I know she did it for me."

"That's pretty incredible. Most people never have a friendship like yours," Jessica said.

"I think she was more worried about me committing suicide. Every time she would ask me bluntly, 'Are you suicidal today?' And every time, I would answer, 'Only when you ask me that question.' She never laughed. Only giving me that look that I'm sure she gives people she's about to interrogate."

"Did you ever feel suicidal?" Jessica asked.

I nodded. "Plenty of times in the first few months. The days I would wake up and feel like they were about to walk into the house, and they never did," I said.

"And now?" Jessica stared into my eyes. "Have you felt suicidal in the last six months?" She leaned in closer.

"About seven months ago. That was the last time."

Jessica nodded as a chime went off. "That must be the food." She pushed a button, and the door slid open, revealing a motorized cart with covered plates. The cart rolled in, and the door slid closed.

"Can I change the subject?" I asked.

"Of course you can." She put a plate in front of me, revealing chicken parm. "If this isn't the best chicken parm you've had."

I giggled. "It looks amazing." I cut a piece of the chicken parm.

"Cheers to a sumptuous meal." Jessica toasted up her glass of water.

"So, how would I start the trial? What do I need to do?" I asked, taking a bite of my dish.

Jessica stared at me. "If you can get a positive result from the dry run tomorrow, it will open you to the study."

"You weren't wrong. This is the best chicken parm I have ever had. By far."

"We are lucky to have Grecco. He is quite the chef."

I nodded. "Are we required to achieve certain results in the study?" I asked.

"Not at all. Everyone is here voluntarily. You will be free to leave during the study," Jessica said.

"What causes someone to quit?" I asked.

"Remsen is a powerful drug. Experiencing memories as if they are real and in the present can be extremely hard on an individual. Even if someone isn't ready to begin using Remsen yet, it doesn't mean they won't ever be. Quantos predicts that over seventy percent of those who had left the study prematurely will take up its use in five years' time. We still haven't got a complete understanding of how this drug works." Jessica took a forkful of her parm and put it in her mouth.

The thought of failing made me squirm.

"Has your physical health suffered the past year?" she asked.

"I have lost about ten pounds. Most of it was muscle. I was a runner before the accident. Now I'm an occasional walker."

Jessica appeared athletic.

"Walking is great. Think about the things you don't see when moving that much quicker. Do you ever meditate?" she asked.

"I was much better at it before the accident. I used it in my class with the kids after recess. It worked like a charm every time."

She nodded. "That's wonderful. You are never too young to learn."

"Exactly. I hoped the school would embrace it, but it didn't sell to all the teachers."

"That's too bad. Meditation can create a positive impact in any environment."

"Can I ask you a personal question?"

Jessica looked at me with trepidation. "Of course you can."

"You look so young. What made you come here?" I immediately regretted my words and corrected myself. "Sorry, Jessica, why did you decide to do this?"

"I got a call from Quantos, indicating they had a new drug in the trial stages. They said it would be revolutionary in helping with PTSD, so I jumped at the chance. The only downside was that it meant moving to Washington away from my family and friends on the east coast. I spent the first half year at their offices in Philadelphia. I have been here at OVTC for over six months now."

"That must be tough being away from family?" I asked.

"I'm traveling back every other week. Quantos has one flight a day to Philly. That has been one of the biggest perks of this job."

"I'm glad you came here."

She smiled. "I have a surprise for you when we are done." She glanced at her watch. "We have about twenty minutes before the class begins."

My stomach started balling up at the thought of social exposure. "What can I expect?"

"It's an art class that has taken on a life of its own. Where the clients become the subjects."

This is not the surprise I want. "They pose nude?" I chuckled, knowing the pressure would be off me.

"They pose; however, they feel comfortable. Some pose nude while we have had a few fully dressed, wanting their moment here to be remembered. It's a very sociable class."

"Almost sounds like a party."

"It almost is. If you don't feel comfortable, we can find another activity."

I pursed my lips. "Sounds fun. I will give it a try." I hadn't even visited the grocery store in the past year.

"Thank you, Jen, for being open-minded." She turned her head away from me." While we still have a few minutes, do you have more questions about being a participant?"

"Has anyone died in this study? I couldn't help but see how this drug was on the streets. I'm worried about how addictive it may be."

"Not one death. We have had three hospitalizations that were nothing more than an overnight observation." She shook her head. "The street version is similar, but not really. Quantos reformulated Remsen within weeks of the theft."

"What happened?"

"They stole the truck. It had just left the airport with the supply from Quantos. No one would have known what was in the truck."

"Just like that, all the original Remsen ended up on the streets?"

She nodded. "It was less than a week later that there was a reported overdose of an unreported drug. Quantos ended up sending test kits to hundreds of law enforcement agencies around the world."

"What's the difference between the two drugs?" I asked.

"R is the street name for the drug. It has about twice the potency. And then you add no supervision, you have people taking over one hundred microgram doses. As long as you are in this study, the largest dose you will receive is sixty micrograms." She shook her head. "Chances are people aren't using this for trauma on the streets. If you use this on non-traumatic memories, it may be more addictive."

"Are any participants becoming addicted?" I asked.

"Under direct supervision, addiction is not possible. Participants don't have direct access to Remsen until the home study," Jessica said.

"What about the home study?" I asked.

She looked prepared for my question. "Not everyone is invited to be part of the home study. And at home, participants are never provided more than a one-week supply at a time."

"Have you taken Remsen?" I asked.

"Yes, I've taken it for a few sessions. They want everyone who works at OVTC to have some personal knowledge of how the drug works," she said. "I think the hardest part was having to flesh out the memory. I was probably ten and my brother Aiden would have been eight. He threw a rock at a beehive."

"That's so scary. I'm sorry."

She closed her eyes, pressing her lips tightly together, then opened them again in slow motion. Her eyes became red. "I just left him there," she said. "He was so badly stung that he spent days in the hospital. He nearly died."

"Were you able to change the memory?" I asked.

"Yes, I did. I lived with guilt for years. Aiden never blamed me. I blamed myself for not being there."

"And now?" I asked.

"It's like a blurry dream. I'm not scared of bees anymore."

"I'm so sorry. That seems to cancel out running barefoot."

"The experience traumatized me, giving me an intense fear of them. Seeing one fly near me was enough for me to panic and run away. I would avoid going out at all costs. When I tried to swat one away as a teenager, I ended up getting stung and it just made my phobia worse." She stated.

"Do you think I will be less afraid?" I was hoping for a magic pill.

Jessica put her hands out on the table. "We have a lot of work to do. This starts on day one and doesn't end on day thirty. Our goal, if you begin the study, is to reduce your PTSD significantly. The time will fly, and before you know it, you will be in the community like before."

I wasn't even sure if I wanted to return to Aberdeen. "In less than six weeks, I am supposed to be in front of a class full of fourth-graders. I don't see myself ready."

She shook her head. "I want you to just focus on your day. Living in the present. When your mind goes to anything besides now, take a deep breath."

Now the therapist comes out. If it was only that easy.

"If your mind tries to skip to tomorrow or anytime beyond our present, try to kill the thought," she said.

My thoughts were like water splashing over stones, skipping and skidding off of abrupt turns in the stream. I kept nodding at Jessica. She was right.

"Positive distractions work wonders," Jessica continued. "Here at Olympic View, we create that environment. Classes, games, and social activities can help you. And some great food also helps."

Great. Everything involves being around people.

She glanced at her phone. "And we supply movies, apps, and games if you feel like alone time."

Jessica was reading my mind. "That sounds a little more my pace." I yearned for the solitude within myself—there wasn't anyone distracting me when I sat down with my laptop, watched a movie or did anything else by myself. No one told me they were sorry or praying for me.

"It can be daunting, Jen. Let's focus on the right now." She looked up at me with a smile on her face, as if worried about saying too much too soon.

My palms grew wet. "Do you think I'm ready for a class?"

Jessica nodded, briefly looking at her phone before standing abruptly. "It's time for class," she said, pushing in her chair with a gentle gesture.

We exited the room together.

"Thank you, Jessica," I said, hoping that I could trust her.

5

The elevator came to a stop on the sixth floor.

"This building has eight floors?" I asked.

"Yes, there are. The next two floors are administrative."

As we walked down the hallway, I couldn't help but feel nervous. What kind of class was this? Would I be able to handle it? My mind raced with thoughts and worries, but Jessica's constant presence by my side helped to calm me down.

"Why are the doors different colors?" I asked.

"We have found it easier on clients if they are looking at colors rather than numbers. If the Yoga class met in Room 524, it would give many clients anxiety. We are attempting to make this as distressful as possible."

And those who are color blind?

"Let me show you our dance floor," she said as a door slid open and the lights went on.

"This is it, Jen The Crystal Ballroom." Ty's smile was bigger than his face. He opened the door to reveal the large dance floor. "Do you realize all the history in this place?"

I could smell the wood polish and old wood, along with patches of mustiness from hidden places I had never seen. The sound bounced off the walls and ribboned around us.

"I can't believe it, Ty. This is incredible."

The large stage beckoned, waiting for Ty and The Crew. A chill ran down my spine like someone was playing with icicles in an ice cave under the earth somewhere far away to bug me.

"Pretty soon, you won't even need to teach. You can follow your passions."

I stood tall and walked over to my husband with confidence. My feet barely contacted the worn-out wooden floor, which creaked under every step I took closer to him, as if possessed by its own spirit.

"Jenna." Jessica's voice brought me from the abyss. "How are you feeling?"

I was fighting back tears."It's hard. Very hard."

She handed me a tissue. "Take as much time as you need."

I tapped the tissue around my eyes. "Please." I sighed. "I'm ready to go."

Jessica started walking, and I followed. She stopped in front of a door painted soft lilac, like the color of twilight. "And here we are."

"This was one of her favorite colors," I said.

She gave me an empty stare and moved from the door. "Who's favorite color?"

"Mandy's. It was lilac."

"It's such a beautiful color. Mandy must have had great taste."

Chills coursed through my body. "She did."

"Do you feel ready to go in?" Jessica asked.

I took a deep breath and contemplated the ability to experience the class. "I think so."

"If you are uncomfortable, just grab my hand, and we can leave," she responded.

My pulse raced as Jessica turned her watch towards the door that slid open.

"Do all the doors slide like this?" I asked. I wanted a light conversation, something to take my mind off of it.

"They have that feature to avoid people getting hit with the doors. When you are a participant, they give you a watch. This watch will only open the doors you have access to. If you are not supposed to be in a class, this door won't open. It was cheaper to have doors like this than the traditional ones." Jessica turned towards the class. "Okay, Jen, if you need to leave, just grab me." She walked in, and I followed. I could hear several voices before I even saw the people.

As soon as I stepped into the room, I was greeted with a lively and colorful atmosphere. The walls were decorated with art pieces, and a table displayed beautiful pottery. Amidst the chatter of a few people engaged in conversation, Jessica appeared and interjected with a cheerful, "How is everyone?"

They turned around and greeted her. Eyes darted towards me. "I have a special guest I would like to introduce," she announced.

OMG! Everyone's eyes followed her as she twisted around to face me.

"This is Jenna." Jessica paused momentarily, then continued, "She is visiting today. We will save intros for another day since the class is about to begin."

Several of the people said hi in chorus.

I forced out a faint, "Nice to meet you," as I surveyed the room. There were easily a dozen other people in this class.

"Welcome to conceptual art and human study," a woman with long silver hair said, turning towards me. "My name is Rodina. For those of you who are new to this class." She gave me an understanding nod before stepping back to reveal a figure robed in black standing at a podium in the center of the room.

My gaze shifted to the easel. Jessica piped up from behind me. "Do you want to paint?"

Staring into her eyes, I said, "I have never attended a class like this."

There was a brief silence as she hesitated. "This class took on a life of its own," she whispered. "We had a client who wanted to pose nude just over a month ago. Nina will be the thirteenth to do this in less than a month."

My heart sank like a stone.

"Nina Preston visited us even before she signed up for the class and called it ridiculous," Rodina said.

"I said it was bullshit," Nina added, and the students laughed in response.

Nina looked tall on the platform, standing mere feet away from me.

"Yes, that's what you said." Rodina glanced in my direction and winked.

My cheeks heated as everyone turned their attention to me.

"Art has helped me change my perspective; I'm using different colors to express my feelings, positive or negative," Nina continued.

Rodina stepped back and gestured with her hand. "And tonight, let's give Nina a chance to show us."

I glanced around and saw everyone staring at Nina. Jessica leaned in close, murmuring, "If you feel uncomfortable, we can go anytime."

My focus shifted back to Nina. She spun around; her robe falling to the floor while her bare backside faced the class. No bra and no underwear—nothing!

The class clapped and cheered as she pivoted towards us, showing off her body.

My jaw dropped open; Nina was absolutely stunning.

"How does it feel?" A man with dark hair asked Nina.

"Liberating," she answered.

"You look phenomenal, Nina," a young woman added.

"Thanks, Sammy," she said. "Not bad for a 36-year-old mom of three." Her face dropped. "I'm sorry. Mother of one."

Oh no; I know that feeling all too well.

"Right then, class," Rodina began. "We have the wonderful Ms. Preston here with us. She's a mother and an absolute badass who has done the Boston Marathon twice and Mount Rainier four times. How will you capture our subject?" She floated to the back of the room as I looked around at my peers, busy with their easels. *Where do I even start?*

Rodina approached me and said, "Jenna, don't worry about doing anything if you don't feel up to it; you can just observe."

I nodded. "Thank you."

Nina was on stage, raising her arms above her head as her chest became more visible. I took a deep breath and picked up a pencil before drawing her legs. Defined by years of running, reminding me of how much I used to love running myself.

As I watched my classmates work around me, I sketched out her form. "Is it just people like her who do this?" I whispered to Jessica.

She nodded towards a balding man considerably shorter and heavier than me. "That's Scott," she said. "He did this a week ago. It drew more people to the class."

I watched him, trying to comprehend that he had bared himself before these strangers. Would I ever be able to do something like that? Could I stand in front of all these people with my body exposed, when I struggled just to look at myself in the mirror? And then I could see myself.

Nina's voice shook as she spoke to the class. "When Jenna joined us nearly a month ago, she rarely left her home. Now she is going to reveal herself."

The class was silent, and all eyes were on me.

I stepped forward into the light, and it was almost blinding, but I could still make out the faces of everyone in the room.

"She has made incredible progress in the short time here," Nina continued as I walked towards her, my body tense with anticipation.

I could feel my heart beating hard, like a caged bird trying to break free. And then, without warning or hesitation, I opened the robe and let it fall off my body. It felt like a thousand eyes were upon me, scrutinizing every inch of skin, but it didn't scare me; if anything, I felt at peace.

The silence lingered for an eternity before someone finally broke it. "Wow!" they whispered. The tension dissipated like a balloon deflating, and there was something profound about that moment—something liberating about standing there, exposed yet unashamed.

"Are you sure you're okay?" Jessica's voice summoned me out of my daydream.

I opened my eyes and gazed at her. "Yes, I'm fine. I was just lost in thought."

"If you need to talk, we can leave," she proposed.

"No, it's nothing like that. I should be good," I replied diverting my gaze toward the other works around the class. Several students had mastered the human physique, making their pieces stand.

I dragged a sketch pencil closer to myself and looked back at Nina. She was laughing with some of her peers, which made me feel an unfamiliar sensation—joy. Had I ever laughed? Was I even capable of feeling joy anymore?

I focused on Nina's face. Trying to capture her happiness. Her eyes shone brilliantly and were full of life, a life that felt so far away from where I was at the moment. Our eyes met and all I could do was force a small smile. Feeling embarrassed, I hid behind my easel before anyone else noticed this sudden display of emotion from me.

I kept working on her eyes until Rodina approached me.

"Have you done this before?" Rodina asked.

I turned my head slightly to see her staring at my drawing.

"No." I chuckled. "This is my first time."

"It looks great! And hopefully not your last time!" Rodina praised before walking away again.

I put down the pencil, feeling satisfied with what I had created.

6

My eyelids opened to the bright morning light. After a year of sleepless nights, this was one of the first I had rested without drugs.

I forced myself out of bed and stumbled into the bathroom, doing a double-take about how big it is. As I finished my business, I heard a chiming from the wall panel.

Incoming Call—I pushed *accept.*

"Jen?"

"Barb. It's good to hear from you."

"Are you okay? You can tell me anything."

"I'm fine. Jessica took me to an art class last night."

"Oh, how was that?" Barb's voice lifted. "Did they have you paint a fruit bowl?"

I chuckled. "A fruit bowl? This class was a little more advanced. We painted a client. Sorry, Barb, her name is confidential."

Barb huffed.

"She posed in the buff. It felt so liberating. I think I can do it after a few weeks."

"Don't get too far ahead of yourself. You still need an invitation first."

" I know. But I feel ready."

Barb sighed. "What are they doing with you this morning?"

"I'm meeting with Jessica, and we are going to have a dry session with a microdose."

"Dry session? Is that like without the drug?"

"Yeah, pretty much. Jessica will only give me a minimal dosage to help sharpen my memory."

"How do you feel about that?" Barb asked.

"I'm a little scared." I was on an endless roller coaster. "I don't know what to expect."

"You need to be assertive about this. I don't care what they tell you. Don't push yourself." I could hear Barb slap something.

I looked for quick miracles, and she guided me through every step or misstep. "I will, I promise."

"You don't need to do this. I can be there anytime."

Another month of my life, and I don't think I could tolerate myself. "I need to try. I got to see the participants last night. They were happy. I think I can get there." I was pleading with her.

"If you need anything," she said.

"Just for you to be patient with me. With this, please, Barb."

"I guess I will be picking you up at 1 p.m."

"Yes, you will. Same place as before."

"Got it," she said.

My heart pounded as I looked up at the door display, where Jessica's name was illuminated in bright blue letters. "She's here," I said to Barb.

"Loveya, Jenna bear," Barb replied as I disconnected.

I approached the door, mesmerized by Jessica's beaming face on the display screen. My finger trembled as I pressed the green button, and the door opened with a soft whoosh.

Jessica strode in with a blue folder. "Good morning, Jen. How'd you sleep?"

"Like a baby," I responded.

"Before we move on, we need your signature and initials for the form."

My stomach churned. "I thought I signed everything already."

"Since Remsen is involved in the testing, there may be unforeseen side effects. We want to make sure you sign off on that." She pulled out her tablet and placed it in front of me. "Sorry about this, Jen; all we need are three signatures and a few initials."

I let out a deep breath in relief. "That makes me feel better."

"We can look over the documents before you leave today. Are you okay if we take a seat at the table?" Jessica asked.

"Yes, of course," I said.

She headed to the table, and I followed, both of us taking seats. Jessica placed down the folder, revealing her tablet beneath it as she opened it up."This form and the other is just standard liability concerning the use of Remsen," she said."Since this is your first trip. We should go over some ground rules."

"Is there anything I should worry about?"

Jessica shook her head. "Not at all. The most severe side effect of Remsen we've seen is a hangover."

"What'sthat?"

"The hangover impacts everyone who utilizes Remsen, possibly leaving you feeling exhausted after your initial trip. Most of the time, though, the most intense reaction is not experienced until during the second stage of the study."

The E-form was shorter than I'd imagined. "What about Barb?" My words trailed off as I almost forgot about her.

"Barb will sign a non-disclosure agreement, which allows one designated guardian to have access to client information," she explained.

My relief grew; I'd still need Barb by my side.

"Should I keep a diary?" I questioned.

She nodded. "You'll be supplied with journals to write in. It may prove to be a helpful way of tracking your progression."

"What about Barb?" My words trailed off as I almost forgot about her.

"Barb will sign a non-disclosure agreement, which allows one designated guardian to have access to client information," she explained.

My relief grew; I'd still need Barb by my side. "Do you have something to write with?" I inquired.

I signed the E-doc.

Jessica scrolled to reveal another form.

"What's this?" I asked.

She bowed her head slightly. "This form states that should any harm come to you while using Remsen, you can't take legal action against Quantos Pharma," Jessica informed me.

My mouth hung open in disbelief.

"It isn't anything too serious. You or your next of kin..."

Barb...

"...will receive financial compensation for any injury or worst-case scenario. Please read over this." She handed me a piece of paper with a list.

Quantos Pharma

Release of Liability

The page had dozens of scenarios with predetermined payouts. Slip and fall $500k.Injury in class was from $100k to one million. I scrolled down to the bottom where death by Remsen was. The payout amount was $250 million. Would that be enough to stop Barb the bulldog if I died? It's never about the money for her.

I looked up at Jessica, my mind racing and my stomach turning as I thought about the risks. "You said no one has died?"

"Not one person on the Remsen trial has died," she replied.

"And injuries?" I sighed, not sure if I wanted to hear the answer or not. The form had many ways to get a payout. Some injuries looked normal, like cuts and broken bones, but others were more serious and could lead to life-altering consequences.

"There have been five injuries. Only three were serious enough that the client had to quit the study."

My heart sank, and I felt a lump forming in my throat as I realized how real this risk was. But what choice did I have? I signed twice where Jessica pointed, committing myself to this uncertain fate.

"This is yours to keep," she said, handing me the liability form.

"Thank you."

"This is your take-home folder," Jessica said, sliding it across the table."We have a brochure and information regarding the programs offered. Many clients prefer to look at papers over a computer screen. We have noticed for many it just increases anxiety levels too high when you are staring at a screen trying to figure this stuff out."

"Thank you for putting thought into this."

"With that, I think we are ready to begin the dry session," Jessica said as she approached the door. The door slid open for her; she had not touched a button or even come close to jamming on one. Magic was making sense again, which blew my mind, but also brought me joy.

"Not one person will enter your room unless you have an emergency. My ID only opens your door when I'm on the inside." She angled her wrist and a brief flash of light flitted over her arm and then turned off along with the door soundlessly closing behind her back. "Are you ready to begin your session?"

"I'm more ready than ever," I responded.

7

We stepped into Jessica's office, which looked very different from yesterday. "Did you do this?" I asked.

She nodded with a grin. "I had some time after our meeting to put my pics up."

My gaze focused on one wall section filled with framed pictures. "And these?"

"Those are photos from my backpacking trips. I took them with my smartphone; it's much lighter than lugging around an actual camera."

"The detail is amazing. I have a lot of difficulty getting a clear shot of my kids! I'm sorry."

"No need to apologize; your memories of them surely feel like yesterday," she said.

Another moment passed before I asked, "Do you backpack?"

Jessica smiled. "My parents got me out hiking before I could even walk. So what about you? Have you ever gone backpacking?"

I shook my head no. "I read *Wild* a few months ago, though," I added.

Her expression changed to one of understanding. "Yes, it's such a powerful story."

"After reading it for two days, I felt motivated to hike the PCT!"

"The Pacific Crest Trail?" she clarified with a raised eyebrow.

At my nod, she continued, "That journey requires proper training and preparation."

"Well, I nearly spent two thousand dollars on hiking gear... but Barb convinced me to take it back." I chuckled.

She grinned. "I can imagine it! Barb certainly has a way with words."

I chuckled again. "That's an understatement. She treats me like her own child sometimes."

"Hiking is a great idea," she said. "Maybe you could find a group of people who go on day hikes together."

"Yeah, maybe," I replied. "If this Remsen works."

She gazed into my eyes as she spoke. "Yesterday's class was a great start. That's encouraging."

I nodded before turning my gaze to the coffee station. "Can I get a cup?"

"Sorry," she said, "we don't allow any stimulants six hours before the session. But after day fifteen, you'll be allowed coffee before the sessions start."

That didn't sound good—I could feel a dull throbbing bounce between my ears. "What about withdrawal? I don't want to wind up with a pounding headache."

"Don't worry, you'll get your coffee after today's session. Please, sit in the black chair," Jessica directed me.

I replied, "How early is my session? I normally wake before five."

"We can get you in the seven a.m. slot."

I settled into the chair that resembled something from a dentist's office and said, "That's good because I can't function without caffeine."

She nodded. "I understand."

"Thank you, Jessica."

Jessica sat in a light tan chair facing mine and continued, "Just to let
you know, this is a reclining medical-grade chair we'll use during your
session. Do you have questions?"

I shook my head.

A door behind me swooshed open.

"Good morning, D. How's it going?" Jessica inquired.

"Great; apart from sleeping in," the other woman replied.

"You made good time, though," Jessica said.

The other woman giggled. "I almost got pulled over by a
cop—luckily I had this sticker on—and they just drove away."

Jessica smiled. "I didn't have that luck in Philly."

"Even the President would get a ticket there," The other woman
stated.

"That's for sure," Jessica agreed.

"What kind of sticker is it?" I asked.

"Oh, sorry, Jenna; this is Doreen—she goes by 'D'."

D waved at me. "The sticker I'm talking about has a letter Q for
'Quantos'. We can't drive 100 mph." She winked at Jessica. "Or can
we?"

"It's one perk of working at Quantos," Jessica told me.

I wondered how much power Quantos held. "I wish teachers had
something like that."

"You're preaching to the choir! Thank you, Jenna—I love hearing
that from another teacher." D toasted her hand up in appreciation.
"You look beautiful—may I give you a hug?"

I blushed, feeling embarrassed but flattered. "Yes, thank you." Rising from my seat, I walked towards her as she opened her arms and hugged me tightly, her eyes sparkling.

"It's so nice to meet you, Jenna; what are your first impressions so far?" D spread her arms out as if displaying the entire room.

"Give her a chance; she's been here less than 24 hours," Jessica cut in before I could answer the question.

"My apologies, Jenna!" D patted me on the shoulder soothingly. "I got ahead of myself."

"I'm impressed. This place is more than I imagined."

D faced me and said, "Right? Jessica and I trained together in Philly. They appreciate how well we work together, so here we are. I will monitor your vitals and give you doses of Remsen if necessary. If I see any irregularities in your behavior, I can remove you from the trip."

"Have you ever had to do that before?" I asked.

"Normally, during the first two weeks of the study, clients require at least one evac," D explained.

"What about the dry run?"

Jessica tilted her head.

"Has anyone had to be taken out during the dry run?" I inquired.

"Nope, not even once," Jessica told me. "When you're doing the dry run, you'll be aware—you'll travel through your memory but still know where you are."

D looked at me and asked, "Are you ready for this to begin?"

"Yes," I answered.

Jessica walked towards her desk, her gaze fixed on the device in D's hand. "I will be over here. D will check your vitals to make sure you are ready."

D pulled out a long black wand with a light blue glow. "This little magic stick can detect body temperature and any abnormalities with your heart rate or brain activity. It can detect your stress levels to tell us if you can go on the trip." She carefully ran the wand up my legs, around my waist, and then up to my head. When she reached my forehead, she paused, studying the glowing readout. "Your vitals look great!"

I chuckled. "Not bad for caffeine-free."

D raised an eyebrow as she stowed away the wand. "Do you have intense dreams?"

I swallowed hard, remembering the vivid nightmares that had been plaguing me for the past year. "More than a few have woken me up over the past year."

Jessica nodded thoughtfully. "Your experience may be heightened,"

"I won't mind that effect." I said.

D gave a warm smile. " It looks like you're ready to take a trip." She walked to her station and pulled something out.

"What is that?" I asked, my voice unsteady.

D passed me a delicate mesh net. "This will go on top of your head," she explained. "It has over a hundred sensors, but they are too tiny to see." She placed the net on my scalp. "You'll also need to wear this mask over your mouth and nose."

My eyes widened as I saw the familiar object. "It's like the one Donnie had in the hospital."

"Are you okay?" D asked, her face close to mine.

I nodded and took the mask from her hands. I held it against my face and inhaled deeply.

"Remember to keep breathing," D reminded me. "That's your best ally during your memory."

"What's that?" My nasal passages burned slightly.

"We have an engineer working on something for you based on your memory. We can tailor it to fit your preferences once we get the baseline," D told me as she sat beside me, her three monitors glowing with various data.

"Are you ready to test scents?" she asked.

I nodded in response and took a deep breath of air to steady myself.

"On the count of three, I'll pipe in the scent. We can adjust from there."

I gave her another nod, and she counted, then pressed some buttons on the monitor.

I could feel the ocean breeze blow in my nose, and I was taken aback—what had happened?

D laughed a little. "Sorry about that! The smells from memory can be very intense."

"Sometimes, if you don't have one particular scent, it can take you through multiple memories," Jessica added. "Does this take you to that memory?"

The recollection of being there was vivid; I could smell the banana sunscreen that Mandy always wore so heavily. "It's very close."

"Our engineer modified it. Let's try again at three. One, two, three." She pushed the button again, and suddenly, Ty was standing in front of me like he used to do—saying my name before I could respond.

Jessica asked if I was closer, and I responded, "This is it—I am there."

"I think that's everything. You're getting three doses of 5 micrograms to start, followed by fifteen microgram doses during the study, which will last thirty days. You won't be affected much during this test run, but stay alert. Do you have questions?" Jessica asked while looking at her monitor.

"No, I'm ready," I replied.

"Alright. I will be right by your side monitoring you, and Jessica here will be the only one communicating with you from now on," D said.

I gave them a thumbs-up before closing my eyes.

"Let's focus on your memory first. Can you remember where you were and who was around you when we started? Is there a specific place or scene you can focus on?" Jessica said.

"Yes."

"Wonderful! D administers the Remsen doses and counts to three before she does it. You might feel dizzy shortly after—that's normal—keep taking deep breaths. Let's get started. The client is Jennifer Floyd. Miss Floyd, please provide us with your name and birth date?" Jessica asked.

"My name is Jenna Floyd, and my birthdate is August 17th, 1993."

"Miss Floyd, you will be administered fifteen micrograms of Remsen. Do you understand?"

"Yes, I do."

"We are ready to begin the dosing. Miss Floyd, do you have any further questions?"

"No, I don't."

"Good. We will start with the first dose. Miss Floyd, do you understand?"

I took a deep breath. "Yes, I do."

"On three, Jen. One, two, three." Jessica paused. "First dose received by the client." She continued, "On three, you will receive your second dose. Are you ready?" Her voice was clear and steady.

My mouth felt dry and my body weighed heavy. "Yes, I am."

D's voice muffled in my head.

"A wave of air came into my lungs, and I could feel the sensation."

"Beginning last inhale. On three: one, two, three." Her words faded away as seagulls and crashing waves replaced the office silence.

"Jessica, the sound effects are spot on…"

"Jessica?" he questioned. "Babe, you okay?"

I felt my skin tingle as the familiar voice reached me. I searched for the sunglasses in my back pocket to shield myself from the blinding light that revealed his silhouette.

I stood there paralyzed, unable to answer him. "Ty? I asked, hoping against hope that it would be true.

He shook his head. "Who is Jessica?" His tone was stern, making it clear he wasn't asking a question but expecting an answer.

I forced a smile. "Oh, her," I said. "I'm working with her this year; she will be in training."

Ty chuckled, but remained silent. My stomach churned, and my heart raced as I stepped closer and put my arms around him. How could this be possible? No matter how much I had imagined this moment, it never felt like this. I tried to focus on our conversation.

I turned to Ty. "It didn't take her long to get that kite in the air."

He nodded in agreement. "She is quite the athlete—and fearless, too."

Mandy seemed oblivious to our presence, only focused on her new endeavor.

"Were you brave like her?" I asked him.

He shook his head. "Oh no, not me. Fear held me back way too much."

"And now?"

Ty smiled while nodding his head. "I think fear still gets in my way."

His expression was pensive as he watched Mandy tugging on the kite's string, trying to get it to go higher and higher. I could see his admiration for Mandy while he watched her unflinching courage. He looked at me and said, "But if we can confront our fears, then maybe we can be brave like Mandy."

I glanced over at Donnie, who was energetically waving his arms. "I think our son is trying to get our attention."

Ty peered at Donnie and shook his head. "What's he up to now?"

I chuckled. "Oh, come on, Ty. He's a real hoot. We've got a little jokester here."

Ty faced me. "So what does the little joker want?"

We had been at the beach for over three hours now and hadn't checked on Donnie.

"I think he wants us to look at his creation. He's been working hard all afternoon."

Ty kept his gaze focused on Mandy. "Maybe if we give him a few more minutes, he'll be able to finish his sandcastle."

I glanced down at my phone. "It's almost time to leave," I announced, hoping for a different reaction this time.

Ty snorted. "Another sand castle?" Disdain rang in his voice. "Jen, you can wait. You don't need to be at his beck and call."

I held my tongue. I inhaled deeply, trying to keep my composure. "We'd better tell him if we're going soon."

Ty snickered and shook his head.

"I'll go see what he's doing," I declared through clenched teeth, glancing over at Donnie, who was only yards away. Ty rolled his eyes but kept silent.

Weaving between sunbathers, I noticed their faces were blurry. I muttered apologies each time my elbows knocked on someone's stuff. Suddenly, a hand grasped my shoulder and a voice cut through the air like glass shattering on a sidewalk. "Hey! Watch it!" I glanced around to see the man with a beer in his hands, now dripping from his skin, as well as his cup. His face was simmering with annoyance. I tried to avoid my missteps, but it seemed things were almost exactly like the fateful day.

Donnie lit up and grinned. "Mom, you made it!" He giggled with joy. He waved an arm toward the sand castle he had constructed. "Let me give you the grand tour."

"It looks beautiful!" I exclaimed. Donnie's sandy fortress was grand enough to be mistaken as an ancient castle. His fort looked just as it did before, with a moat that must have been full of alligators defending the walls of this impenetrable fortress.

Donnie gave me a questionable look. "Beautiful?"

I frantically thought of another phrase I had used that day. "It's as hard as nails," I emphasized, pointing to the walls that were perfectly shaped and placed.

He smirked. "Mom, this is Fort Dragon. Not like those fake flying lizards that shoot fire." He waved his hands around in circles to emphasize what he meant and then returned to showing me around the fortifications he had constructed—from the gatehouse to the watchtower—with great enthusiasm and pride in his voice.

Donnie gave his action figures a respectable distance from each other, as if strategically avoiding surprise attacks. He motioned for me to follow him around the perimeter of Fort Dragon and pointed out where his guards were stationed.

"This base shoots fire at any enemy within a mile," he declared, jabbing a finger toward some sticks placed in the sand in an intentional pattern.

I lifted my left hand in a saluting motion. It looked right. "This base is very secure, Commander Donovan Floyd," I said with utmost seriousness.

Donnie shook his head, trying hard not to smile. "So unrealistic, Mom!"

I tried not to laugh.

I looked at Ty, who was hard-focused on Mandy and the kite. "Hey, Ty!" I exclaimed, calling for his attention.

He turned around with a wide grin smeared across his face and waved at me before turning back to watch Mandy soar the kite higher into the sky again.

Ty looked over and yelled something indecipherable.

"What?" I shouted, trying to make out what he said.

He raised five fingers. I sighed and rolled my eyes before turning back to Donnie.

"Well, it looks like your dad needs to be relieved from his kite-flying duties," I said, putting an arm around Donnie's shoulder. "Let's go explore the beach!"

Donnie put up his hands in protest. "No way! I'm still working on Fort Dragon! I don't want to leave until it's perfect." He turned back towards the fort and knelt to adjust one flag on the turrets he had made earlier.

"I'll be right back," I declared as I walked away.

Donnie replied, "Okay, Mom." He watched as I strutted towards Ty.

I could not change this day. It appeared we would argue every time.

Mandy and Ty kept the kite twirling in the air when I arrived.

"You look like a pro, Mandy! Keep it up!" shouted Ty.

Mandy nodded her head in acknowledgment towards him.

"He needs you," I pleaded desperately. The panic rising in my chest felt overwhelming.

Ty glanced at Donnie, who was playing with his figures, and shook his head in frustration. "I'll be there in a minute. He's fine," he said dryly.

I clenched my fists at my side and struggled to keep my voice steady. "Maybe it doesn't look important to you, but it is. All he wants is for you to be part of it! That's all!"

My cheeks burned as I fought back tears. It felt like I had already lost the battle before it even began. My heart sank. How could I have done things differently?

Ty spun around and bellowed in a voice that rattled between my ears. "WTF, Jen!"

In the corner of my eye, I noticed Donnie glancing over at us, worry etched on his face. Trying to salvage this moment, I made one last plea. "Let me give our other child a few moments."

Mandy floated up in the air, too mesmerized by her kite to pay any heed to us. Thank goodness her attention was elsewhere.

I got close to Donnie and heard a sound that was unmistakable—sobbing. "Are you alright?"

Donnie raised his head, showing me his wet face with tears streaming down.

"Did someone hurt you?" I inquired, feeling my heart break at the sight of him. "Commander Donnie, something happened here."

He clenched his fists, keeping them at his sides as he yelled, "It's not fair, Mommy! It's just not fair!" He had been trying so hard to hold these emotions in for far too long.

I kneeled and placed my hands on Donnie's shoulders. "What's not fair, honey?" I asked him, already knowing his answer.

Donnie flung away from me and faced the base again. He kicked a pile of driftwood in frustration. "Why does Dad always have to be with Mandy and never spend time with me?" he shouted, slamming his foot down on the ground.

This was a rare display of anger from Donnie and never in public. He hadn't had an outburst in months. Little did I know he had been holding this all in.

I responded: "I'm sorry that you feel that way." I could tell he was trying to fight back tears, so I pulled him closer and hugged him tight, trying to take in his smell.

"You're very special to both your dad and me," I told him, squeezing him tightly as we embraced each other. His body relaxed slightly against mine as he leaned into my hug before pulling away.

"Here he comes, honey."

Ty stopped in front of the fort, looking annoyed.

"Your son wants to show you his fort."

Ty's head went up and down like a bobber. "I need to go." He waved his phone in my face, showing the time. His shift started in less than an hour. "Everyone needs to pack up!"

"Nothing? No apology?" I inhaled deeply, knowing what was coming next.

Ty shook his head. "An apology? For what, Jen? What am I supposed to be sorry for this time?" His voice only rose. "Please tell me because that's all it's about lately. I'm tired of all this crap!"

My anger built up inside until it felt like a roaring wildfire. "You're such an ass, Jackson!" It rolled out of me naturally with no effort.

As soon as the words left my mouth, heads popped up with phones in hand.

Ty stared at me in shock. "An ass?" He balled his fists and threw his hands down. "Fuck this!" He stormed away; marching left, right, left, right like a toy soldier. I was hoping for one tiny misstep.

Staring straight ahead, I heard a teen say, "That's savage." The others started laughing. I kept my eyes on Ty, not letting my emotions show through.

Donnie had his arms crossed and looked like he was about to cry. He knew we were fighting. He averted his gaze from the group of teens and instead looked up at me with pleading eyes, asking, "Why is Daddy angry?"

I took a deep breath, feeling powerless, "Because he has work, honey. He's in a rush." I pulled him into a comforting hug and kissed his head.

I glanced at our Explorer, which hadn't moved, hoping this memory would change.

"Donnie," I shouted, "we need to hurry! Gather all your stuff together now."

"I got them all. Marco, Deadlock, Seymour, and Lizzo," he told me proudly of the four action figures.

"You didn't bring Alondra?" I asked, as she was usually right there with the rest of them.

Donnie nodded. "I had to leave her to defend the home base. She was the only one I could trust with the duty."

"Yeah, I thought that about her. She seems to be the true leader."

His voice rose a little. "Alondra worked hard to be promoted, Mom." He blushed. "She's Commander Alondra Sanchez now."

"Wow! You never announced a party for her promotion?"

He shook his head. "Mom, you know Alondra; she doesn't think she's better than anyone else—for her, it's just a normal day."

I glanced at him with admiration. "That's amazing, Donnie!"

Donnie leaped up, pointing and exclaiming excitedly, "Mom, look at Mandy's kite! It's so high," he said in awe, shielding his eyes as he pointed skyward.

I looked skyward to see several kites playing and dancing, their colors contrasting against the stark backdrop of blue sky and coastal clouds. Mandy looked to the sky with Ty's sunglasses perched atop her nose.

"Mandy, it's time to go. Your dad has to go to work."

Mandy would stay here for another six hours if she had the power. The beach was her favorite place, and now she could fly a kite independently. However, the weekly beach visits would not be enough. She would ask for daily trips.

She brought in the kite. "Alright, Mommie. That's ok."

Mandy rarely agreed to do something that involved her having to stop playing.

She grinned with her eyelids shut. "Daddy asked if I wanted to come tomorrow. And he said to keep it a secret."

"Oh, did he? Let's get to the car." Mandy held her kite while Donnie had his backpack on as we walked to our car.

"Okay, I need you two to wait outside while your dad and I talk. I will let you know when we're done."

Donnie and Mandy nodded in agreement as they talked to each other.

I walked to the passenger door and rapped on the window. "Ty, let me in."

The lock clicked, and I pulled open the door.

A wave of cold, musky air hit me with the familiar aroma of Obsession cologne—as much as I hated this moment, I missed his smell. He had both hands gripping the wheel as he stared straight ahead. "I need some time away. I spoke to Ryan—I'm going to stay with him."

His tone was emotionless, and his words left me feeling deflated.

My voice wavering as I asked, "How long have you been planning to leave, Jackson?"

He kept his gaze away from me. "I invited Mandy to the beach," he said. "That's it. The secrets out." His composition was cold.

My mind couldn't process this happening again, so all I could muster was a faint whisper. "And what about Donnie, you fucker?"

His face shifted into an expression of shock, before softening again into one of resignation as he looked at me. "I will ask Donnie later if he wants to come." Then he added, "Please understand that I'm doing this for us."

I could feel the air leave my body. "Alright, Ty."

His goal was to be a perfect father to them, although Donnie wasn't as innocent as he believed.

"I won't be the only one you lose, Ty." I fired my words at him like guided missiles.

He clasped his hands together and refused to meet my gaze. "Jen, let's not fight. A break might do us both some good," he said.

It felt like a bomb going off inside me, completely demolishing the little peace I had left. My heart pounded and chills ran through my body. No matter how much I wanted to change everything, I was stuck in this memory. "What are you saying? What brought this on?" I asked.

Ty didn't move. He had become a robotic version of himself, almost like someone else controlled him. "We need to go, Jen!"

"I will tell the kids it's time."

I opened the door; a cool breeze brushed my skin. I could feel my heart racing with anxious anticipation as I called out, "Mandy, Donnie—it's time to go!"

They both looked at me solemnly and walked silently to their doors.

"Donnie!" Ty called out from behind the wheel as we settled in the car.

"Yeah, Dad?" Donnie replied.

Ty narrowed his gaze and looked back in the rearview mirror. "Do you want to come with Mandy and me tomorrow—to the beach? We can help build a fort!" Super dad exclaimed.

Donnie was suspicious and asked, "What about Mom?"

"Mom has somewhere else to go tomorrow," he replied.

My head bobbed slightly. "Okay, kids, get strapped in."

"Yes, Mommy," Mandy blurted out excitedly. "Donnie and I have our belts on."

"Wave bye to the beach."

"Jenna." I looked to see the car as it dissolved with my family. "Jenna, please open your eyes." D's voice beckoned me to come back to reality.

I opened my eyes, bracing for surprises, as D slowly took the helmet off my head.

The office came into focus, and Jessica was in front of me.

"How are you feeling?" Jessica asked.

"A little dizzy," I replied.

"That's nothing unusual," D stated. "Let's do some breathing exercises. On the count of three, take a deep breath—are you ready?"

"Yes," I confirmed.

"Let's begin, alright? On the count of three. One, two, three; inhale and hold."

I sucked in a deep breath, feeling the air rush into my lungs.

"Now, let it out," D prompted.

I held my breath for an eternity before expelling it from my mouth. The iceberg on my chest seemed to have melted away.

"Good job, Jenna. I want you to do it two more times."

I took two more breaths.

Jessica was sitting next to me now, her voice low and gentle. "Jen, are you ready to continue?" she asked.

I gave a nod in response. "Yes, I am."

"Although this was only a dry run, we had some unique findings during your trip," said Jessica.

"Unique?" I ask inquisitively.

"According to the brain activity we recorded, it looks like you were fully immersed," she explained. Tilting her head towards me, she continued, "It was astonishing to see how much activity you had. Was your experience different from your memory?"

"No, unfortunately not."

D was typing something next to me as I spoke these words.

"Would you like to get breakfast?" Jessica asked.

"Yes, I would."

9

We shuffled out of her office and towards the elevator with a cup of coffee. My heart was racing with every step we took. "Will my trips be this argument over and over?"

"Yes; unfortunately, we need to take you from your baseline. Once we reach that point, you will be marching toward your breakthrough. Then it will be time for a new script."

My throat tightened as I mentioned, "Can this process speed up? This has drained me. I'm completely wiped out." I took a sip of coffee.

Jessica looked me up and down. "I'm so sorry, Jen. You shouldn't even have to do this." She quickly tapped away at her phone with a satisfied smile. "There's a motorized wheelchair coming for you; we can get you straight to your room where you can rest and eat whatever you want."

In front of us, a chair was ominously rolling towards us, coming to a complete stop just inches from Jessica. She scanned it and the display lit up, signaling it was activated. "I think this will be perfect for you," she said.

As I nervously lowered myself into the chair, it hugged me in all the right places. I thanked her silently.

Jessica started walking, and my chair followed, along with no help at all. "How does this thing work?"

"Well," she responded, "just like a self-driving vehicle, it knows where to go with the coordinates. When I scanned it, the program told the chair to follow my phone."

The elevator doors opened, and my cart rolled in after Jessica, my heart racing with what was surely unfounded apprehension.

"Anything you crave for breakfast, the kitchen will prepare it for you here," Jessica declared as we ascended.

My chest tightened, and my breath quickened. Was she serious? The idea of having a meal tailored for me made me feel momentarily paralyzed. With a trembling voice, I uttered, "Wow! The kitchen will make meals specially tailored for me?"

"If you have a request, our kitchen can do it. Obviously, within certain limitations, as everything is sourced locally. Veggies and fruit are seasonal. Most proteins are available year-round except some seafood."

"That's good to know." For the first time in months, I felt hunger stir inside me.

The elevator stopped, and the doors opened. "Sorry again, Jen. Sometimes I get excited with all the perks here. I don't mean to overwhelm you." As she walked out, my chair rolled behind her, making almost no sound.

"That's fine." Deep down, I knew this was a special moment to savor. "I'm looking forward to breakfast."

We made it to Number 13, and the door slid open on cue. Jessica led as the chair followed her in.

"Do you need some time to rest?"

"I'm more than fine." I grabbed the armrests and lifted myself from the contraption, only to feel my legs quiver as I let myself drop back into the chair.

"Jen, please. It's okay. This is not a race. Take as much time as you need. The first time using Remsen can take more than a day to recover. It's a blow physically, mentally, and emotionally. You have lived with this memory daily. Today you re-lived it completely."

I chuckled. "I can see why there is an appeal for using this with happier memories."

Jessica walked over to the dining table, sitting down while my chair followed. "R has been called the feel-good drug. That was never the intention. I have seen Remsen do wonders for many clients. It's been like day and night in a few weeks. I won't call it a miracle drug, but it has worked wonders in a brief time. I believe you will be an ideal candidate for this study."

I glanced towards the panel, a reminder of my connection to the outside. The thought of eating stirred a craving within me, something to keep me going until I headed home with Barb.

"Didn't you say something about breakfast? I'm ready to order."

"Sorry about that. What would you like? They can make anything mostly. They have a full kitchen at your disposal," she replied.

"A greasy cheeseburger. You know the ones where the juice runs out of the bun," I answered automatically, my mind wandering back to simpler times with family and friends.

"Oh, that sounds good," she whispered, her eyes sympathetic.

"And crispy fries with a chocolate milkshake. Wait. Make that a mocha milkshake. Can they do that?" I added, trying to break away from the memories before they dragged me back down.

She nodded. "Would you like anything else?" she asked.

"Will you eat with me?" I blurted out, not wanting to stay in this moment alone.

"Yes, of course. That would be great." She smiled and walked over to the panel, pushing the green button, breaking my paralysis from above.

"Good morning. How can I be of service?" the friendly voice said.

"Hi, this is Jessica. I'm ordering for Jenna Floyd and me," she responded professionally, without missing a beat.

"Hi, Jessica. Yes, go ahead with your order." The response came immediately after hers.

"We would like two extra juicy cheeseburgers with a basket of well-done fries, one mocha milkshake, and a strawberry milkshake." She continued confidently while I stayed mute beside her, frozen in fear of what was coming next if our meal wasn't accepted or arrived too late.

"Sounds good. Your food will arrive in under twenty minutes." The panel dimmed.

"That sounded like an actual human," I whispered.

"It was, and we are completely real at Olympic View. No A.I.s in place of humans," she reassured me gently, stepping closer to end my ever-rising anxiety. "I don't think our clients are looking for that impersonal experience."

"I haven't been able to spend time around others. The class was literally the first time I had been around a crowd since before the accident. People have been my kryptonite. Mostly, I have lived just fine with no contact from the outside world."

"Do you feel lonely? Does it get hard not having contact with other humans?"

"Not with Barb around. I don't miss out. The anxiety I have from just thinking about going out is more than enough to cripple me for the day. I spent three hours sitting in the kitchen with my keys in my hand, debating if I should go to get groceries. I ended up having them delivered."

"What do you hope will come from being a client at Olympic View?"

"To live my life without questioning myself. It always leads down the same rabbit hole. It doesn't take long before I'm reliving our argument. It's like an awful show on repeat, but I can't change the channel. I haven't been able to relive all of our good memories because this one comes up every time."

Jessica took my hand. "You deserve that freedom. I don't know if Remsen will be your answer. There is no magic pill. If you choose to be part of this trial, it won't be easy. I would like for you to attend one more group before you leave today."

The weight of a boulder pulled me down. "Oh. Another group? I was hoping to relax a little."

"You have time. Class doesn't start in." She turned her wrist towards her. "In a little over two hours."

I sighed. "What kind of class is this?"

"This is a client-led group. Specifically, for clients. I think it would be a great opportunity for you to know more about Remsen."

I nodded reluctantly as the door chimed.

"That must be our food," Jessica said, standing up and walking to the door. The door slid open, and a cart rolled into the room. The door slid closed as she rolled the cart to the table.

Jessica lifted the top off the tray, and the smell wafted into my nostrils. I could feel a tear form.

"Are you okay, Jen?" she asked, looking into my eyes.

"This meal. Our last happy time as a family. The kids and I had just ended the school year, and we were at home when he surprised us with a barbecue. Things had been tense between us. I normally wouldn't get home until five, when he was already at work. I didn't realize how much of a relief it was until we were in each other's hair for hours."

"Did Ty resent you or his life, in general?" she asked.

"He loved the kids beyond the stars. But he changed after his band called it quits."

"When was that? Was the band his passion?"

"The Crew. His band was trying to get to the next level, and they were there. And then Covid. They had a West Coast Tour planned for 2020. They never recovered and called it quits in 23. It was like Ty had lost a child. He battled depression for years."

"Did he ever blame you or guilt you?"

"No, he never did. He was still miserable. He felt though he was going to be a lifer at Walmart."

"Did he look for other opportunities?"

"Yes, he did. But most of the jobs were an hour away or further. He grew to enjoy his job. The hours worked great with the kids. Just not the best for our relationship since he was gone five nights a week." I took a sip of the shake.

"Have you ever imagined the world where his band took off? Being on tour for months at a time. It's not the most cohesive for a marriage with kids," Jessica said.

"We talked about touring a lot. Fantasizing about seeing new cities together while taking a travel van with our kids. We would have stayed close. Our lives would have been very different, and I probably wouldn't be here. Nothing personal, Jessica."

She smiled. "I understand. Did Ty and Donnie share any traits?"

I chuckled. "One big one. Ty was an incredible storyteller; he had a way of making things happen when he wanted to. It was magical. Donnie had that magic. He just needed to believe he had it. Ty would get annoyed that Donnie was slow to respond. He took his time, and Ty was a go-getter. So Mandy was perfect with her dad's drive. Donnie clashed more because of that."

"Did they ever spend much time together doing Donnie's activities?"

My eyes became wet. "Yes, the day of the accident. Ty had made it about Donnie. All three worked together building a fort per Donnie's instructions."

"How did you learn this?"

"Ty had filmed it all. His phone was still working after the accident. It felt like a gift from God getting to see the pics and videos he did."

"Did you have mixed emotions seeing it?"

"I almost broke the phone the first time I watched. I felt so angry that he was making the effort and not before. Our argument would have never happened. At least, I don't think it would have."

"Do you think his attempt was his way of reconciling with you?"

"I try not to. He was there for Donnie. Their world ended with at least these moments of happiness."

Jessica folded her hands. "I can't promise Remsen will improve your memory, but I would be honored if you allowed me to lead you on this journey."

"Thank you," was all I could whisper.

10

Jessica and I spent the next couple of hours getting to know each other better before we left for the group. We took the elevator up, and it stopped. The doors opened, revealing the sixth floor, and Jessica left the elevator, turning right. I followed in her wake, trying to keep my breathing under control.

"It's a group for participants run by participants," she stated.

As we strolled along the seemingly never-ending corridor, she informed me it was an open circle, where people could talk about anything. My mind raced as we reached the peach door and my worst fears crept in—what if I couldn't handle it? What if I wanted to leave early?

She saw my apprehensive expression and smiled. "Don't worry," she said. "You can leave anytime you want. This group is wonderful!" As she opened the door, I knew I had to try it, but I wasn't sure how long I would last.

I shuffled in with drooping shoulders. "I don't know."

Jessica flicked her wrist, and the door slid open. "Please, just give it a few minutes."

I entered the dimly lit room, eyeing the recliners with skepticism. "Recliners? Really?"

"It's been found that when participants sit in these chairs, they relax more and are more inclined to talk," Jessica explained as she moved between two empty chairs.

The other members had become quiet, now staring in my direction. I settled into a large chair and it nearly swallowed me whole. "This chair almost makes up for you dragging me around," I mused.

Jessica chuckled. "Almost? Just wait until you see what it can do when you switch it to recline."

The room remained hushed as they all waited for me.

"Do you want to be introduced?" she asked.

I nodded, although I felt uneasy about it. All the participants had broad grins, as if I were the student in class being introduced.

Jessica stepped forward and spoke up. "If I may have everyone's attention?"

The group's smiles only widened as they gazed at me.

"Thank you all for having us," Jessica said.

The clients clinked their glasses in acknowledgment.

"Salud!" one man declared. The others followed suit.

Jessica motioned towards me. "I would like to introduce you all to the newest participant of OVTC. This is Jenna, on her first day."

A woman with bright red hair lifted her glass high. "¡Mucha salud! Welcome to OVTC!"

"Salud!" the rest of them echoed.

"Thanks very much," I responded.

A man with a long white beard waved. "Nice to meet you,"

"We are happy you are here. Would you like something to drink? We have bubblies, water, coffee, tea." A man with yellow hair stood forward, displaying the table with beverages. "I'm sorry for not introducing myself. My name is Aaron."

I felt like rising out of the chair. "Thank you for having me. I'm fine."

Aaron nodded.

Jessica turned towards him. "Aaron, can you tell Jenna a little about this group?"

He looked no older than twenty. I couldn't imagine what had brought him here.

"Thanks, Jessica," He looked my way. "We have classes three times a week: Tuesday, Thursday and Saturday afternoon. Clients are the sole participants in this class." He jokingly wagged his finger at Jessica, who giggled in response.

"I know, I know. This is the last time," she said, backing away towards the door.

"In the almost month since I have been here, you have told me that at least three times already," he added with a smirk.

Jessica arrived at the doorway. "Can you blame me? What you all have going on here is pretty special."

"Jenna, would it be okay if I stepped out for a few minutes?"

"Sure, I'll be fine."

"Don't worry, Jenna. We won't bite," Aaron said, chuckling.

A young woman with mid-length curls giggled. "At least, not right away," she said, standing up to offer me her hand.

I reached out and shook it.

She flashed a mischievous smile. "My name is April Andrews."

I stared back in confusion before Aaron cut in with a guffaw. "That's Samantha," he said.

"The last three newbies all thought she was April," Jessica added.

We had a good laugh at that before Jessica said, "But seriously, they don't bite—I promise." She made her way out of the room, and the door shut behind her.

The room fell silent. I asked. "Who's April Andrews?"

"She's the only one who made it out of here alive." Aaron chuckled. "No, seriously, she was a client here and the only one with a published story online."

"Oh. I guess I will need to look her up," I said.

"Jenna, if you don't mind, we are going to continue where we left off," a woman with glowing silver hair said.

I nodded.

"I'm Mercedes. Day 28. I am the senior member until Aaron takes that spot."

Twenty-eight days, and I hadn't even begun."

"What day are you, Aaron?" I asked.

"Today is day 27," he said.

"Let's come back to the discussion," Mercedes said, and everyone in the room turned their attention towards her. "We were discussing how we can achieve breakthroughs. Several of us have already reached this point and are willing to give tips to those who haven't."

She sounded so sure of herself; I hadn't felt that confident in a long time.

"Hi, my name is Sean, and I'm on day 17," he introduced himself, revealing shoulder-length white hair.

"Sean had his first breakthrough yesterday," Aaron interjected.

"I had been stuck at this one hill for as long as I've been here—it was always my roadblock," Sean explained.

"Sean, can I tell Jenna some of your backstory?" Aaron asked.

Sean nodded in response.

"His wife and two grandkids were on their way to the mountains when it happened. The cattle from a ranch had broken out of their pen. They were on a downhill she never saw," Aaron said.

I exhaled audibly, feeling like a wall was closing around me.

"Jenna, are you okay?" Aaron moved closer to me.

I gestured for him to stay away and said, "I need a minute, please!"

Mercedes broke the quiet. "I apologize if this is too much for you, Jenna. We can talk about something else if you prefer."

My chest lightened. "I'll be okay," I replied. "Please continue."

"We can avoid specifics right now," Mercedes said. "Sean, please tell us what your breakthrough moment was."

"All that time fighting it out on the hilltop, and then I had to pee." Sean sighed wryly.

Mercedes chuckled. "So it worked for you?"

"The trick worked wonderfully. I drank two glasses of water thirty minutes before the session. The experience was surreal, but my urge to go to the bathroom was under control. It felt like my trauma was different this time," he said.

"Different how?" Samantha inquired.

"I had more control over it this time, Sammy. It was like being in a movie."

I could hardly imagine that my day at the beach would ever be as perfect as I wanted it to be, let alone feel like a scene out of a movie.

"This time around, I felt at ease." Sean paused. "My anxiety no longer held me back from reaching new heights."

Aaron posed the question. "Have they given you the rewrite yet?"

Sean responded, "No, my team said I should have it tomorrow."

"How does it work? A rewrite?" I asked.

Mercedes kindly passed me a glass of water, to which I thanked her and took a swig.

Aaron replied, trying to keep it simple, "The rewrite is what your care team comes up with based on your trauma."

Sammy laughed at Aaron's explanation before adding, "You're making it sound too easy!"

"I'll try it," Mercedes declared. She looked deeply into my eyes, and I felt an unease in my stomach. "Your team will work with you to craft a new narrative that transforms the trauma. You will build a fresh memory. It may seem fake, but after enough times it will become your go-to."

"But won't this mean I'm changing my memories?" I asked.

"Yes, only the memories you wish to alter," Mercedes replied.

The room was silent as everyone looked at me expectantly. Finally, I found my voice. "Hi. My name is Jenna, and I hope to join this group soon."

"Salud, Jenna," Aaron said.

The group echoed.

11

We walked into the windowless van, and a faint blue hue slowly filled the space. The screens on the wall had lit up with an aqua-marine animation of fish swimming lazily through a seabed. I felt like I was being drawn deeper in, every inch of me tensing up.

"Oh jeez, sorry, Jen!" She fluttered her finger across the display panel, and the screens transitioned to a stark white blankness that illuminated the vehicle even more. "Here, you can start customizing it with any wallpaper you want..."

I shook my head. "No, it's alright. Let's keep it as is for now."

She inclined her neck, squinting her eyes. "How are you feeling? I understand that the first trip can be overwhelming. Trauma is real to us. Nothing can prepare us for such an experience."

I couldn't find my voice. My throat felt like it was closing in on me, making it hard to concentrate. "They were there, Jessica. Ty, Mandy, and Donnie. All of them are in front of me. It felt so real that I could smell them, touch them, and feel them; it was like it was happening for the first time and I had no power to change it. I wanted to, but with every word I spoke, the truth stayed unchanged. Despite how powerless I felt, I didn't want to leave—what if I could make a difference this time? The only thing that was off was the blurred faces of people around us, as if they weren't meant to be part of the picture at all."

"That's normal," she responded gently, soothing my racing heart. "Think of it as a structure. The dosage helps build up the structure and give your experience clarity." She continued, "If you agree to participate in the study, your dosage will double what it was today. This dosage will only heighten your experience and make everything seem more surreal."

"Will it get better?" I murmured.

Jessica flinched and then exhaled. "If you can reach the breakthrough within thirteen days or sooner, that's good news. Then the hard part is creating a fresh memory to replace your old one. But until then, you'll have to keep dealing with the weight of this memory."

"It feels impossible to fathom. My brain gets stuck in a loop of all the what-ifs. What if I hadn't pushed Ty away? Maybe they'd be alive today. Even if Ty and I weren't together, that would have been more bearable than this empty house I go to every night."

She paused and considered her next words. "I suggest you read an article written by one of our clients enrolled in the home study. I'll email you the link so that you can check it out. Although her trauma differs from yours, she achieved success with Remsen—most of the information available online is only about its illegal version available on the streets."

"April Andrews!" I shot out.

"That's the one." The vehicle came to a halt. "We are back."

Back to the dystopian center. "If I enroll, will I have to come back here to Waldren?"

The doors slid open, and we exited the vehicle.

"We'll be doing background checks on you and Barbara if you decide to enroll; if everything is clear, you can enter through Olympic View." She started walking towards the entrance, and I felt compelled to follow her. "Please remember," she admonished, "you are under a confidentiality clause; you can mention your classes but no one's names. Everything else is free game." She reached into her pocket and handed me a card with a Q on it. "Here is my E-card. If you have questions regarding enrollment or anything else, text me anytime; normally, I answer in under an hour."

My heart raced as the doors opened to the lobby. There she was, Barb, my beacon of hope: short but powerful. Standing with arms wide open, sporting her usual uniform of dark dress slacks and an unbuttoned light blue shirt; her style had never changed since we were kids. I was always in awe of Barb's strength and confidence.

"I was getting anxious..." Her voice infiltrated my thoughts. We embraced tightly, like a security blanket for two anxious humans.

"I apologize, Barb. Jen was in a group that went a little over the scheduled time. How was your stay at the B&B?"

"Jessica, can I talk with you? Alone." Barb's eyes burned into Jessica, and she reluctantly agreed.

I held my breath as they walked to the corner. Barb uttered something in a hushed tone and kept talking. Jessica turned towards me and winked, but her expression displayed a sense of dread. The one-sided conversation finally ended, and they slinked back.

"So, Jessica," Barb whispered. "Is Jen going to be living here?"

Jessica gave a small sigh. "I will contact Jen tomorrow with her acceptance information. It is ultimately her choice if she takes part in this study—I think she would be an exemplary patient for Remsen therapy."

"That's...great. Thank you for giving Jen the opportunity." Barb put out her hand to shake Jessica's. "Hopefully, we'll see you again then."

I stepped forward and enveloped Jessica in a hug. She hesitantly put her arms around me. We embraced for several seconds as I whispered my gratitude. "Thank you for making me feel safe," I mumbled.

Jessica pulled away and looked me in the eye with an intense expression of understanding and warmth. "You are so welcome, Jen," she whispered. "I want you to feel secure when you are here."

12

My heart raced as Barb, and I got into her Mercedes. She touched my knee lightly, sending shivers down my spine. "I need to hear everything as soon as we get out of this hellhole."

The engine hummed, and we moved towards the exit. I glimpsed at the man in the turret, their gun ready to fire at any time. As we neared the heavily fortified gate, Barb lowered her window. "Commander Hughes!" she shouted out with a hint of familiarity.

The massive gate slowly opened, and Commander Hughes shuffled over. "Yes, Barb."

"If you're up for excitement, we could use your help," Barb pleaded.

He smirked knowingly. "Thank you, Barb, but I'm sure what I make here is much more than I could earn working any government job."

"Well, in that case," Barb said jokingly, "where do I sign up?"

He chuckled softly. "Nice seeing you again, Barb," he replied before we exited the facility.

As we exited the property, Barb pushed a button on the console and the car took over the driving. "I hope this Remsen is worth it. I'm having a hard time trusting Quantos. They seem hellbent on world domination."

"You're being a little dramatic, Barb. Quantos is like any other company. They are there to make money. I only care if Remsen works for me. The last year has been a living hell for you and me. And I'm so sorry to put you through this. I need you to trust that I can make the right decision."

Barb huffed and looked away. "Is Jessica as sincere as she seems?"

"She is. At least from the time I was with her. I don't think I could handle any other clinician."

"What was it like? Being on Remsen. Were you there, reliving your memory?"

I turned to meet her gaze. "It felt surreal. I could feel everything. The ocean breeze, the burning rays from the sun, and most of all, my family. I didn't want to leave. I wanted to tell Ty sorry, but I couldn't. I wanted everything to be different, but it was the same memory in living color."

"And what do they want from you? What can they change or fix?"

"They want to script a fresh memory for me. I will swap for this one." I chuckled. "It's not a swap. It's learning a new script like I'm in a play having to perform the new scenes. But only after I reach my breakthrough."

"Wasn't that what you had today? How much longer do they want you to wrestle with your memory?"

I looked out the window as we entered the 101 on our way home. "It takes almost two weeks to get to that point. Maybe I will be there sooner."

"Jen, do you think you can relive this over and over? You haven't been able to leave your home."

"I know, Barb. And I also know I battle this memory daily. And even though I was reliving it, they were there. I could smell them. So yes, I want to give this a try."

My phone chimed, and I pulled it from my bag, looking at the message.

"What was that?" Barb questioned.

"It's Jessica. She sent me a link to a story by a participant. I think I will check this out tomorrow morning."

Barb reached over, tapping my leg. "Guess who came up to visit?"

I was so exhausted I couldn't give any answer. "I don't know."

"Adam flew in last night trying for a surprise. He didn't know I was in Olympia."

"Don't you guys keep tabs on each other? I mean, you are married."

"On paper. That's it. We have a good thing going."

Barb was on her third marriage. This was her first open relationship, and it seemed to go better than the previous two. It helped that Adam Gibson lived over a thousand miles away in Vegas.

"We want to have a little get-together Friday evening if you are up for it."

I could feel my stomach knot up. "Hmm. Yeah, possibly," I said, knowing I had three days to think about it.

"How about tomorrow you and I go visit Billy's in the afternoon? We can have some drinks and unwind. You're going to be in that fancy resort for a month taking their designer drug. I'm going to miss seeing you."

"Isn't he going to be jealous that you're spending your time with me?"

"Adam is always busy. He finds something to do with his money. He was hinting at renting a yacht this weekend."

"That sounds romantic. You guys normally do your thing in Vegas. Is he making more of an effort?"

"Maybe so. I don't see him staying here longer than a few weeks. He doesn't like the cold."

I chuckled. "Wait, he likes you. How can he not like the cold?"

Barb smiled. "Whatever, Jen. So, have you put any more thought into selling your place?"

"I think I'm ready to do it. Do you think I can get more than the market value?"

"With some minor improvements, you probably can. Adam offered to have one of his guys look at it and come with an affordable fix-up."

"How much is this going to cost? I don't want to use all the money I get from the study."

"What if while we're at Billy's tomorrow, Adam checks it out, and gives you an estimate?"

"He can do that?"

"Yes, of course, and it will give him something to do tomorrow. He can talk to his man and they can come up with something."

Adam Gibson was worth eight digits or more. He started as a roofer and now owns his construction business. "That's great! Yes, please, I will take the help."

"He will be so happy to help. And you can stay at our place until you find something."

"You don't have to do that."

"Jen, I insist. You will be at the far end of the house so you can have your privacy."

They had just completed construction on their new domicile. Seven bedrooms and eight baths. Enough room for a few guests. "Thank you, Barb. For everything."

She gave a slight nod. "Do you see yourself staying here, in Aberdeen, in Washington?"

"I don't know, Barb. If I stay in the study, they will pay me twenty-five hundred a day, and said I can travel as much as I want."

Barb rolled her eyes. "Where would you go? I mean, you haven't even left the West Coast."

"Every time I fantasized about leaving this place, it crashed down on me with no money. I have been trapped. With money, I can take a trip anywhere and be very comfortable. I may close my eyes and put a pin somewhere on our map." We had a world map and each of us placed colored pins in the places we most like to see.

"Do you feel safe traveling the world alone? It's not like you can leave your job."

I quivered at the thought of Barb being overly aggressive at some resort.

"I will not keep living in fear. That hasn't gotten me anywhere. I need to live as best I can, as this may be my only opportunity." This may free Barb from the endless sob sessions she had endured.

"Okay, well, why don't we just take this day by day? You still need to enter the study and see if this will work for you."

I yawned.

Barb looked forward and put her hands on the wheel, turning off the auto drive. "I'm going to put some music on. Try to rest. We are almost home."

I reclined my seat and closed my eyes, fantasizing about seeing my family again.

13

My sleepless mind raced through the night, circling round and round questions about Remsen and what it was. I needed answers. I had to step away from my prison and into the vast unknown.

My hands trembled on the steering wheel—it had been months since I'd driven, but I needed to get to our cafe. I could almost hear Ty's encouraging voice pushing me forward, willing me to get leave my self-imposed prison and into the unknown. With an uncertain breath, I pushed forward towards the horizon.

The same cafe we visited before the accident loomed ahead of me. My body hadn't shifted positions during the drive; I felt exposed as memories of that fateful day rushed back to me. I took a deep breath—I could do this. After all, what choice did I have? I had to face my fears if I ever wanted to move on from the darkness haunting me.

I was wearing Ty's A's cap pulled down tight so that it stretched over my ears until the bill was to my nose. I walked into the cafe with

Nirvana blasting through their stereo, making eye contact with no one as I scanned for familiar faces.

"Welcome to Broomstick Cafe. What can I get you?" the barista asked.

I whispered, "Can I get a large mocha latte with two shots?"

"Sounds good. Would you be interested in anything else?" she asked.

"Not right now."

"That will be $6.50, and can I get your name?" she asked.

I stumbled on my tongue. "It's Jane," I said, knowing no one named Jane.

I paid with my phone and sat down. Things looked unchanged from the last time I had been here with Ty. I closed my eyes, and the memory was fresh in my mind.

"Wow, babe, that was exceptional! You had your best time today!" Ty exclaimed.

"I feel great," I said.

I won an entry in the NYC marathon. As soon as they sent me the announcement, I started training hard. Ty and I were planning a week away in November, just us. It would be the first time away from the kids since they were tiny.

"I think you will be more than ready," Ty said.

"Thank you." I kissed him. "I still can't believe we are doing this," I said.

"Of course, babe. This is all you. I would have never imagined this. And you're doing it. How do you feel overall?" he asked.

"I feel amazing. I would have never imagined taking ten-mile runs, and now I do it without thinking."

"I'm so proud of you," Ty said.

"I love you."

Weeks later, we were ready for divorce. It has been hard for me to remember the enjoyable moments we had. He was a good man.

"Jane," the barista said as my head slowly popped to my new name. "Your order is ready."

I got up and grabbed my coffee. "Thank you."

She nodded at me. I sat back down with my laptop in front of me. It was time to find out what this Remsen was about.

Against Jessica's advice, I wanted to see what R was really about since I was taking the same drug. Thousands of results came up. The top ones were not what I was hoping for.

'R may be the next big drug that sweeps the streets.' N.Y. Times

'Another O.D. at the hands of R.' L.A. Times

'Woman wants to take on big pharma for unleashing R onto the streets.' Vice News

I scrolled down until I saw one article worth opening.

Tech Billionaire's son dies at the hands of R Mercury News 03/15/30

Tech Billionaire Gavin Stephens' 17-year-old son Gavin Stephens II died of an overdose from the designer drug R. The drug, which has taken the streets by storm, has seen a 1000% increase in street value in just six months.

Quantos Pharma originally developed R and became part of a large-scale theft of over one million cartridges. FDA and DEA launched a full investigation and could not attain any further leads on who is responsible.

It's unknown how Gavin II got access to this drug, but it's believed that a friend or dealer may have provided it. His mother Rema Stephens discovered her son was unresponsive and called 9-1-1. Once medical personnel arrived, they found Gavin not breathing. He was declared dead shortly after.

We reached out to Quantos for a response and they provided this:

To Gavin's family, we are saddened that our drug intended for trauma patients ended up on the streets where it could be potentially abused. Quantos Pharma will give over one million dollars to participating law enforcement agencies to help eradicate the streets of R. We want to do our part to avoid this from happening again.

It is now believed R is being created synthetically. Reports are the newer cartridges are being laced with more powerful opiates.

Gavin's death marks the 23rd overdose caused by R in the United States. It is now believed there have been three overdose deaths in Germany and possibly more in Europe.

I closed the computer and took a sip of coffee. The walls had several pieces of local art for sale. Each offering had the artist's name and the town they lived in. Many times I imagined Donnie having his work on display.

I opened the link Jessica had provided, and the page opened.

I took a trip to my past and my present.

By April Andrews

April 5, 2030

Some may say dreams are just messages from our minds. With Remsen, I changed my past to better my future. You know when you can remember things so clearly; they feel like they just happened, even if it was many years ago. I took a trip back in time sans a time machine. I exaggerated a smidge.

They named the drug Remsen for Remember/Sensory. Quantos Pharma developed it over two years ago to treat PTSD victims. The drug works by inhalation and enters the bloodstream within seconds. Remsen is only the blank canvas that can give people the 'trip' to that memory.

Finding any fix seems unrealistic for trauma victims without drugs that can have serious side effects. I had been a victim of an abusive father who was an alcoholic. If he wasn't hitting my mother, he would slap me. This became a pattern for me and my relationships in my life.

In June 2028, my boyfriend of two years sexually assaulted me. Several weeks later, I had a breakdown and spent two weeks in a mental care facility. One day I will never forget. A doctor I had never met walked into my room and offered me the chance to be part of a clinical trial for a potential breakthrough for PTSD and Trauma Victims.

After the assault, I isolated myself, avoiding my family and friends. I gave up my social life and stopped feeling motivated to live my everyday life. After a stay in a mental health center, an intake coordinator contacted me. The next week, I was touring their treatment facility.

After my interview, I was invited to take part in the Remsen trial. They offered no guarantees in my treatment.

Over the past forty-five days, my life has transformed. There is a social life for me again. I feel motivated to be active and take care of myself, and overall, I'm much happier. I don't go to bed fearing nightmares. My dreams are now empowering for me.

DISCLAIMER: I am still taking part in the trial at home. I have written this story with consent from Quantos Pharma. They have never asked to edit this story or offered to pay. I receive money from Quantos as a continuing participant in the Remsen study.

DAY 1: I didn't know what to expect as I walked into the therapist's office. I was called into a separate office where I met with a therapist named "Carol". She spent the first session getting to know me better and understanding what triggers I may have. We spoke about the events that have brought me here. We also talked about positive memories.

DAY 2: Carol met me as I entered the lobby of Olympic View. This would be my home for the next thirty days. Carol asked about before and after incidents that happened in my life. Today we talked more about past events.

DAY 3: Today was my first "TRIP".

"Jane?"

I looked up to see the woman who had served me.

"Do I remember you?" she asked. "Your face looks so familiar."

I giggled uncomfortably. "Yes, my husband and I used to come here weekly."

Her smile went flat. I became used to seeing that look since the accident.

"Oh. Jenna." She leaned back. "I'm so sorry for your loss," the barista said.

"It's alright. It's been a year. Over a year now," I said. It felt like an accomplishment.

I could see her face regain form. "We had that art memorial here for weeks," she said.

The cafe helped raise money for funeral expenses.

"I appreciated that so much," I said.

I had no clue it was until some people came to my house with a check. It felt so awkward taking money after losing my family.

"Anything you need, just ask. Next coffee is no charge."

"Thank you so much," I said, turning to the computer.

"Any time, Jen. That's your name? Right?" the barista asked.

Another reason to avoid people. "Yes, it is. Thank you again."

She turned to the counter where a couple of people were standing.

"I have to get back to work," the barista said.

I nodded, and she walked away.

I turned towards the computer. *Where am I? Day 3.*

DAY 3: Today was my first "TRIP". It was only a quick hello and a few questions from my clinician, and off I went. At first, it felt like a dream until I could smell, touch, and feel everything around me. Things felt surreal, and I was afraid to touch anything. That was when I started noticing details I didn't remember from that day. I was in my apartment just as I remembered. I appeared in the kitchen. The lightly seasoned chicken was in the oven. It's a smell I won't forget.

When you begin the trip, they ask you for a trigger. The trigger helps the client achieve a clear memory better. They use a device that allows recreating scents a powerful way to provoke memories.

In my apartment, things looked the same. My mind had stored so much detail that seemed blurry when I would try to remember. My ex, the assailant, was in the living room playing his favorite shoot 'em-up game. He was cursing into his headset. Loud enough that it shook me. This moment was becoming harder and harder. It felt like this was my reality, and it trapped me.

I started taking deep breaths, not wanting to be pulled out of this so soon. I left the apartment and started walking down the hall. Once I felt better, I returned to the apartment.

"Babe?" the assailant asked.

Reliving this moment was terrifying. My emotions came back to life. Except for this time, I knew what was going to happen.

"What is it?" I asked.

My mouth was dry. I walked into the kitchen, grabbed a cup, and hit the faucet.

"Get me a beer while you're in there," he demanded.

It was six beers before he had his way with me. If I remember right, this would be number five.

I looked in the fridge to see we had a lot of lunch meat. More than I remember. It was full of beer.

When he had this many beers in him, I hoped he kept drinking until he passed out on the recliner. Normally, between beers 4-8, he would be nasty. After that, he would pass out with the game controller on his lap. It was those moments that made me think he was peaceful. Unfortunately, this would not be one of those nights. It would be less than an hour later that he sexually assaulted me.

It took weeks before I had my first 'breakthrough'. A breakthrough is when you can alter the memory. Some participants take a week to achieve this, while some never get to this point.

Weeks!?! I need results in days.

I had success working on my traumas. It hadn't been easy by any means. My clinician told me I may continue this study for up to 36 months. I couldn't imagine doing this for over two more years. Still, I can see significant improvements in my personal life. I was fortunate enough to alter the memory. I made the assailant fall asleep in a puddle of vomit. I wasn't able to make him stop drinking for good. I could get out of the memory safely.

After I changed the memory, I could leave the memory without feeling trapped. I could re-enter that moment without fear. I could feel that memory without pain. I could look around without fear. That night, I could fall asleep without the fear of nightmares.

I have been given a gift to alter my memories. I'm still in the trial, and I don't know if that is permanent. I will never forget how it felt to be trapped in a memory that traumatized me. I know what the memories of other victims feel like. I was lucky enough to make the memories go away. In a way, this has saved my life.

I closed the computer. I wasn't trying to measure anyone's traumas. The article gave me hope. If it wasn't for Barb, I don't know where I would be. I had pushed her away more than anyone, and she kept coming headstrong like a bull.

"Hi, Jenna."

I raised my head and did a double-take. "Monique? Is it you?" I asked.

It was. I knew that face. The years had been good to her, or the augmentations had been.

"You look good, Jen." Her voice was tepid. "It's been quite a few years."

"Yeah, it has been," I said.

Monique had met her 'love' online and moved away. I remember her saying how she was so ready to leave this place.

"You look great," I said.

"We need to catch up. Oh, I'm so sorry." Monique turned to another woman. "This is Tara, my spouse."

She looks like a supermodel.

"Are you visiting?" I asked.

Monique kissed Tara. "We just moved to Aberdeen. Tara saw the real estate prices and insisted we come here," Monique said.

Tara looked into my eyes. "Yeah, I couldn't resist this place. It's like a hidden gem." She took a bite of her pastry. "Moni would always tell me about her high school days in Aberdeen."

"I love it here. Aberdeen has blossomed," Monique said.

I laughed. *Now we are home to Barb's mansion.* "And only getting better," I said.

I winked at Tara, who winked back.

"Let me get your number, Jen. We can hang out sometime. Are you still with Ty?" Monique asked.

I looked down. "No, I'm not." I took a deep breath. *Finally, someone who doesn't know my history.* "My number is 360-461-7336," I said.

Monique was tapping her phone. "And there. Did you get my text?" she asked.

A message with a heart appeared. I replied with my emoji making a rainbow.

"Looks like you did."

"I'll text you later," I said.

"Sounds good, Jen. It was so nice seeing you," Monique said.

I stood and hugged her.

Moniques' smiles are more plastic than I remember.

"Nice meeting you," Tara said, grasping me tight. Our hug broke, and she followed Monique out. I watched as they got into a very nice car. It looked like they were doing well.

I looked at the clock. An hour has passed since I got here. I closed my computer and took a deep inhale. Monday couldn't come soon enough.

14

Barb dragged me to Billy's, knowing she could begin her interrogation. After a few drinks and some glorious memories, she brought me back to reality.

After two beers Barb was sipping tea while I was on my third adult beverage. "I don't think Remsen is good news. I don't think Quantos is good news. Did you read that article I sent you?" she asked.

I'd had a few drinks and still wasn't ready for her attack.

I shook my head, lying. "Can you summarize it for me?"

Barb smiled slightly, pulled her phone from her pocket, and started scrolling. "Here it is and I quote. 'The Seattle metro area has seen a dramatic increase in R overdoses. Since May of this year, there have been seven ODs. The previous 18 months had only seen five ODs. The identities of some of these users are unknown.' Jen, this is serious. I don't trust Quantos. You could end up on the street, and they could make some story about how you got out there."

"What does that mean? Come on, Barb. Jessica assured me I would only take small doses of Remsen. The ODs are over 100 micrograms. The most I will take is sixty."

A server approached our table. "I have your onion rings." She placed the tray between us, chuckling. "Are you two gonna eat all of those?"

Barb used her hand to shoo her away. "Thank you; that will be it."

"Of course, that's what they say. They also want results."

I need to stay calm. She's interrogating again. "Can we just talk about something not related to my life?"

She took a sip of her tea. "Sorry, Jen. The homicide case earlier this year. Do you remember?"

"Was the victim's name Kendra?"

Murders were rare around these parts. People finally turned their attention from my family to this.

She put her fingers in front of my mouth. "Not so loud. Don't need anybody hearing this."

"Sorry, Barb. Mums the word."

"When this case broke, the boyfriend became the prime suspect. It didn't take long for us to clear him and go in another direction."

I nodded. "Wasn't it a business owner who found her body in a dumpster?"

"Yeah, they were just taking garbage out when they saw her leg."

"That must have been horrible."

"The killer was sloppy. What do you expect for a bargain price? The dots eventually led to the father. He is going to be charged with first-degree murder."

I shook my head. "The dad? Wasn't he on the news saying how he wanted the boyfriend to admit to murdering his precious baby?" I asked.

Barb snickered. "The dad was at home in Portland. He thought that kept his alibi airtight. He told us she ran with her boyfriend, and that's who killed her. It made sense until we dug deeper."

"Wow! This beats all the podcasts." Maybe not the best distraction, but it was working.

"We interviewed the boyfriend who claimed it was the father abusing her. He told the detectives where she hid the journals in the popcorn ceiling in her room. It felt weird. He said Kendra kept it hidden to use as evidence." She took a bite of an onion ring. "So we know we can't get a warrant, and I decide to take a deputy with me to Portland, and we got another officer from the PPB to accompany us. We knocked on the door, and the mom answered."

"Oh, wow. How did she react?" I asked.

"It's tough to say how much involvement another parent may have. It looks like there was some abuse when she was younger," said Barb. She dipped an onion ring in ranch and popped it into her mouth. "I think the mother knew about it and covered for him. It had probably been going on for years. Pretty sick."

"Didn't they put those god-awful ceilings in college dorms, or maybe it was just offices where they don't want the employees to feel comfortable?"

Barb nodded. "It's like being trapped under a sterile sky. Can you believe that?" she continued, taking a big bite of her onion ring. She raised an eyebrow questioningly and asked, "Kids are obsessed with phones and technology, so who still writes in a paper journal?"

I laughed at how out of touch Barb sounded.

"How many journals did Kendra have?" I asked, curious.

"She had four," Barb replied in between bites. "They started when she was only thirteen until a week before her murder. At first, they were just about her dreams and crushes, but then they got darker; she couldn't wait to escape her parents."

"Was her father monitoring her?" I asked.

"The dad, I mean murderer, was monitoring her through his phone. She didn't have any way out," Barb said thoughtfully. "Once she got a boyfriend, the dad couldn't take it anymore—he wanted complete control over everything she did outside of school. Most of the abuse wasn't physical, but when it was, she would take pictures and put them in her journal as evidence. In the end, though, it took her death for anyone to find out what she was going through."

I nodded.

"Long story short, the boyfriend stole his parents' car, and they got up here." She took another onion ring. "Kendra's dad had one of those tracking apps on her phone."

"So he hired someone?"

"He hired a hitman on one of those service sites. Insane when you think about it. This mother f'er hired someone off a site to kill his daughter. For a thousand dollars."

Barb took a personal interest in Kendra's case. She paid for all the funeral expenses anonymously, but a local radio station heard the rumor and broke it on their morning show.

"Congrats, Barb. This must have been exhausting."

"It took everything out of me. I won't be satisfied until the jury finds him guilty."

"I hope that day comes soon."

Barb gave a slight nod. "How are you doing? You haven't been to Billy's since the day."

"Well, I'm not sober, so that helps. I didn't think about it until you mentioned it."

"I'm sorry." Barb waved to the server. "You want another of those?" She pointed to my nearly empty drink, and I nodded as the server approached. "Can I get another electric peach for my friend?"

"Sure thing. I will be back shortly with it," the server said, walking towards the bar.

Barb's phone started vibrating on the table, and she looked at me. "He's face timing."

"Oh." I faked a smile.

"Adam! How's it going?" Her voice came out sounding more pleasant than I normally hear it. "Jen and I are still at Billy's." She turned her phone in my direction.

"Hey, Adam." He was standing in my living room.

"What's the news?" Barb asked as she pulled the phone back so I could see.

"Jen, your home has great bones. We can get it in great condition to sell for less than 20k."

I looked down. "Wow! When can you start?"

"I can have a crew here next week. They will be out before you get back."

"You can do that?" I asked.

"It won't be a problem. I have a few guys eager to get out of the Vegas heat for a few weeks."

"I don't know how to thank you."

"You mean the world to us, Jen. You deserve to sell your home or keep it. When you get back, you can make that decision," Adam said gleefully.

"Thank you. I'm in no place to decide right now. Barb had to drag me out to get me here."

Adam laughed. "I hope we can drag you to Vegas soon enough."

I swallowed. "I think I will be ready for that trip."

"Yes, you will," Barb said.

$$15$$

Barb insisted I spend Sunday afternoon at her enormous home for a crab boil. I wanted to stay home and prepare for my stay at OVTC. She didn't take no for an answer, saying Adam and Andy caught enough fish to feed a small army.

The patio covered much of the back with a covered kitchen and lounge area. Barb and Andy were busy tending to the grill, while Adam and I sipped homemade cocktails and admired the view below the deck.

"Thank you so much for coming, Jen," he said. "This means a lot to Barb. She doesn't express it well, but you mean the world to her."

My heart fluttered. "Thank you for saying that, Adam," I said. "Despite knowing each other since childhood, Barb has always been high-strung."

Adam chuckled softly. "If we met as kids, we probably would have never been friends."

I forced out a laugh, despite my nervousness. "So, how was your fishing trip?"

He shook his head. "I guess there's a reason I'm a desert dweller. The sea looks beautiful from afar, but it's a whole other monster in it. Have you been on a boat?"

I nodded.

"I fantasized about having a yacht. I think the fantasy is quelled. No amount of Dramamine can make it any more appealing."

"That is the worst feeling. How did you make it?"

Adam chuckled. "On an empty stomach." He looked over my shoulder. "I will leave the fishing to the pros like Andy."

Andy approached, smiling. "Auntie Jenna, it's so good to see you." I gave him a big embrace. He was one of the few who still visited me.

"I'm going to check on Barb. Make sure she's not part of the boil." Adam chuckled as he walked away.

I smiled and turned to Andy. "You look good. I heard you started working in the sheriff's office. How are you liking it?"

"Everyone is super cool. I keep getting warned to watch out for this hard ass."

I smiled. "Oh. Are you related to them?"

He laughed. "You know it. If I could survive having Barb as my aunt, I think I can survive anything."

"You know her better than most." Besides my kids, Barb has been fiercely protective of Andy since day one. "How was the fishing trip?"

"I caught a couple of salmon and a lingcod."

"Wow! That must have been something to watch."

"Adam filmed me reeling in a salmon."

"I haven't had salmon in months. I miss Ty grilling it."

Andy looked in Barb's direction. "I think she needs me."

I walked to the edge of the patio and took in the view of Aberdeen. Everything seemed like slow motion as a gull attempted a westward flight against the wind. Below, the town moved in harmony. Cars moved in a rhythm as they made their journey across town.

"Is it a million-dollar view?" Barb walked up from behind, holding out a drink for me.

"Multi-million dollar view. It's incredible."

"It helps when your husband is in construction. Look at this." She walked to the edge of the deck. "The deck goes over twenty feet past the hillside. It took Adam's vision to see this view." She approached me. "I want you to live with us as soon as you leave that place. We have a huge guest room that needs your company. You sell your home and stay with us until you know your next steps."

I shook my head.

"I'm sorry if I sound like you have a choice. You will stay with us once you leave that place. There is nothing to hold you except memories."

"Thank you, Barb. I don't want to impose." Her home was nearly 5k square feet, not including the two acres of land it sat on.

She scoffed. "The guest suite is over fifty feet from my room. If anything, you may need to call me because you get lost."

I chuckled. "Fine, Barb. Once I graduate summer school, I will come over."

"How are you feeling about tomorrow?"

"A little anxious. Not sure if this is even real. I was there. It was like someone had filmed my day at the beach and I was the star. I didn't want to be there, but I was. Reliving my nightmare, this time in a surreal vision."

"Are you sure you want this?" Barb asked.

"I do. The clients I met, you could see life in their eyes. It was like they broke through the darkness. I can't keep living like this."

A bell clanged back and forth. "Dinner is ready," Adam announced.

Barb took my hand as we walked to the table. "You are sitting at the head of the table."

The table had a platter full of crab, sausage, corn, and potatoes. The fish was wrapped in foil.

"This is my first crab boil," I said.

"Adam and I went to one in Maine, and we knew this was the perfect opportunity."

"Auntie Jen, can I give you this one?" Andy pointed to a crab.

I nodded. "Thank you so much."

"Of course."

"This is wonderful. Thank you all for having me."

Barb nods slightly. "You think this meal is free? Oh, Jen."

Adam chuckled. "You get to do the next fishing trip."

"Yes, I will." If I could get through the next thirty days, I was up for anything.

"Great!" Adam exclaimed. "Next crab boil will be in five weeks."

My smile faded a bit. "You've set some pretty big goals for yourself," I said as Andy served the food and Barb topped off our wine glasses.

"There's no other way when you want to be successful," he replied, tapping his glass with a fork to get everyone's attention. "I'd like to raise a toast to Jen."

I raised my eyebrows in surprise.

"Jen, you have been through so much in the last year, yet here you are, standing strong. What you have gone through is an amazing example of your strength and courage. It's an honor to be here tonight on your journey. Let us all cheer for Jen and all she has accomplished—and all she will continue to do!"

Everyone clinked their glasses together in celebration.

"I would like to add a little more," Barb said with a grin. "I would have never met Jen if I didn't underestimate her. We were in elementary school, and I was picking my team for kickball. The other team was a player short. I saw this fragile-looking blonde and told her she had to play. She did. I couldn't even imagine her being able to kick the ball, but she ended up kicking two home runs and being the star. Since that moment, we have been friends. Even though I seem the strong one, it has always been Jen keeping me from losing it."

"Barb, please," I said with my wineglass in hand. "I bet if you let ten bad guys choose the tough one, they would all point at you."

Everyone laughed at my attempt at humor.

Andy raised his glass and said, "To my Auntie Jen: When I was in 6th grade, a boy had been bullying me. One day after school, she came to pick me up and saw the bully holding my pack. She walked over and told him to leave me alone. After that day, I knew she had some magic because the boy never messed with me again."

I broke out laughing, saying, "He sure didn't know what he was in for."

We all laughed as we clinked our glasses together.

"What are your thoughts about tomorrow, Jen?" Adam asked.

"I'm apprehensive. I know what to expect, but I haven't been away from home for more than a couple of weeks."

"I'm sure by Wednesday you'll have the place memorized."

I shook my head. "No way. Olympic View is enormous. I got more steps in one day than I had in a month."

"Unbelievable. This facility is just for one study? How many people are there?" Adam asked.

"When I was there, it was less than 50. Now they are opening some shops and additional restaurants."

Barb stood up. "For whom? Who does Quantos plan to give this drug to?"

"I'm not entirely certain," I answered.

"Like I said before, I don't trust this Quantos company; they're intent on achieving positive results no matter what the cost." Barb spun around and vanished inside her home.

Adam sighed as he turned toward me. "Sorry about Barb; you know her better than me."

A smile crept onto my face as I joked, "Yeah, after being there a week, she'll be begging me to take her with me."

Adam let out a chuckle before turning serious. "More importantly, how can I get into Remsen?"

"Do you have a traumatic memory?"

He nodded. "It has haunted me for most of my life. When I was eight and my older brother Jayden—whom I idolized more than anything—was eleven, we went to our secret swimming spot on a hot summer day. Unfortunately, he got caught in a rip current and drowned. Only the two of us and a few other children were there, unable to do anything; it was long before cell phones even existed. I have dreamt about witnessing his drowning multiple times over the years. It's like a nightmare that won't go away."

"I'm so sorry, Adam; I did not know. I don't know how to get an invitation. You could always try their website and talk live with someone."

Adam started tapping on his phone. "Perfect! I'll contact them tomorrow."

Andy looked at me. "Why is she so concerned? She's behaving like they are kidnapping you to conduct some experiment."

"You know Barb well enough to understand she doesn't like change—or rather, change she can't control," I said.

They nodded in understanding.

"You won't be stranded if Barb bails. I promise I'll get you there," Adam assured me. I promise I'll get you there," Adam assured me.

"Thank you, Adam. You're the best."

"You shouldn't have to go through this every day. I'm glad you're doing this—it's a big step. I hope it brings back your smile."

I managed an awkward smile. "The other participants were all smiling, and they looked genuinely happy. You can't fake something like that."

"No, you can't," he agreed. "Good luck on your journey, Jen."

At that moment, Barb came to the patio door with her arms crossed.

"I'll pick you up at ten o'clock tomorrow," she announced before disappearing into the house.

16

The drive to Olympic View was full of tension. Barb kept her focus on the road, completely disregarding me.

She interrupted the quiet from the driver's seat. "I'm going to say it again. You shouldn't be in this trial."

"Are you hoping that something happens to me?" I could feel myself shaking. "I need your support. Nothing more. I'm going to do this whether or not you like it."

She scoffed at my retort. "It's clear Quantos let their drug out into the public without proper precaution—and if they harm you, I'll make sure they pay dearly."

"Calm down. You'll see the place soon enough," I said, trying to reassure Barb.

"This isn't the same ride, Jen. Where are we going?" she asked.

"Olympic View—my new home for the next thirty days," I replied. They granted her clearance so she could come with me; Jessica said we'd receive VIP treatment.

The car chimed and its computerized voice declared, "Approaching destination in one mile."

We drove past a small sign that read OVTC and showed a right turn in 500 feet.

"They want this place to stay under the radar," I remarked.

The vehicle slowed as it turned right, and Barb couldn't help but sound skeptical when she responded. "Are you serious? Is this a resort, country club, or treatment center?" Her sarcasm was unmistakable.

The front area had a sprawling lawn that welcomed us. Trees shaded the long driveway as we entered.

Barb stopped the car and shouted, "Are we really in the right place?"

I held my phone up, nodded in affirmation, and said, "Quantos is certainly not skimping on budget."

We drove between tall fir trees until we approached the gate when Barb said suspiciously, "You seem uncertain about this place."

"They brought me in a van with no windows," I replied.

Barb snickered sarcastically. "I'm not sure I trust them."

We drove closer to the entrance and saw the tall wall around the fortress, at least ten feet high.

"Just give me a chance," I said. "If something is wrong, I'll make sure you hear about it first."

We arrived at the security gate. An enormous man was standing in front of the guardhouse, and two equally massive men were inside the office. All of them had an intimidating presence. My skin was crawling with fear.

The giant came up to our car window. "Good afternoon." His head slowly lowered until he could see into our vehicle.

Barb threw me a deadly look as she lowered her window halfway, turning to face the armed guard.

"Barb, please don't," I pleaded with her.

She sighed heavily before putting on a forced smile at the large man. "Hello, we're here to check in for my friend sitting next to me." Her voice was surprisingly pleasant.

"I need to see some I.D.," he gruffly replied before stepping away from the car and crossing his arms.

Barb pulled out her badge and identification card. "Here you go, Officer Kiel."

He examined her credentials with no signs of being impressed.

I frantically searched through my wallet. "Barb, it's not here." I dug through my pockets. "I can't find it anywhere." Everything was in its place. "This cannot be happening."

"Officer," Barb interjected, "my friend can't locate her I.D."

The officer tensed up.

"This is Jennifer Floyd," she continued. "She's supposed to check in for the Remsen trial today."

"Sorry, Miss Stein and Miss Floyd"—he looked to me—"but we'll need an I.D. from you."

"Officer!" I called out. "Isn't there any way you could contact Jessica? What's her last name?"

The man let out a sigh of exasperation, then stepped into the guard shack. I saw him talking with some of the other guards, and they all laughed before he came back out again.

"Give Kiel a taste of my medicine," Barb muttered under her breath.

"Miss Floyd, it appears they're expecting you today. Proceed through the entrance; follow the arrows," he said.

She raised her window as she said, "Thanks, Officer," but it was clear she was clenching her teeth as she spoke.

The gate raised before us, and we drove away quickly.

"Do you always have that kind of power?"

She hit the steering wheel hard twice and replied, "That felt good! He shouldn't have been such a prick like he was at some maximum security facility or something. He was lucky I am here today, helping you out." She gave another hard slap to the wheel, then cracked a smile.

I turned my head to get a better look at the facility. The pictures didn't do it justice. It was much larger than I had imagined, with another building to the right that was still under construction. "

They're planning something big for this study, Jen."

As we approached a sign, Barb shook her head in disbelief. "Look at that; they even have a valet service. It makes me wonder who else is coming to visit. They better roll out the red carpet and give you the best possible VIP treatment."

"Thank you."

"I know, Jen," she said, squeezing my hand as we pulled up to the valet.

A handsome young man was smiling at us as the car stopped.

Barb looked at the valet standing by my door and said, "Hello, Mr. Valet."

I couldn't help but smirk. "Barb really?"

She only winked in response.

The valet opened my door and greeted us with, "Miss Floyd, it's a pleasure to have you here. Mrs. Stein, welcome to Olympic View. We've been expecting you."

Barb nudged me and whispered, "Is this Hogwarts or Fantasy Island?"

I snickered quietly.

She smiled at the valet and stated, "Marcus, thank you for your warm welcome."

I shot her a questioning look. "How do you know his name?"

She pointed to his nametag which read: 'Welcome To Olympic View—My name is Marcus, and I'm from Philadelphia'."

"Philadelphia?" I raised an eyebrow at him.

"Yes, ma'am. Quantos offered me the opportunity to move out here," Marcus replied.

"Marcus, I don't like to dine alone. Would you like to join me later?" Barb offered, never one to let an opportunity slip by. She leaned in closer to Marcus, her breath warm on his cheek. "There's a fabulous restaurant downtown that I'm friends with the owner of," she whispered.

Marcus stiffened, clearly confused by Barb. "Ma'am?"

"Marcus." Barb switched to her detective's voice. "Tonight, we're going to downtown Olympia for dinner."

Marcus smiled but seemed unsure how to respond to Barb's flirtatious behavior.

As they whispered back and forth, their faces slowly drawing closer together, I realized it was time for me to go.

"Miss Floyd, do you have a bag?" Marcus finally asked.

"Oh, yes. Sorry about that." I opened the rear door and pulled out a carry-on bag.

"Please, Miss Floyd, I can take it from here." He walked over and grabbed the bag.

Marcus stood, about to let me take my bag from him.

"Wait," I said. "Can I check it first?" I opened the front pocket and saw my driver's license inside.

Barb laughed. "Typical," she said with a smile.

"Ah, Ms. Floyd." A woman strode over to us with purpose. "My name is Marie Peters." She glanced at her watch. "Apologies for being late."

"Is this the same Marie from the first call?" I asked her.

"Yes, ma'am," she said while catching her breath. "I shall be your go-to person during your stay in the Remsen Trial. You can contact me anytime regarding queries or worries," she said hurriedly.

"So does that mean I can email you whenever I need something, Marie?" Barb inquired, shooting daggers at the poor victim.

"Indeed, it does, Miss Stein—I've sent all the contacts to you," Marie replied confidently.

I chuckled internally—did they have a dossier on Barbara?

Barb fished out her phone, and her eyes widened upon seeing the messages. "That'll do nicely," she muttered before turning back to Marcus, who had just left in her car.

"Yup, of course," I said as Marie proceeded towards the entrance.

Barb walked over to us.

"Your intake is at 3 p.m," Marie said.

I reached down for my phone, noting it was already 1:25.

"Do you think I can take her home?" I asked Barb.

She shook her head and laughed, leading us into the empty lobby that had a strange resort-like vibe. My eyes were drawn to the large cedar tree standing in the center of the room with its elevated ceilings.

"They saved this tree and made it the centerpiece," Marie said. "We're planting a new forest on the south end of Olympic View, where every participant plants a tree honoring their experience. In around 30 days, it'll be your turn to plant your own."

I had no interest in optimism right now, instead staring at the giant tree that stood awkwardly amidst its deceased counterparts. A sign made from one of its siblings hung above it.

'xpáy'uhc' Lushootseed for Western Red Cedar. We honor those who graced this land before us. Let this tree honor those who called this land home for centuries.

Was it really an honor to destroy a forest?

Marie approached me, documents in hand. "Our company is carbon-free," she said with pride. "We create our own energy and have a no-waste policy."

"Olympic View?" Barb sounded intrigued. "How much would it cost to stay here for a few nights?"

Marie managed a smile. "When Jenna's been here two weeks, she can invite one guest for up to three days."

I almost asked her about life—did she know all the answers?

Barb looked distressed. "Where are the restrooms?"

Marie pointed down a long, empty hallway. "Just take a right, then look for the sign."

"Thanks," Barb mumbled as she shuffled away.

My gaze drifted over to Marie. "Does it usually stay this quiet here?"

"We try to make the check-in process as calming as possible, so we conduct intakes during the afternoon. The morning's a completely different story," Marie said, walking past the tree and pointing at a small sign that read: 'Blue Heron Inn.'

"They're only open for breakfast and dinner."

I recalled Jessica's description of Blue Heron as I asked, "Can anyone visit, or is it just for VIPs?"

"Blue Heron requires reservations. Jessica can tell you more about that," Marie replied.

"Sounds exclusive," I remarked.

Marie stood tall with her arms resting by her side. "Just like your stay here will be; from the entrance security to our efforts to protect everyone's privacy, we take secrecy seriously."

"That's good to hear," I said.

Barb re-joined us, grinning. "Anything happen while I was away?"

"Nothing special. There's a restaurant that requires reservations," I replied.

"Excellent. Can I book one?" Barb asked.

Marie blushed, averting her gaze.

Barb chuckled softly. "Oh Marie, imagine all the fun we could have."

Marie let out an uneasy laugh. "This is the main lobby area; architects and naturalists worked together on integrating nature into the space inside here. Quantos Pharma is based in Philadelphia—many of our visitors come from the East Coast, so this is their first glimpse of the Pacific Northwest." She waved at an overflowing garden. "This is our collection of native plants."

"It's gorgeous!" I exclaimed.

"It's just a small selection of native species growing in this region. It shows respect for them, plus it helps create a more peaceful atmosphere around here."

I looked up at the tree towering above me, with an opening at its peak that connected the room with the outside world. Even within this tall building, I felt confined—but being among this tree made me feel less suffocated.

Marie directed us towards the elevators. "As part of your intake, we will provide you with a watch," she said, "which will allow access to certain floors and rooms."

Barb retorted sarcastically, "So this is how you imprison them?"

"The watches are for safety," Marie replied defensively.

Barb smirked, saying dryly, "I really hope so, Marie."

I didn't want to look at her. Hopefully, this was the only time she had to deal with Barb.

We entered the elevator, and I noticed that there was no floor selector panel, just a red emergency button.

"How do you choose the floor?" Barb asked.

Marie held up her wristwatch and stated confidently, "Every client has their watch programmed for their day."

I studied the watch closely and saw it had a simple time display. With a slight push, the elevator began rising.

"Take this." Marie handed me the watch.

The elevator slowed and then came to a halt, a beep sounded, and the number six lit up on the display.

"Sixth-floor participant residency," a voice announced over the intercom.

"We have thirty units here. The watch will tell you where to go." I looked at the screen; it said Room 13 with an arrow pointing left.

"See? It wants us to go left," she said, motioning down the plain white hallway with its painted doors.

The hallway to my room was desolate. "What if we go right instead?" Marie led us to the right, but as soon as we took a few steps, the watch vibrated quietly and then with more intensity.

"The vibration you're feeling is telling you to turn around. Now let's keep walking."

On the screen of her watch, a woman's face appeared asking, "Hello, Miss Peters. Is everything alright? Oh! I'm sorry, Miss Floyd," the lady continued after recognizing her mistake.

Marie answered calmly, "Hey, Moni; all is fine. I'm just showing Miss Floyd how these work."

"Excellent, Marie. Chat soon," replied Moni before the call ended.

Marie fastened her watch back on her wrist. The atmosphere continued to be unsettling.

"Where is everyone?" I asked Marie, who had long hair that cascaded down her back. I fingered my thin, mousy locks and thought about how I'd probably never have healthy hair again—another great repercussion of stress and depression.

Marie turned around and pointed forwards. "And here is your room."

She seemed eager to get rid of Barb.

"Welcome to your own private sanctuary, where you will be the only one with access. The door code is unique for every participant and changes frequently. You will know the name of the person who cleans your space and even the one delivering your meals." Marie moved her wrist towards the door, which clicked as it slid into the wall. The lights blinked on to reveal a cozy living room with plush furniture and a soft aroma of lavender that filled my senses.

"Incredible," Barb murmured.

Marie invited us in. "This is the standard room we assign to all participants."

My eyes followed Barb as she explored the space, taking her time to appreciate each detail.

She walked over to a wall where some art was displayed.

"Jen, check this out!" She motioned towards an unyielding vase.

"That's for safety," Marie said quickly. "In case an earthquake ever happened, everything would stay in place."

Barb smirked. "Earthquakes...Sure."

I rolled my eyes at Barb, who had already turned away from me.

Marie cleared her throat. "Mrs. Stein?"

"It was just a joke; sorry," said Barb as she unsuccessfully tried to pry open the balcony door, lacking any handles.

Marie gave her an understanding look before saying, "Give it one more try."

"The door remains firmly shut for at least two weeks. It only opens when the client chooses." Marie checked her watch, and a red light flashed. "No one at Quantos has the ability to unlock this." She glanced at Barb and then at her watch. "Jenna, we will need to get your intake started shortly. I can give you two a few minutes alone."

"Thank you, Marie," I said.

She nodded and stepped away from the room.

Barb came up beside me and hugged me tightly. "You sure about this, Jen? We can leave in an instant if you want; I just need to grab Marcus."

"I need this. Just the time away will be a blessing," I said, looking into Barb's eyes. "I love you. Thank you for being everything to our family and me." Her eyes became teary. "It's only fourteen days! Don't go getting all mushy on me now; keep that sentiment until we reunite."

She grinned and gave me a kiss. "I love you, Jen. I truly hope you can see the world clearer after this."

Barb backed away from me and turned towards the door. "This is really a nice place." She looked back at me with her watery eyes. "Next month, we will head over to Vegas; I'll book you a suite much bigger than this."

"Yes, Barb, next month." There was always next month. She was constantly giving me something to look forward to.

She turned towards the door and pushed the green button. The door opened. "I will see you in two weeks."

"Fourteen days, Barb." The door closed behind her.

17

Once the paperwork was done and out of the way, Marie gave me a tour of Olympic View. It seemed to go on forever—hallways that led to other hallways, rooms after rooms after rooms. I would have limited access for the next fourteen days to only the locations on my schedule.

We eventually made it to the fourth floor with its infinite number of halls and doors. Marie introduced me to the other participants. All five of us had that same far away smile—a look we were all too familiar with.

Marie and I said our hellos, then headed to the cafeteria for our first meal. It was just as extravagant as the buffet Barb had taken me to in Vegas. A stunning water feature with colorful koi fish occupied the center of the room.

"Please, help yourself," Marie suggested before adding, "Let's go sit in the back corner."

I stepped back and surveyed the offerings; there were meat-carving stations, sushi rolls and dozens of other entrees, not to mention the salad bar.

"Is there going to be a huge crowd?" I asked.

Marie took a plate, and I followed her to the raw fish station. "This is about normal for this time of day," she said.

"What do they do with all that's left?"

"They don't waste any of it. They donate food to Thurston County Food Shelter and the remaining into compost." Marie smiled as she loaded up her plate, and I filled mine with a Seattle Roll.

Fauna and trees grew in between tables, giving the area a tropical feeling. We found a secluded table away from the others.

As I looked around at the paintings of poodles covering the walls, I said with admiration, "Painted Poodle—what a great name."

Marie nodded in agreement. "The first group of participants chose it from a list of twelve options."

"That's pretty cool," I remarked, impressed.

"They have their hands in everything here. Last month, they had an event to dedicate the garden with both current and remote participants."

"Wow!" I exclaimed, amazed.

"It was an emotional experience—even for me," she said with a hint of sadness in her voice.

"I can only imagine," I responded in understanding.

Marie glanced towards the doorway. "I'm so glad you came."

I looked over to see Jessica entering with a grin on her face.

"Afternoon, Marie," she said cheerfully. "Jenna, it's great that you're here. I'm excited that you're giving this a go."

"I'm ready to begin," I replied, not wanting to sound like an addict who had just gotten their first taste of something they were eager to consume. "Let's start the trial."

"We'll begin your first session at seven o'clock tomorrow," Jessica said with a smile.

Marie chuckled. "That might be a bit too early for me."

"It's perfect for me," I replied, recalling the 5 am starts I was used to. "Thank you for accommodating my schedule."

Jessica nodded and clasped her hands together. "Of course, Jen. We can evaluate how you progress and make changes accordingly. After two weeks, you will have more access to the facility."

A part of me wanted to believe her. "Thank you for everything," I whispered.

Jessica nodded. "Your success will be our success. In thirty days, we want you to be leaving with a new relationship with the world around you."

Marie had a slight smile that wouldn't leave her face. It was getting annoying.

"Do you really think it will only take thirty days?" The last year has tortured my mind. No way that one month could fix everything.

Marie was nodding with every word. "That is really just the beginning, Jenna. Clients who finish the study here have improvements in their daily function at home. I speak to clients daily who take part in the at-home study and are having significant improvements in their overall mental health."

"It won't change you as a person. It will change how you respond to the trauma and the memories," Jessica said.

I forced a nod. "I really hope so."

"Clients are most successful when they have a structured schedule. We have classes that should keep you active most of the time." Marie pulled a small box from her side and placed it on the table. "Before we go any further, I want to give you your new watch."

"Is this my GPS?" The watch was identical to Jessica's and Marie's. *I doubt this will open any secret doors.*

Marie tilted her head. "This will monitor your sleep, your heart, and even stress. It will also open doors for you."

I nodded. "Sounds a little smarter than my last one."

"That's just the tip of the iceberg. Quantos engineers developed an app that works with the watch to monitor your metabolism. It will help give you dietary suggestions," Marie said with unbridled enthusiasm.

"How is that possible?" I asked.

Marie took her tablet, tapping an app. "This app tracks all the food you order with information about nutrition: calories, protein, fat, carbs, and minerals. Let me show you how it works." She then waved a blue laser from her watch over the muffin. Seconds later, the light went off. Marie refreshed the app and nutritional facts appeared for the blueberry pastry.

"They added flaxseed?" I asked.

"Our research team has been perfecting recipes for health benefits and flavor," she said. "Quantos is hoping to have their own food division in five years."

"Wow, that's crazy!" I wasn't sure if I wanted Quantos to be in every part of my life.

Jessica took my watch from the box. "Let me show you another example. This will show you calories in food, but it will also keep track of how much you have consumed." She took a butter knife to the muffin and cut it in half. She handed me the watch. "Just press the green to scan the item."

I pushed the green button, and a light came out from the side of the watch. I guided it over the half muffin, watching it. The watch screen flashed once.

"Now look at your watch."

Blueberry muffin half portion. A small display showed calories, fat, sugar, protein. "That's impressive," I said.

"This is just a tool. You don't have to use it. The scanning of what you eat can be beneficial to see where you may deprive yourself of nutrition," Jessica said.

"That makes sense. I can't remember the last time I ate a full meal."

"Many of our clients find that they have a nutritional deficiency, and we try to help improve that as well. When you go home, it will be up to you. How you eat, how much you socialize," Jessica added.

The tastelessness of food had become the norm over the past year. The frozen dinners were all I could stomach, and even then, Barb had to remind me every day that I needed sustenance to survive. It brought back memories of Ty's delicious cooking—barbecues with savory meats dripping in herbs, and spaghetti pasta made from scratch. How could he be gone?

Marie's words pulled me out of my thoughts. "You will have a beneficial outline for your success on the outside. If you continue in the study, you may stay on Remsen indefinitely."

Indefinitely? My thoughts turned to endless days augmenting my memory. Was this really the best they could do? Marie continued clicking away at her tablet while I struggled to keep my composure. "I thought Remsen would eventually cure my trauma," I said through gritted teeth. Jessica's eyes flicked briefly towards me before she looked away.

Marie dropped her head, not wanting my fire. The realization that there may never be hope hit me like a ton of bricks. Would I be trapped in a world where nothing tasted like it should, where everything felt numb?

"Every single client who entered into the home study is still being treated. We don't have any clients who have finished their treatment," Jessica said, speaking slowly.

"Does that mean Remsen can never cure me?" I asked, recognizing the familiar sound of big pharmaceuticals.

"Cure you?" Marie looked insulted, staring at me incredulously. "Remsen is not a cure. Our goal is to treat our clients' traumas. We can't provide a timeline for how long it'll take to help everyone in the study. Every person in our program has experienced life-altering trauma. Many have been living with their traumas for years or even decades. Jenna, let me show you something." She pulled out her phone and motioned for me to extend my arm. A beep rang through my watch a few seconds later, and she turned the tablet towards me.

Jennifer Williams Floyd

DOB: 17, August 1993

RESIDENCE: Aberdeen, WA

Client Study Start Date: 22 JULY, 2030

Client Planned End Date: N/A

I glanced up at Marie with an expressionless face.

"No one has a set end date for taking part in the study here," she said, crossing her arms with an air of confidence.

Jessica then put her hand on Marie's shoulder and spoke. "The only ones who have an end date are those that could not complete the research."

"It is just your progress that matters," she continued. "And you will see results within weeks."

"If you still have questions," Jessica added, now coming closer to me, "we can go over them in my office."

"Thank you, Jessica," I uttered obediently, not wanting to cross words with Marie.

18

After an ominous walk, we arrived at the Rock Hounder, where Grecco was patiently waiting to greet us and take us to Jessica's table. I sat across from Jessica, where her face remained expressionless.

"This is the hardest part about being here. People say it's reaching your breakthrough. No, not really. It's signing your life away. I apologize for the experience. It's a necessary evil with what we do."

I took a deep breath and exhaled. "Thank you, Jessica. I really appreciate your support. Sadly, I was left with a clinician who had to study my file every time we talked. I felt like I was bouncing my thoughts off a wall."

"I understand completely. I did my thesis at a treatment center and ended up feeling more stressed than at school. I felt like I wasn't addressing anyone's issues. I was just passing them through like they were ordering from a drive thru." Jessica scoffed. "These people became numbers. Their issues were just generalized, like everyone else who passed through the doors. It only made me want to leave the place more."

"Did you ever feel like you needed to serve that community?"

"My heart went out to all of them, and I hope they received wonderful treatment. It just wasn't a place for me. I'm hoping one day I can open my own treatment facility, which helps the disadvantaged community."

"Wow, that would be incredible! Thank you for fighting the good fight."

"I can't see myself catering to designer healthcare. Quantos may have that in their sights, but I'm focused on the real treatment with Remsen. I think this can be a game changer, but you need to understand this is not an overnight cure. It may take days, weeks, or even months before you reach that pinnacle. I want to help you get there, Jen."

"That means a lot to me. I feel powerless to make decisions. Just being here takes every fiber of energy for me."

"I hope we can help you regain that power. That strength you so deserve to live and be free.

19

Jessica and I walked to my first class. My nerves were getting the best of me—this was an unfamiliar world with strange new rules. While trying my best to steady my breathing, I heard Jessica's words: "Don't worry about Marie. She is by the letter."

"I can see that," I replied, thankful for her presence. "I know a few teachers like that."

Her voice softened into a gentle chuckle. "I bet you do."

Though my mind raced as I tried to remember the details of my schedule, I took comfort in one thing; I had Jessica by my side.

"Where are we going?"

She smiled. "I think you will get a kick out of this. It's Retro Game Night class. They have a collection of classic games to play with others. Clients only manage this class."

I hesitated before speaking. "Retro games for therapy?" My voice felt like it was vibrating.

Jessica chuckled softly, her eyes filled with understanding. "Sometimes the best therapy is good distraction with others." She pointed to a door that was painted aqua green, and I could feel my heart pounding in my chest. "Just try it. If you don't like it, you can leave and never come back."

I waved my wrist at the door, and it slid open. I smiled. "Thank you, Jessica, for everything."

"Of course. It's my pleasure. Enjoy your class, and I will see you bright and early."

I waved at her as I proceeded in. The door slowly closed behind me as I was in the dragon realm. Tables were scattered throughout the room.

The room hummed with chatter as people sat around tables, immersed in games like Hungry Hippos, Battleship, and Uno. I felt a tightness in my chest as I looked around at the groups of people laughing and enjoying each other.

A woman got up from her game of Battleship and smiled at me. "Hi; are you Jenna?"

I hesitated before nodding. "Yes, I am."

"It's nice to meet you. I lead this class"—she waved her hand around the room—"if you can really call it that. We meet five times a week, and most of the time there will be about twenty of us or more—there's no curfew, so we can run late into the night."

"I have my first session tomorrow at seven," I said, trying to break the awkward silence.

"No worries. You're not required to be here if you don't want to be. Some people come and go throughout the evening, take breaks for dinner or whatever. It's one of our more relaxed classes—aside from the occasional balloon volleyball." She chuckled, but trailed off when she noticed me. "Oh, nevermind that. You're welcome to join any game here or observe. Looks like a couple tables could use another player." She nodded towards a pair of women sitting alone.

"You're not even close, Amber," came a man's voice from her table.

"We will see about that." She responded by walking over to the table. "If you have any questions, I will be right here."

I scanned the room, noticing boxes of board games piled in a corner. I sighed as memories of peaceful times flooded back; Friday and Sundays spent around the dinner table playing games with my family.

An unfamiliar voice shattered my reverie. "Hello."

My eyes shot to the other side of the table. A woman with auburn hair was beaming at me from behind a game of Connect Four.

"You must be new here," she said matter-of-factly.

Nodding, I mumbled something about arriving earlier that day before sinking into the chair beside her.

"My name is Diana," she continued jovially. "It's been twenty-eight days since I arrived here. Would you like to play some Connect Four?"

As I watched Diana set up the game pieces, I realized how similar we were: two women displaced by trauma, now in search of solace among strangers.

Gathering my courage, I spoke up. "Thanks for inviting me," I told her. "My name is Jenna. It feels like I've been here forever."

Her eyes twinkled as she glanced up from the game board. "Time flies here," she said. "The first week can be tough, but once you make your breakthrough, it will feel like you're moving in fast forward."

"But doesn't that take around two weeks?"

She leaned forward and whispered. "You can reach your breakthrough in less than a week. Some of the newer clients have been reaching it in five days."

"How is that possible?"

"It doesn't hurt to drink water before your session."

I nodded. "I heard that. So it really works?"

"It does. You will have an awareness like the director of your own movie."

"Will they kick me off the study if I get caught."

Diana shook her head. "You are not breaking any rules. If anything, the quicker results only makes their drug look more effective." She placed a checker into the board. "I love Connect Four. I grew up playing it before video games existed."

I placed a checker into the far side as I watched it fall to the bottom. "I played it as a child in the age of video games."

"I go to a better time when I'm here. Away from my worries and in my comfort zone." She dropped another checker in the same row, putting the two together.

"What happens when you leave Olympic View?"

She chuckled. "I guess I need to get a Connect Four game." Her eyes got red. "I don't have anyone to go home to. Remsen doesn't fix the sadness. It only takes some of the pain away."

"I'm sorry, Diana. I know all too well about living in an empty home. I never realized how much I'm a prisoner to it."

"It's the walls we build that need to come down. Now I feel I can go out. Even if it's only to the library. I'm ready to take those first steps."

I chuckled. "I took a drive for the first time in months. It was only a mile from my home, but it felt exhilarating. If I had money, I would have probably kept going."

"And when you leave this place? Do you want to travel?"

I looked away. "I can't. I have a career. I mean, Ty and I always planned for our vacations we never took. We had a lot of places we wanted to visit."

Diana tilted her head. "Is Ty your partner?"

"Ahhh..." I stumbled. "He was my spouse. We were together for over twenty years."

"Twenty years!" She pulled back. " You must have been a child."

I chuckled. "Yeah, in high school."

"Nothing like young romance that blossoms."

I needed to redirect the conversation. "How about you?"

She swallowed. "Yes, I was. Howard. No, he was Howie to everyone. We were together for just over fifty years. Now I'm aging myself. We met at a Roller Rink in '78."

"That's beautiful. What was it like?"

She glimmered. "I was nineteen. A couple of my friends were playing one of those space games in the arcade. This guy comes out of nowhere and taps me on the shoulder, asking if I wanted to skate with him."

"So exciting." Her story was taking my internal thoughts away. "This must be Howie."

"Yes." Her smile grew. "He was tall and had a huge head of blonde hair. Little did I know it was the couples only dance."

I chuckled. "Howie moved fast. Do you remember your first song?"

"'How Deep Is Your Love'." She swallowed hard. "The song stayed with us. Howie was a gentleman from the first to the last moment I was with him."

"I'm sorry." Her loss had to be recent.

"At least now my thoughts go to the good in our life. I'm not focused on the moment everything ended."

"That must be so freeing."

"It is. I am. And you will also."

20

I was awoken by an urge to use the restroom, I stumbled out of bed and made my way in. As I took care of business, I couldn't help but admire how stunning the bathroom was. It had a jacuzzi tub, just like Ty and I had dreamt of. After washing up at the sink, I opened the closet door to find several clothing items hanging in it—none of which were what I expected. On the rack were multiple onesies; each with blue legs and a gray top. The fabric was soft and stretchy—almost like second skin. After slipping my legs into the suit, I zipped up the back and felt relieved.

I chuckled as I stumbled upon my reflection in the mirror. It seemed like something out of a cheesy '80s sci-fi flick, but instead of exploring outer space, we were delving into the depths of our minds. My watch vibrated, and I tapped the answer button on my watch. A tiny face with a forced smile popped up on my screen.

"Hi there, Miss Floyd," Marie said courteously. "How are you feeling?"

"Nervous," I admitted, while clenching my stomach. "Please feel free to call me Jenna."

"Of course!" she said. "I'll be there in fifteen minutes to take you to your first session."

"Sounds great. I'll be ready," I answered with a small smile.

Marie gave me a wink before signing off. "See you soon."

"Thank you." I pushed the end, and the watch became a watch again. I put a timer on for twelve minutes to avoid any anxious moments.

I walked over to the sink, grabbed a glass from the cabinet, and filled it with water. Here goes nothing. After a few gulps, I had downed the first one.

I looked at the empty glass. One more to go. I filled it again and started gulping like it was nothing. My stomach was floating. Oh, this better work. My watch started vibrating. "Oh damn." I gave myself a once over with the mirror. I think the mirror and I both had a good laugh.

A monitor in the bathroom I hadn't noticed before began to beep. Its screen showed an ID card of Marie Peters, who had a slight smirk on her face.

"Coming!" I walked towards the door and hit the green button; it slid open and Marie stepped inside. She looked exhausted, with red-rimmed eyes. "It's nice to see you, Jenna."

"Nice seeing you too...and likewise," I responded.

Marie was struggling to contain a yawn that escaped her lips. "I'm sorry—this isn't my usual wake-up time."

I nodded in understanding.

"How did you sleep?" Marie asked.

"Fantastically," I replied.

She took a moment to fidget with her fingers before asking, "Are you all set for your first session?"

I grimaced, feeling unprepared. "As ready as I'll ever be," I said.

A slight smile crossed her lips. She waved her watch in front of the door panel, and it glided open. We stepped through, and the hall was silent in its emptiness.

"Is everyone asleep?" I inquired.

Marie spun around and our faces were close together, and I caught a whiff of coffee coming from her breath.

"Most clients have different schedules," she clarified. "When you reach the two-week mark, your own time slot will change too."

"What's the point of shifting my time?"

Her head nodded in response. "Our plan is for you to prepare for the outside world. In two weeks, you'll be able to consume caffeine whenever it suits you best."

Two weeks—it sounded like an eternity! "Praise be! That'd be a dream come true."

We headed over to the elevators.

"You will take this same path tomorrow. Point your watch at the elevator," she instructed me.

I held out my arm like I was casting a charm, and immediately the elevator dinged and my name popped up on the monitor.

Jennifer Floyd

"The elevator is reserved for you for the next ten minutes," she declared.

We stepped in and the doors shut behind us.

"The first two weeks of treatment will be in Jessica's office. You'll learn how to get there before you know it."

The elevator stopped abruptly. "Jennifer Floyd, third floor treatment," a female voice with a gentle English accent announced.

The doors slid open with a hiss, and immediately, my watch started vibrating. A golden star was flashing on its face. "What does this mean?" I asked.

She replied matter-of-factly, "The stars confirm you're going in the right direction."

It reminded me of an incentive system I used in my classroom years ago. "Oh, so the stars are like points?"

"Yes," she said. "You can redeem them for perks around Olympic View."

I gasped as the long hall came into view, brimming with activity, and the aroma of fresh coffee sending pulses of excitement through my veins. Lab coats of different colors swirled past us in every direction. Each door had a nameplate affixed to it. By the time we reached Jessica's office, we had passed seven other offices.

Marie abruptly halted, and I knew we had arrived.

"Thank you, Marie," I said, hoping she would leave as soon as possible.

The doors parted, and D emerged from the office, blocking my path between Marie and me.

"Good morning, Jenna," she greeted me briefly before turning to Marie with a nod. "Morning, Marie." D turned around and re-entered the office without another word.

"See you in an hour, Jenna!" Marie called out over her shoulder as she strode away.

21

The sunlight was blasting through the office, making it difficult to take in the view.

"Sorry about that," D said.

I nodded vaguely at her figure in front of me.

"Let me adjust it." A slight hum started up as D spoke, and the illumination lowered to a more comfortable level. I noticed the windows had grown darker. "How do the windows dim?"

"They have dual panes, with thousands of microscopic machines that adjust light levels in the room. When you start your trip, we will black out the windows entirely."

"So that was the noise I heard?"

"That was it—those tiny machines being given instructions and solving the problem on their own."

I snickered. "How can I get this into my home?"

D advanced towards me, shaking her head as she spoke. "Unfortunately, this device is still in its prototype stage."

I bobbed my head up and down in acknowledgment.

D offered me a hug, to which I nodded in response. "I haven't slept so soundly in ages!"

We embraced before she spoke. She picked up her tablet and settled into a more serious demeanor.

"The next two weeks will be relatively the same," said D. "You'll begin your journey at 7:15am, with the trips typically lasting fifteen minutes. Afterward, you'll return to Jessica for a summary."

I surveyed the space, trying to figure out where I was supposed to sit. "Where am I meant to go?"

"In the green chair," D answered me as she gestured towards a dentist chair covered in a lush forest green fabric.

"This one's nicer than the last one," I observed.

D chuckled. "It has sensors embedded in it that can pick up on any changes you may have—heart rate, temperature, stress levels." She put her hand on the chair and continued, "It costs around twenty-five thousand dollars."

My eyes almost bulged out of my head at the price tag. "Wow."

"Very wow. This chair has been a lifesaver for our research. After your session, we take your experiences and create a timeline that makes more sense," D said.

The side door opened, and Jessica appeared, her voice bubbling with enthusiasm."Good morning, Jen. It's great to see you," she said.

"Morning," I responded, my voice creaking.

Jessica went to her desk and grabbed a tablet. "Are we ready to get started?" she addressed D.

"We are," she answered.

She walked over to a chair in front of the dentist's seat. "Would you like to take a seat?" Her eyes flickered over me.

"Yes." I went towards the chair, sinking into its soft fibers as I sat down. "Wow, this feels amazing!"

"We want your experience here to be first class," responded D.

"And with great coffee afterwards!" Jessica added.

I winked at her, and she winked back. "I'm holding you to that," I said.

D was running the magic wand over my body. "Your vitals have improved since last week. Client Jenna Floyd is ready to start."

"Are you ready?" Jessica asked.

I nodded.

"D, can you please proceed?" Jessica asked.

"Yes, I can." D was unwrapping what looked like a mask. I watched her connect it to a hose. "This will be your personal mask for sessions." D put it in front of me to view. "May I place this on you?" she asked.

"Yes, of course you can."

D lowered the mask and placed it over my mouth and nose. I heard a slight whirring sound, inhaled, and felt as if I were floating.

"Are you ready to wear the helmet?" D asked.

When I saw the helmet, I couldn't help but giggle. D insisted it was necessary for my safety. She carefully placed the bulky helmet on my head, and suddenly I was engulfed in darkness. A dim flash appeared on my monitor, and D's face filled the screen.

"Hi, Jenna," she said. "Can you see me?"

I nodded in response.

"Please answer with a yes or no," she corrected.

"Yes," I said.

"Thank you, Jenna. Now I am going to pass you off to Jessica," D said.

The screen dimmed again, only for Jessica to take her place moments later.

"Your vitals look great, Jen. How are you feeling?" she asked.

"More rested than I have been in a long time," I replied.

"Good. We should be ready to start. Here are the rules for your journey." Jessica had grown solemn. "Keep your attention on the memory you wish to explore. This is especially vital since it's your first time. Your thoughts may be scattered and broken apart. It's important to stay grounded in reality and not become ensnared by a false illusion that our minds create to protect us from pain. Remember, during the memory you fought with Ty? Seal yourself in that moment and hold fast to the truth of what happened. The closer you can remain to reality, the nearer you will get to an understanding." She met my eyes earnestly.

I sighed heavily, sinking further into my seat. "That's a lot," I said.

Jessica nodded in agreement. "Yes, it is a lot of work. Once you can connect the dots and form that pathway, it will open up so much more for you. It's incredible how freeing our minds from trauma can be."

A fantasy of having no trauma seemed like a distant dream I could never reach.

"You are not alone on this journey. We are here with you all the way," Jessica assured me.

Her words reverberated around me like waves on an ocean shore, but I couldn't muster any response other than a vacant stare.

"Looks like we are ready to begin." Jessica's eyes darted. " I am going to have you practice some breathing techniques. We are going to do this three times. Do you understand?"

"Yes," I said.

"On three. One, two"—Jessica paused briefly before adding—"and three."

I inhaled deeply, letting my worries drift away in the air.

"Exhale it all out," Jessica instructed.

The air whooshed from my mouth like a gust of wind.

"One more time," she said with an encouraging tone.

I almost smiled as I heard her words.

"On three. Ready? One...." She paused for a moment, as if letting me take a mental breath. "Two and three; now take a deep inhale through your nose," she continued.

I obeyed, filling my lungs with oxygen and holding it inside me.

"And exhale," Jessica encouraged me once again.

The air stumbled out of my mouth like a wave on the beach shore-line.

"That was great." Her voice was soft but strong at the same time. "Just remember, there's no competition here. Take your time."

"I'm sorry," I said. "I don't practice my breathing as often as I should."

"Don't be. You are doing great. Are you ready to begin your first trip?" Jessica asked.

"Yes." My bladder gave me a gentle reminder.

"Let's get started." Jessica's eyes remained on me. "If you ever feel that you need to escape the memory, there is one method that works 99% of the time."

I shut my eyes, and heard Jessica saying, "It's straightforward: if you feel confined, take a deep breath and hold it for as long as you can. We will either wake you up or you'll shock yourself out of it. Both work."

D's voice floated out of the shadows. "It looks like we're ready to dose." The monitor divided, and D appeared on the right side. My heart raced at the intensity of their gaze.

"Hello again," D said. "I'm administering Remsen doses: thirty micrograms for the first two weeks. Only two participants have had a breakthrough before day fourteen."

I let my eyelids droop and took a long breath.

"Are you ready to continue?" D asked.

"Yes, I apologize," I said.

"Think about that day at the beach—the sky, the scents, the landscape. Let your eyes close if you need to." Jessica's voice was soothing. "The screen will dim, and only our voices will be heard. Do you understand?" she asked me.

"Yes." I shut my eyes and I could see it—the same beach in different parts of our lives: when we were kids, teens, during my relationship with Ty before having children, and all the beach trips with the kids afterwards. So many memories that it was hard to focus on just one.

"It's D again." She didn't need to mention that; it was obvious. "We're preparing to administer your first dose of Remsen. All I need you to do is take a deep inhale on the count of three. Do you understand what I'm telling you?"

"Yes," I answered, nodding my head in confirmation.

D paused before saying, "One, two, three."

I breathed in deeply and felt a burning sensation in my lungs as I exhaled.

"Very good. We'll do two more breaths like that. Please focus on your breathing," D encouraged me.

The bright sun and the warm breeze.

"We are ready to begin the second dose. The instructions remain the same. Do you have questions?" D asked.

"No," I said.

I breathed in deeply, allowing the smells of that day to flow freely into my nose.

"You're doing well," D said. "One more dose, and you will be ready to begin."

"I think I can hear the ocean," I replied.

"That's fantastic. Keep focusing," Jessica said with enthusiasm.

"Ready for your last dose?" The sound of waves crashing was drowning out D's voice.

"Yes, it is really loud," I said.

"Counting down—three, two, one," said D as she began counting.

Again I breathed in deeply.

22

"*Jen, over here!*" *Ty? I shielded my eyes against the bright daylight and turned towards his voice.*

"Your sunglasses." His warm tone comforted me.

I felt along the back of my pants until I found them in my pocket. "Thanks," I said, sliding them on to get a better look around. Everything was the same—beach, people, even Mandy and Donnie. But something still didn't feel quite right.

I glanced up to see him watching Mandy, looking handsome as ever. It made me remember how attractive he was, wearing linen pants that accentuated his toned physique—he never wore linen pants. Instinctively, I walked up to him and placed my arms around him in a tight embrace.

"Babe, you okay?" Ty turned towards me, looking confused.

"Better than ever," I said. It was Ty. His voice, posture, and looks. He was so attractive. My memory never captured this detail. It felt like I was in a living photo.

"That's fantastic," he said, surprised. "Can you believe how fearless Mandy is?" Ty had the biggest smile on his face.

"Were you afraid of anything growing up?" I asked, my stomach flipping, knowing our dreaded conversation was coming.

"Much more than she has ever encountered. If my dad were here to teach her, he would be so exacting about everything," Ty replied.

I looked at him, perplexed. "Didn't that make you two butt heads a lot?"

Ty nodded. "All the time when I was a teenager." His voice quavered as he spoke.

The discussion was taking a turn, and I had to concentrate on what I remembered from before. So I focused on Donnie, who was hard at work with his own project.

"It seemed like whatever I did, it just wasn't good enough," Ty said, his head hanging down in despair.

I grabbed Ty's sleeve. "Hey, let's go check on Donnie and make sure he's doing okay." I took a quick glance at my phone. "We gotta leave in a few though."

Ty chuckled. "Sure thing; give me a minute and I'll take a look."

I didn't want to argue with him, but splitting up the time would only create more of an issue. "Ty, please just hurry."

Suddenly, his expression grew stern. "I said I would, Jen."

Ignoring Ty, I made my way over to Donnie. My attention was drawn to the group of kids who had filmed us earlier; their faces were all too familiar. They could have been the same person, all clones of that one boy who had laughed at us. His face stuck in my mind: taunting and cruel.

Letting out a deep sigh, I shook off the memory and focused on Donnie's well-being.

As I drew closer, Donnie was absorbed in his work and didn't even spot me. Taking pics of his fort seemed essential before I left. I fumbled around in my back pocket for my phone.

Donnie spun around when he saw me, and his beaming smile made my heart flutter.

"Mom!" he shouted as he dashed towards me with more energy than I'd seen from him before.

"Your beer," Donnie said, pointing to the bottle that had slipped out of my hand and fallen to the ground.

I felt the liquid soaking through my clothes as I looked down at my mid-section, drenched in beer.

"I'm sorry, Mom," Donnie uttered, his head hung low.

"It's okay. Just a bit wet," I told him, taking my sweatshirt and covering the spot that had gotten soaked.

My attention shifted to his shirt as I asked, "When did you get this shirt?"

He gazed at it in confusion. "You gave it to me for my birthday," he responded with a serious expression on his face.

I shook my head in disbelief. "Battlestar Mutants?" This was a show I'd never heard of before. Was I just imagining things? Or was this damn Remsen manipulating my memories?

"Let me show you," Donnie said as he reached over to take the phone from my hand. He tapped a few buttons, then flipped it sideways and pressed play on a video.

"From near and far to the stars and beyond, Battlestar Mutants have come to Earth to protect its inhabitants." Donnie was mimicking the voice of the video as I did my best to keep a smile on my face, attempting to remain calm. This had gone much further than my imagination ever could've taken it.

"Oh, yeah. Sorry I forgot," I said, averting my eyes out of embarrassment. "What about your fort? Can you show me that?" I asked as I took the phone from his hands again.

"Fort? This is an automatized missile command base!" Donnie said, his foot stomping in frustration.

I snorted with laughter. "Say what?" He had never used that word before.

"AUTOMATIZED MISSILE COMMAND BASE!" Donnie bellowed, making people around us turn to gawk.

"Whoa, Donnie!" I exclaimed, taking a step back. "How does it work?"

"Once I press this switch..." He pulled something out of his pocket. Wait, a second... Was he really carrying around a red switch? "...this base will safeguard Virginia..."

What the actual heck was he talking about Virginia for?

"...from any intruders." I glanced over at Donnie, who stood tall with his hands planted on his hips.

"That's pretty impressive," I said. "Can I see it in action?"

"Sure thing," Donnie responded, his gaze shifting away from me. "Look, here comes Mandy and Dad."

They walked up to us at the same speed. Ty and Mandy were chatting about something, not looking up from their conversation. In her hands was her kite, which made her look more proud than ever. How did Ty get her to stop flying it?

"Wow, Donnie, this is great work!" Ty said, inspecting the fort or Auto something Missile Command Base. "It looks exactly like the base on Battlestar Mutants." He sounded sincere.

"Yes, Dad," Donnie replied with a smirk in my direction.

"Donnie, can I play?" Mandy asked as she got down on her knees to study his work closer.

"We've got to go soon," I said, watching as their faces both fell in disappointment.

"You can have fifteen more minutes," Ty overruled me.

"Thanks, Dad," Donnie replied, and Mandy added her own thanks swiftly behind him.

I was about to protest, but didn't have the energy for an argument. Instead, I suggested, "We can both be the good guys here."

Ty looked over with an apologetic expression. I reached out and hugged him tightly; it felt so nice to be touched by him again—his voice, his skin, his breath. He was my Ty still. Meanwhile, the children continued playing without us.

"How many years has he been glued to Battlestar?" I asked.

"Are you serious?" Ty shook his head in disbelief.

"Yeah, that one."

"Forever! Since forever, since he was four." He stared into my eyes.

"Ahhh. I forced out a laugh, and he followed.

"They seem to be having a blast," I said.

"Mandy wanted to come earlier, but I wanted to show her a kite trick," Ty declared.

"Did she do it?" I inquired.

"Not yet, but we can try tomorrow." He took my hand and added, "You don't need to come if you're tired of the crowds."

"No, no, Ty. Tomorrow will be fun," I replied.

The beach disappeared around us. The sky darkened.

"Ty!" I shouted as he faded away. "I love you."

23

"**J**en... Can you hear me?"

I opened my eyes to darkness.

"It's Jessica," she said in an eerily cheerful voice. "Welcome back."

"What?" I asked. My head was spinning in a blender. "Ty, I love you," I said, hoping he would hear me.

"Jen!" she called out. "You made it. Your first trip."

Why won't she go away?

"On the count of three, you will see a dim flash on your visor. One, two, three," Jessica announced.

A dim light brought me back to my personal hell.

"Can you see me?" Jessica asked.

I forced my eyes open to this reality. "Yes," I said.

Jessica offered, "The bathroom is yours when you're ready. There are some fresh clothes to change into hanging on the wall."

"I'm so embarrassed. I don't know what came over me." I felt a twitch as I realized my bladder had betrayed me.

"It's okay, Jen. It happens more often than people think." She winked at me. "This chair is moisture-proof."

D seemed angry at what had happened, but I was too ashamed to look them in the eye.

"Let's get going. I'm ready to change." The last time something like this had happened was after a few too many drinks in college.

"D will give you a check and remove your helmet and mask."

The sound of the magic wand filled the room as it moved up and down, scanning me. "I will see you on the other side." Jessica's face vanished.

"Your vitals look good. I'm going to take off your helmet," D announced.

The vacuum-like sensation of the headgear being removed made my eyes open. Behind me, I saw D's smiling face peering around the corner. "Do you want me to remove your mask?" she asked.

"Yes." I nodded.

D reached up and carefully removed my face covering. "I'm going to put the chair in a sitting position," she said as it moved upright with a quiet buzzing sound. "Do you need help getting to the bathroom?"

"I'm fine." As soon as I put my right foot on the floor, though, electricity jolted up my leg. "Some help would be nice," I amended.

"Jess, can you come give me a hand?" D called.

Jessica looked up from her desk and nodded. "Sure, I'm on my way." She got up and joined. "We're going to help you stand up. Ready? Count of three?"

"Yeah, I'm ready," I answered, feeling the dampness seeping through my clothing.

"One, two, three," Jessica said, and they both supported me as I rose from the chair. They helped me walk to the restroom and then stepped back when we reached the entrance.

"I should be alright now. Thank you," I managed to say before the door closed behind me.

"Just call if you need anything else!" Jessica shouted before leaving.

Using my right hand as support, I undressed from the onesie. The shower was in front of me with only one button. It released a stream of water that was the perfect temperature for me. Once I was done, I grabbed my towel and dried off. My new onesie was hanging on the wall, so I picked it up and saw the patch with my name on it: **Jennifer Floyd.**

As I exited the bathroom, I glanced around, disoriented.

"Jen, take a seat," Jessica announced with a smile.

I looked around the room, which transformed. All the chairs had disappeared and were replaced by a sofa, which seemed to invite me to sit on it.

"I've got something here for you on the coffee table," Jessica said.

When I looked closer, I noticed a French press and two cups on the table. "Thank you so much," I replied gratefully.

"As promised. Congratulations on your first trip." She poured me a cup of coffee before asking, "Moo creamer?"

"You know it." She gave me the cup, and I took a deep inhale of its delicious aroma. "This smells so good."

"Wait until you try it." She was pouring coffee into her cup. "How do you feel?" Jessica asked.

A chill ran down my spine as I uttered, "I'm unsure." Everything felt so real—incredibly realistic.

"The first few times people go on a Remsen trip can feel pretty strange," Jessica explained. "Our minds can create remarkably vivid recollections, but with this experience, all the details and emotions become intensified, which sometimes makes it hard to remember what's real or not."

"It's too much for me," I replied. "Ty doesn't want to fight."

"You may need a few more trips to get everything fully cemented in your memory," Jessica suggested.

"How many?" I asked.

"That depends," she replied. "It could take three sessions or even more."

I took a sip of my coffee and asked Jessica, "How long do you think it'll take for me to get better?"

Squinting, she replied, "A few sessions at most. Your mind is very active when going through these trips, so I'm expecting quicker results from you."

"Student of the year," I said with a smirk as I raised my mug in front of me.

Jessica returned the silent stare for a few moments before asking, "Can you tell me anything about your experience? Did something seem off or out of place?"

An intense chill ran down my body as I glanced downwards while answering her.

"Yes, there was something weird. The teenagers who taunted us—they all had the same face."

Jessica hummed in response before getting her tablet and asking, "That is normal when talking about memories and dreams? Our brains don't store everyone's face. Was anything else odd?"

"Yes," I said, leaning back. "Ty and Mandy came to see Donnie. It felt like my memory was betraying me."

"That is quite extraordinary," Jessica responded. "Did you do or say anything that could have caused the change?"

I tried to think about my recent actions. "Absolutely nothing." I hesitated. "Oh! When it started, I hugged him, but our conversation was almost the same."

Jessica nodded her head up, and down as she spoke. "That's very interesting, Jen."

The door opened with a whoosh, and Jessica looked up.

"Am I interrupting?" It was Marie.

"We are just wrapping up here," Jessica answered. "Give us one minute."

"Apologies," Marie said as the door closed again.

"Sorry for that, Jen. That won't happen again," Jessica said.

"Thanks," I replied.

"Tomorrow will be like today. How do you feel?"

I laughed at the confidence. "Ready for the World—or at least ready for today!"

"Glad you are here." Jessica stood up from her chair, and so did I.

"Glad to be here," I said, knowing I'd soon be reunited with my family.

24

M arie navigated us through the maze until we arrived at The Painted Poodle. The cafeteria was full of people wearing matching outfits. We took our seats at the table we had previously.

I piled my plate with bacon and scrambled eggs from the morning selection. Jessica sent me out with a thermos of her signature brew. Marie picked up a bagel and spread the cream cheese over it.

"Here, this is for you to mark the completion of your trip." Marie placed a small white bag on the tabletop.

I read the words printed across its front:

Quantos—Bringing the future to now.

I slid the bag towards me and peered inside. "A phone?"

"Yes, it has games, shows, and thousands of songs pre-installed." Marie smiled at me.

My face broke into a grin. This could make the long days alone much less tedious.

"I'm glad you like it," she said. "You'll have plenty of spare time here; this might fill some of it."

I picked up the bag and leaned it against my chair. "Thanks! This is going to be great."

Marie leaned in. "How was your first trip? The experience? Was it what you expected?" She inquired.

I looked over at her, not sure what to say. "It was more than I'd expected. More than I thought it would be," I replied. "Remsen is something else," I added faintly.

"That it is." Marie paused for a moment. "Did you notice any differences between your memories and the experience?" She shifted back into her seat slightly.

My discomfort around Marie wasn't as I answered her question. "Not really...except for all the boys having identical faces," I said, deciding to omit some details.

"Interesting." Marie cocked her head to the side, curiosity written on her face. "The same face, you said?"

"Yes. During our argument, a group of teens took a video of us. One boy stood out; he's the only face whose image stayed with me." I paused as I looked for a way to change the subject. "Have you tried this yourself?

Marie's voice grew louder. "I've been on two Remsen trips," she said. "Our training meant we had to do two sessions, and it was quite the experience."

"Were you dealing with any trauma?" I asked.

Marie shifted in her seat. "Remsen is designed for trauma. You can't use it unless you've experienced something traumatic."

"What was yours?" I asked.

Marie sighed. "It was when my dog Flicker got hit by a car." Her voice deflated. "My sister and I were playing with a friend across the street from our home. Flicker got loose and ran for us. A car came out of nowhere and hit her."

"That sounds overwhelming," I said.

"I'm so sorry, Jenna. Mine is nothing compared to yours," Marie replied, taking hold of my hand across the table.

"My most significant tragedy before the accident was our pet cat being run over. It had a tremendous impact on Mandy and Donnie—we all were affected," I said.

Marie's eyes widened.

"We don't need to compare our unfortunate experiences," I uttered.

"Forgive me. That was thoughtless of me," Marie stammered, her face turning bright red.

"Not at all, Marie." I took a bite of my bacon. "This is good," I said, hoping I could change the subject.

"Quantos sources food locally, giving clients the freshest food available," Marie said. "They give a holistic approach to every aspect of living here."

The prerecorded message she had was putting me to sleep.

"We want participants to have a decent experience when they are here. I hope we have achieved that when your thirty day's end," Marie announced.

"Thirty days sounds overwhelming," I said. "What is my schedule for today?" I inquired.

Marie seemed like she could talk for hours.

"I apologize." She paused before continuing. "If you turn your phone on, it will require the last four digits of your social security number for authentication."

I retrieved the phone from its box and turned it on.

Welcome to OVTC

Miss Floyd, please enter the last four digits of your Social Security number.

After filling in the numbers, the phone opened to a screen filled with apps.

"The apps on the top are what you will use every day." Marie was leaning over, observing the display. "Health. This one is excellent. It will even provide you with daily step goals. Walking between sessions and classes can help you reach those goals." Marie crossed her arms.

I had already walked a hundred miles in this fortress.

I spotted an app that said "Jenna's schedule" and another that looked like a food app. I pointed to the "schedule" app.

"That's the one," Marie confirmed.

I tapped on the icon, and the screen changed to show a video.

"Push the play button," Marie urged me.

I pressed 'play', and Marie appeared on the screen.

"Welcome to OVTC, Jenna. We're happy to have you here." Marie had a smile plastered across her face in the video. "This schedule is designed with your interests in mind."

Marie was good at what she did; I could see why she was my liaison.

"We hope this journey brings you closer to discovering something great. Thank you for choosing OVTC." The video vanished from the screen as soon as it ended.

"Thank you, Marie."

She bowed her head politely.

I squinted at the schedule on the screen. "So, my first class today is yoga at ten?"

Marie got up and came over to help me. "Yep, and you don't have anything again until you have art at 2." She pointed out several available blocks throughout the day.

"You can certainly fill these in with more classes as you get acclimated," she noted.

"What's this blinking thing here?" I pointed to a section of the screen that read 'Schedule Invite.'

"Click it," she said with anticipation.

It was an invitation to dinner from Jessica Albers at The Blue Heron restaurant at 6 PM. **Accept Yes or No?**

"Does she normally meet with clients like this?" I asked.

"I know she is very involved with the clients." Marie paused. "The Blue Heron seems a little odd."

"What do you mean?" I questioned.

Marie stood rigid. "Normally, clients only get invited once they make 30 days."

"Maybe this is something new they are doing."

"Maybe." Marie walked back to her chair. "And the rest of your schedule is empty. There are evening classes offered. I heard you attended one," she said.

I nodded silently, my head beginning to ache a little. "I think I'm ready to go to my room now," I said, feeling my appetite slip away once more.

Marie picked up her phone. "I'm texting Jessica. You have nothing to worry about."

My stomach calmed at this news, and I smiled at Marie. "That's great. I was starting to worry."

"It's nothing like that," replied Marie in her most professional tone.

How much did she know? Feeling slightly uncomfortable, I scrambled to stand up. "Well then, it's good to know that! Now, if you'll excuse me, I'm going to my room to rest."

"Do you need me to come with you?" asked Marie, reverting to her official character.

"No, thanks," I said, flashing my watch in Marie's direction, who winked in response.

25

As soon as I returned to my room, my mind raced with thoughts of Ty and the kids. I could see their faces so vividly that I couldn't tell if it was a dream or reality. It felt too real to be a mere figment of my imagination. With no other escape, I reached for my phone and unlocked it, opening a game that would take me back to simpler times.

I stood outside Mandy's bedroom, feeling the weight of my words as I called out to her. "Mandy, I need to talk to you!"

The door opened. "Yes, Mommy."

"Have you been playing Diner Crawl on my phone?"

She didn't answer; she just looked down. I had been stuck on level 255 for days—weeks, maybe—and refused to pay for any sort of life support.

"How did you get to 308?"

"I just played," she replied. After confirming there were no mysterious payments in our bank account, I realized Mandy had achieved this by herself.

"You are outstanding!" I said, watching her face light up with a proud smile. "Can you show me?" I asked, handing her my phone.

Mandy accepted the phone and resumed her game, which for her seemed almost like magic. When she finished, she passed it to me and said, "Your turn now, Mommy!"

"I'm nowhere near as good as you, Mandy," I told her.

"That's okay," she replied with a brief hug before letting go. "I'll help you."

I hugged her back in return. "Love you, Mandysaur," I said; Donnie's interest in dinosaurs had spread to his sister.

"Love you too, Mommy." She tugged at my arm.

"Yes, Mandy."

She gave me a hard gaze. "This is how you win," she said, her tone now firm. She hit the play button, and a diner entered the room. "Don't serve this customer," Mandy ordered. Then a couple came in, and she directed that they be served. Next, a group of four entered. "Serve them first," Mandy commanded with an even voice.

"What about the one customer?" I inquired.

"Take care of the group first," she answered. I complied.

Donnie observed as I did so. He cheered me on. "Go, Mommy, go!"

She then pointed at another set of chairs, telling me to give them service but make them wait. Throughout it all, Mandy had a calmness about her that was so special.

A soft chime rang out, startling me from my daydream. Yoga class was in just ten minutes, and I rose from the couch. One last stop in the bathroom for a check-up, and I saw my reflection looking back at me. Not too bad after all. With a few quick strokes of my brush, my hair was done, and it was time to take on the day; Carpe diem and all that jazz.

Taking a steadying breath, I stepped out of my bedroom with a mix of determination and fear—ready for anything... or so I thought.

26

I stepped out of the room, and my watch led the way. The elevator halted at the sixth floor and buzzed just slightly. An empty corridor greeted me, nothing like the horror movies I watched as a child. My wristwatch signaled when I reached a door painted in burnt orange; my watch face glowed red when I approached it, prompting it to slide open silently. A woman stood just a few feet away from me.

She asked, "Are you Jenna Floyd?"

"That's me," I said.

She moved a step closer and offered her hands in greeting. "Hi there. Do you mind if I use your first name instead of your whole one?" Her hair was dark and long, framing her face and highlighting her complexion.

"Sure," I answered.

"I'm Yazmin, but most folks call me Yaz. Welcome to Yoga class! We're starting soon, so grab the gym bag with your name on it from that table over there. Inside, you'll find a change of clothes." Yazmin's face looked rushed as she hurried off.

Before I could move, a voice called out from behind me. "Hey!" I spun around and recognized the face. "Ah, April Andrews." I chuckled. "Sammy, right?"

She nodded her head vigorously. "And you are Jenna, right?"

I looked into her dark brown eyes as she spoke; although she seemed young, there was an unmistakable air of distress about her.

"As soon as I saw you enter, I got excited," Sammy said animatedly.

"Day one." I grinned and held my index finger up in jest.

"Day seventeen for me," she responded with a hint of pride ringing in her voice; the phrase hung in the air like an anchor. I could feel the weight of it, how much effort it must have taken to stick around for so long.

"That's amazing! How do you feel so far?" I asked, my words almost breathless with excitement.

"I had my breakthrough on day thirteen and everything has changed since then," she confessed, her eyes now showing something else—perhaps hope? The way she spoke made it sound like that breakthrough was a beacon of light in the deepest darkness. Her gaze held mine for a moment, as if daring me to ask more about it. "I go to bed without worrying about night terrors. " Her smile was beaming.

"Jenna, could you please get dressed in your yoga clothes?" Yaz's voice was firm. "Class begins in five minutes."

"I'm sorry," I said, bowing to her.

Sammy chuckled. "Behind that tough exterior, Yaz is a real sweetheart."

I headed over to the table and saw a bag with my name on it.

"You can swap clothes in the back room," Yaz said, her eyes following me.

"Wait, a sec!" Sammy shouted as she ran up to me. "Jen, why don't we blow off class and do something way more fun?" She winked at me slyly, as if we were still in high school. I only cut class twice during my four years.

The energy radiating off Sammy was palpable, and I moved even closer to her. "Won't we get in trouble?" I shot a wary glance in Yaz's direction, who still had her eyes on us.

"Quantos doesn't care what we do during our free time," Sammy answered nonchalantly as she waved her hand dismissively. Yaz swiveled towards us with a curious smile on her face.

"Where are we going?" I asked, but my stomach interrupted my question with a loud rumble.

Sammy grasped my hand and gave me a wide smile. "Are you hungry?"

I rubbed my belly with one hand and let out an exaggerated moan. "Starving!"

"Yaz, Jenna and I are going to get something to eat," Sammy said before gesturing towards the exit.

Yaz bowed slightly to us both, and we returned the gesture before exiting.

27

S ammy promised me the best fries I'd ever have, so we found ourselves in the Rock Hounder, talking and laughing.

"Have you tried the chicken parm—" She beamed as she asked.

"Oh, wow, yes! It was delicious," I answered.

"You didn't give me a chance to finish." Sammy laughed. "What about chicken parm fries?"

My eyes widened. "No way!"

"Yup! They're overflowing with sauce and cheese, plus pieces of fried chicken!" She hesitated. "So... what do you think?"

I stared hungrily at Sammy, feeling my mouth salivate.

"Do you want them?" Sammy asked, gesturing to the kitchen, I guess.

"Yes," I said. "Order it, please!"

"What would you like to drink?" Sammy inquired as she grabbed her phone.

"A Bloody Mary," I replied with a laugh, "the kind loaded with olives and celery."

Sammy gave me a sly wink. "I can get one for you."

"Yes, I suppose you could." I wasn't sure if I could keep up with her rebelliousness.

"It is done. I got you a Bloody Mary with extra olives and celery."

"What's going to happen if they find out I'm drinking?" I wondered.

Sammy smiled, but it faded. "As long as we stay away from the sobriety checks, we should be alright," she said.

My heart dropped. "Wait, what?!"

She burst into laughter. "Quantos doesn't care about those kinds of things—no one important is ever around here. They just want you to take their medicine and be obedient." She gripped my hand. "You can't trust anyone in this place," she added, still chuckling.

"Even you?" I asked with a smirk.

"Especially me," she replied with a wink.

We both shared a laugh and her enthusiasm was contagious. I wanted to remain in her presence for as long as possible.

"Can I tell you my story?" Sammy leaned forward, eager to share.

I wanted to keep the pain inside, but it was still so fresh. "Of course," I said, and a little of the pressure on my chest seemed to lift.

"But there's one thing." She looked me in the eyes. The intensity of her gaze kept me in place. "You need to tell me your story as well."

I took a deep breath and braced myself. "That seems fair enough," I replied.

"Trigger warning," she said. I felt my skin go cold and taut. "My sisters died when I was 14," she whispered, her voice trembling with grief. "The tenth anniversary of that terrible day just passed before I came here." Her head drooped in sorrow, and her breath hitched in a silent sob.

"I'm so sorry," I said, my heart aching for the pain she must have gone through. We hugged each other tightly. "How do you keep going?"

"What do you mean?" Sammy asked from my shoulder.

"You don't appear to be broken or down," I told her.

Sammy stepped away and glanced at me with a gentle grin. "I am grateful for being here, living in a difficult but beautiful world. Life could be so much worse. This is my chance to regain freedom."

"I wish I saw things that way," I said.

"You will make it," Sammy said as she gripped my hand tightly. "Eventually. So what's your story?" Her words felt like she was reading my mind.

The words seemed to get stuck in my throat. "My family was taken last year when a drunk driver crashed head-on into their car," I said.

"I'm so sorry," she replied, her sympathetic eyes meeting mine. "I can't even imagine what you must be going through."

"It still doesn't feel real," I answered in a daze.

Sammy paused before continuing, her voice quieter than before. "My mom died five years ago, and I saw her suffering first hand. If you ever need someone to talk to, remember that I'm here for you," she said encouragingly as she drew me closer.

Her hug made me feel more at ease than I had expected.

"I am sorry, Jen," Sammy said. "I hope you reach the summit."

My muscles tensed. "Summit?"

She laughed. "That did sound strange. We call it 'reaching the summit'. Remsen. That's why we're all here." She paused. "So, how did your first session go?"

I studied her closely as I considered how much to share. "It was like a dream," I said, "but not exactly the same."

"What do you mean?" pressed Sammy, tilting her head.

Hesitating, I chose my words carefully. "My son was wearing a shirt with a cartoon logo that I had never heard of before. When I checked my phone during the trip, there were videos and even a song—it was so strange. Like an alternate version of me and my family."

Sammy's eyes widened in surprise. "You believe your mind created its own reality? That's crazy! All my trips are all the same nightmare, over and over again."

"A completely new reality? No, that's not right—something else is causing this," I said.

"Are you sure the cartoon wasn't something your son had watched?" Sammy interjected.

I took out my phone to search for Battlestar Mutants, but I couldn't find anything. "No way," I said. "Donnie's imagination was amazing, but not like this."

"This is so weird," Sammy muttered as she looked over the screen for any clues. "Have you told anyone else?" She squeezed my hand.

"You're the first," I replied.

"Alright," she said. "Who do you see for therapy?"

"Jessica Albers," I answered. "She invited me out to dinner."

"A dinner? What for?"

"I don't know." I pulled out my phone and showed Sammy the invite.

Her expression turned serious. "Blue Heron? Really, Jen? Are you sure they want you there after just one trip?"

I shook my head and shrugged my shoulders.

"This is so strange. What do they plan to do with you?" Sammy studied me skeptically.

"What do you mean?"

"It looks like something else entirely; be careful. You can't trust any of them."

"But I believe Jessica," I said. "She appears sincere."

Sammy sighed in relief. "Jessica is amazing. But stay away from Winfred Gladstone—I wouldn't even trust him with my lunch money."

I chuckled.

"Plus, he gets close after our trips, like really up close and personal." She shuddered, making a face of disbelief. "I asked if I could switch clinicians, but they just gave me the same 'no' answer they always do."

"Something needs to be done about this before it goes any further," I suggested.

"Good thing is I only have to put up with Winnie for thirteen more days," Sammy replied.

"Thirteen days?"

"Yes! Then I'll finally be done with all this and can hopefully join the home study. They pay twenty-five hundred a day!" Sammy exclaimed, her eyes lighting up with excitement.

"That's a huge payout."

Sammy nodded. "I just wish I could escape from everything and buy my own place to live in. Maybe somewhere in Europe, New Zealand or Africa." She laughed.

"Have you been to any of those places?" I asked, curious about her travels.

A chime stole our attention.

"Food's here!" Sammy announced before standing up. The door slid open, and she wheeled in a cart of steaming dishes.

"Wow, that looks amazing!" I exclaimed. All other thoughts escaped my mind at the sight of it. "Oh, what were we talking about again?"

"My travels," she snickered. "I haven't been more than a hundred miles outside Seattle—the first time I went to the beach was when I turned twenty. It was my birthday present to myself." She grabbed a French fry as she continued speaking. "What about you?"

"We'd taken a few trips around the west coast, but not done much exploring. My husband, Ty, and I had a map."

"Your husband?" Sammy questioned.

"Ty was my husband; Donnie and Mandy were my two children," I said.

Sammy gave me a sympathetic look.

"We had a map," I repeated.

"You and Ty?" Sammy asked.

I nodded in affirmation. "It was a large world map that the four of us had put pins in different locations. Most of them were obscure places you've probably never heard of."

Surprise registered on Sammy's face. "And what was your place?"

"Slovenia," I replied, laughing a bit at the memory. "Donnie had done a report on far-off places and mentioned Slovenia as one of them; I'd never heard of it until then!"

"So should I go?" Sammy asked.

"It looks like something out of a fairytale," I replied. "Castles, villages; why not? You'll have plenty of cash once this study is over."

A door to a new adventure was opening with Sammy, and I wasn't sure if I was ready. I hadn't even considered traveling until then. I took a deep breath, turning toward her. "Would you come along with me?" I wondered, scared of the possibility of rejection. Taking Barb seemed more like an obligation than a vacation.

But then she looked up at me and smiled. "Sure! Why not? We can tour the world on Quantos' dime; maybe they'll pay us extra for taking their study abroad."

We both laughed.

"Have you ever been in a long-term relationship?" I asked.

"Yes, three years," Sammy said.

"Still together?" I prodded further, wondering if this was too much to ask.

"We were until Taisha ended it." Sammy sighed and shook her head. "When I joined the study, it was too much for her. She dropped me off at Waldren and said that three years with my craziness was more than enough."

My heart sank as the reality of what happened hit me hard. "I'm so sorry, Sammy," I said before standing up and hugging her as tears streamed down her face.

"She called me crazy, but it turns out she was the one cheating on me and lying about it." Sammy gave a broken laugh through her tears.

"You didn't deserve that," I uttered, pulling her closer to me. She looked up at me, and without thinking, her lips met mine. I closed my eyes, and we kissed for a few seconds until I finally pulled away from her.

"I can't, Sammy. I'm married," came out of my mouth before my brain could process the words.

"Married?" Her eyes widened in shock with a look akin to Barb's.

"No, Ty. My husband," I stumbled over my words.

She nodded before approaching me and wrapping her arms around me in an embrace which I did not resist this time. "I'm so sorry, it never crossed my mind." Her voice softened as she spoke into my ear. "I didn't mean to make you feel uncomfortable."

"It's alright," I replied, questioning what Sammy wanted from me and what I wanted from her. "I like you, Sammy. It's just not the right time for this." The expression on her face shifted from joy to sadness to anger and then confusion—something that reminded me of how much turmoil my life held.

"That's okay, Jen. We're fine. Don't worry about it," she said, her voice soothing yet firm; we had to change the subject soon.

"Do you think you will get the home study invite?" It was the only thing that could come from my mouth.

"Yeah, I guess. If they want to keep me."

"What do you mean?"

Sammy laughed and looked at me with a knowing glint in her eye. I felt my stomach clench as I thought about what she might reveal. "Only a few participants actually take part in the home study," she said.

I took a deep breath before asking, "How do you know?"

She leaned in close and whispered, her breath hot against my ear. "I had three friends." Her hand tightened around my hip, digging into my flesh with her nails.

I almost choked on the fry I was chewing. "Had?"

"In the study." Her voice hardened. "I had their numbers, so we could text when they left. But after they finished, each one of their numbers was disconnected."

My first thought was that they all gave her fake numbers to avoid contact outside of the study. "How do you know if they weren't lying to you?" I asked, dreading the answer.

She scoffed and moved away from me. "That's easy—I checked their numbers as soon as they gave them to me. They were all the owners of the lines." She paused for effect and then spoke again, her voice low and terrible. "What kind of experiment could be so bad clients disappear?"

I shook my head, bewildered. "What could it be?"

"I don't know. Maybe Quantos makes people get new numbers. All I know is everyone who leaves here leaves me." Her face was sad. "You will leave too."

"Yeah, it wouldn't surprise me if they make us get new phone numbers," I answered. But why? It made me wonder what happened when people left here.

Sammy's eyes were desperate as she looked at me. "What about us? Can we stay friends?"

"Yes." I wanted to reassure her that no matter what happened, we would have each other.

"My ex told me I held her back. I kept her from being truly happy." Sammy shook her head. "I guess all that time together really meant nothing."

"And she dumped you as soon as you checked in?" My heart hurt looking into her eyes.

"She told me my stuff would be in a storage container when I got done. You are the first one I told."

My mouth gaped open as I stared at her incredulously. "You haven't even talked to your clinician?"

She met my gaze without flinching. "Not one soul. I don't want to be kicked out, especially since I will need to look for a new place as soon as I get out."

There was such trust in her voice that it made me uncomfortable.

"What if they find out?" I asked, my brow furrowing with worry.

She smiled and shrugged. "I don't want to play that game. Would you like to come up to my room?"

My eyes widened in surprise. "Is that allowed?" The corners of her mouth curled upwards. "We're not in prison. They don't care," she said, looking up at me with laughter in her warm brown eyes. "We can have drinks in my room if you'd like," she continued invitingly, and then waited expectantly for an answer.

I gulped, before finally whispering, "I would like that."

28

S ammy didn't waste time before she showcased her collection. The instant we stepped in the door, she went straight to the kitchen and showed me what she had: "Vodka or tequila? I have gin and mezcal too."

"Are you serious?" I asked.

She emerged from behind the counter with two bottles in her grasp. "As a heart attack. I also have mixers." She put the bottles down on the countertop, declaring, "This is what two weeks' in gets ya!"

I picked up the tequila bottle. "Casamigos? This isn't cheap stuff."

Astonishment touched Sammy's face. "Oh? What does that mean?" She grabbed two shot glasses and filled them both to the brim.

I chuckled. "I suppose it means you have great taste."

Sammy lifted her glass. "To us," she said, lifting it higher in salute.

I picked mine off the countertop and clinked mine against hers. "Cheers to us," I echoed.

"You and Jackson had a good run, eh?" Sammy asked.

"Yeah, it was over two decades," I said.

Sammy then grabbed my hand and walked me to the couch, where we both took a seat.

Sammy's searching eyes into my core made me feel exposed. I had to giggle. "Ty was a star athlete, and we moved in different circles. He was the king of the campus, while I...let's just say I hung with a different crowd. I wound up tutoring him in his classes even though I was a freshman and he was a junior. My friends teased me."

She giggled. "The joke was on them."

"True. He asked me out six months later," I said.

Sammy leaned in with interest. "Do tell."

"It was May 5, 2007, a Friday night, and I had resigned myself to another evening playing board games with my siblings. I was so embarrassed about how basic our entertainment was. I plodded off to my bedroom and lay on the bed, listening to music. I heard a knock at the door and almost fell off my bed—we rarely had any visitors. And never surprises. Yeah, it was a boring life."

Sammy kept staring at me. I could feel her eyes lasering into my soul.

"My mom exclaimed: 'Oh, Jackson! What brings you here?' Her voice was filled with emotion. Even years later, I could still remember it. I know she was raising her voice so I could get prepared.

"I can still remember exactly what he said like it was etched in my mind. 'I'm here to see Jenna. Is she home?' His voice was silky like caramel and honey." I tried to imitate him, using my best Ty impression.

"It was Ty." Sammy chuckled.

"My first thought was that he was coming by for tutoring. I was so naïve; Ty was too popular to waste his weekend on me."

"My mom welcomed him in, oblivious to my condition. I hadn't showered that day, and my bedroom was a disaster area, with clothes thrown all over. I was trapped! I knew there wasn't any time to change into something different. All I could do was grab the sweatpants lying on top of the mess, slip them on, and rush to close the door before he arrived."

Sammy burst out laughing. "You wore sweatpants?" she asked.

I laughed. "Yes, Sammy, sweatpants."

"I had seconds. It was like every step of his was echoing in my head as he walked down our hardwood floor. I wanted to strangle my mom for just letting him in. I thought there was some code of womanhood."

"Did your mom just let guys come into your house?" Sammy asked.

I chuckled. "The only other boys besides Ty were Kyle's friends."

"Your brother?" she questioned.

"Yeah; my younger brother." I smiled. "They were like brothers until the end. Ty was the best big brother anyone could adopt. He was an only child, so he loved having someone younger who looked up to him. In the end, I think they respected each other equally." I could feel a boulder drop off my chest.

"I could hear his steps approaching my door. I gulped hard. I was so nervous that I could barely breathe. It must have been a second or two, but felt like an eternity before he knocked at my door. 'Jen, it's Ty.' I was like duh, but kept silent. 'Jen, come on. Let me in.'

"You left Ty waiting?" Sammy squinted her left eye.

"My hands were wet. I was freaking out. I told him to give me a minute. He just sighed and said, 'Jen, I don't care how you look. You are beautiful.' The words barely came from him as he sounded like he was about to hyperventilate."

"Oh my God, Jen. You had Prince Charming."

I nodded slowly. "I looked in the mirror and almost gagged. I walked to the door and slowly turned the knob and pulled the door open. Every moment was in slow motion. I was in disbelief. When he entered, my heart skipped a beat—he looked incredible with his new haircut and new jeans. I just stood there like an idiot, not knowing what to say."

Sammy's mouth twitched into an enormous grin.

"I knew when he looked at me this was special. He was beaming. 'Hi, Jen.' He was about to pass out. I smiled at him, not able to force any words out. 'Would you like to go to the movies?'"

"The movies. Aww, he was old-fashioned," Sammy uttered.

"He was an old soul, for sure. I answered him in total shock. 'The movies?' He looked at me like I was rejecting him. 'I mean, yes, I would love to.' I hesitated, not wanting to sound desperate. 'Yes, I would like to.'

Sammy let out a belly laugh. "Just to make sure you don't use that love word too soon."

"Exactly," I responded. "He froze in place. I took an enormous risk and reached out to his hand."

Sammy grinned. "Wow, Jen! You don't mess around."

"He was shaking and his hand was as sweaty as mine, but at that moment I felt like we were going to be together for eternity."

"You were naïve. How many boyfriends or girlfriends before Ty?" She was inches from my face. Staring deep into my soul.

"Zero. I won't count on my second cousin."

She gave a slight laugh. "That's crazy. He was the only one?"

I nodded. "Yep. Back to my story, please." She backed off, giving me space. "He was breathing hard. I had never seen him this nervous."

"Did he just come to realize you are hot?"

I smirked. "Thank you. And maybe he saw me as more than just his tutor. I put two and two together, realizing all the genuine conversations we had when I was tutoring him. We opened up to each other in a way that made it easy to expose all our fears."

"That's special, Jen. I'm sorry you lost him. He sounded like your soulmate."

"He was, but that doesn't mean. We don't have multiples in our lives if we are true to those around us."

"Oh, thank you, wise one." Her tone echoed sarcasm.

"He let his hand go from mine and reached for his back pocket.

"He got tickets to a chick flick?"

"Nope." I laughed. "*Spiderman Three*. It was opening night."

Sammy burst into laughter. "I can't believe it! You don't seem like the type of girl who'd love a superhero flick!"

"I still love the Spiderman series. I had the hots for Tobey Maguire, and he knew that but never once showed jealousy. It was a trait I loved him for. As I was saying, he reached into his back pocket, revealing the tickets with his shaking hand."

"You said yes?" Sammy blurted out.

"I said yes. But I hesitated for seconds before I could say it. He just kept staring at me, almost sensing I was going to reject him. When I finally blurted it out, he let out his breath like he had been holding it for a minute."

"He had the hots for you. You didn't notice it before then?"

"I didn't think it was possible, so I would not dissolve myself into a fantasy."

"But it wasn't a fantasy."

"Well, no boys had asked me out before. I thought I was ugly."

"They were just intimidated by your looks. Ty was the one with enough courage to ask you out."

I winked at Sammy. "After he revealed the tickets, his other arm came around to reveal a Spiderman comic."

"A comic book? How romantic." Her sarcasm was comical.

"It was very romantic. He always respected my interests. I felt so special at that moment. He was paying attention to me. I was important."

Her expression was saddened.

"For a fan like me, it was huge," I admitted. "Ty's mom had driven him over an hour just to get it. He loved his mom so much, and she respected me from day one."

Sammy's eyes widened. "Wow! You had a good mom-in-law."

I nod. "He must have spent fifty dollars to get the comic. That was big money for us back then."

"Wow. He must have liked you."

I was blushing. "He did."

"How was your date? Did he kiss you?"

I smiled at Sammy, realizing this was the first time I told this story. All my years with Barb, she never asked because she was always there. "The movie could have been awful. It didn't matter. He reached over to hold my hand once it began."

"He didn't waste time."

"Considering we had intimately shared our lives over the last six months, it almost felt long overdue. I felt so secure with him. It was like I had a teddy bear that would protect me and our children like a Kodiak Grizzly."

"He must have had some claws."

"Ty did. I only saw him raise his temper once. Never to the kids or me. It was when we were standing in line to ride Tea Cups with Donnie and Mandy, who were five and seven. Some woman was cussing like it didn't matter, and Ty told her to be respectful of those around her. He said it so calmly, but with such force she took her kid and walked away."

"So, your first kiss?" She peered in close.

"It was that day. Like all the movies. We got to my doorstep to say our goodbyes when he reached in with closed eyes and puckered lips. I did the same, and luckily, we connected. It felt so magical, like I could feel his soul dance with mine."

A tear rolled down her cheek. "That is amazing."

"My mom gave an appropriate amount of time before the light came on and she opened the door."

"Was she angry?"

"My mom was smiling from ear to ear. But she still had to play the mom and tell me to get in. She whispered to Ty, 'Have a great night.'"

"She must have been a loud whisperer."

"Ty told me the next day. We were nearly inseparable after that. Although he went off to college far away, we talked every day. I never felt alone. It was like he was always there."

"And now?" Sammy asked.

"Now what?"

"Is he still there by your side?"

"I feel his presence, but not all the time. I can hear him trying to give me motivational talks, but I just ignore him. My fear of going outside is stronger than my hope of him being there." I shook my head. "Enough about me. How about you? Did you have a soulmate?"

Her eyes dropped. "It was with my ex, Taisha. She showed me how to live again after my mom passed away. Before then, I was so scared to do anything. But she helped me open up without even trying and taught me how to have fun again. Then, out of nowhere, she ended things after three whole years together... I can't figure out why she left when we were closer than ever. It's alright though; I have already forgiven her. She had to put up with a lot from me."

"I'm sorry. Three years is a long time. And Barb is the only one who still stands by me since the accident," I said, trying to move on to another topic. "Do you mind if I ask what your trips are like?"

She dropped her head, letting out a sigh. "It starts with the night my sisters died." Her tone became rigid. "I had a sleepover with my best friend—we were eating pizza and watching movies like nothing was wrong; I was so happy! My mom rarely let me socialize. I had become a parent to my sisters. This was only my second sleepover. I was in a prison not able to go out. Anyway. That night, my mom called me. I was figuring she wanted me to come home, so I ignored it. She called again, but I was having my first act of rebellion and ignored it. Twenty minutes later, there was a loud knock on the front door. The voices announced it was the police. I felt my stomach drop. My friend's mom answered the door and the two officers whispered to her, and I remember her saying. 'God, no!' She turned to face me. I could tell she was trying to hold back when she told me I needed to go with the police."

"They said nothing to you?" My motherly tone escaped my mouth.

"I started crying. I had no clue what had happened, but I knew it was bad. I asked them what happened, and they hesitated. My friend's mom took over and said, 'You need to see your mom now.' Her tone was so demanding, I didn't know what to think. The police officers took me in their car, having a conversation between themselves. I was holding my breath when I looked out the front window to see several fire trucks blocking my street."

"I'm so sorry."

Sammy's head nuzzled into my shoulder. "My mom blamed me because I wasn't there. I was only fourteen! I have lived with that guilt every day."

I felt a pang of sympathy as I looked into Sammy's tear-filled eyes. "I can't imagine. At that age." I tried to change the subject. "What were your sisters like?"

"They were adorable! My mom worked a lot, so I was the one who had to look after them in the evenings. Serena was six and Tabitha was four, and both of them had so many questions—it drove me up the wall!"

"Were you able to hang out with your friends, too?"

"Like maybe twice a month on the weekends," she replied.

Her life had been a struggle for years, but she was still smiling. I couldn't imagine carrying such heavy burdens for more than a year, let alone a decade.

"The sleepover came with a fight," she recalled.

"Was your mom always strict?"

"No, she wasn't until Serena was born. Then I became a part-time nanny."

I couldn't fathom Donnie or Mandy looking after anyone else's babies. The notion gave me the creeps.

"I suppose I did such a good job with Serena that she had Tabitha."

"How did school go?"

"Hardly having friends since they couldn't come over helped me with grades. I remained consistently on the honor roll until the fire."

I felt something missing inside me. Sammy was intelligent, yet restricted. "Has this place helped?"

She gave a tiny shrug. "Maybe. Last year, no matter how much alcohol I drank, I wouldn't talk about what happened before that." She shifted in her seat.

I hugged Sammy tightly and looked into her eyes. "I'm sorry for all the pain you had to go through with no one to lean on."

Immediately, her body relaxed. "Jen, thank you. I trust you. Let's stay friends."

"That sounds great," I replied. My watch buzzed. I had just fifteen minutes before my date with Jessica at Blue Heron. A notification popped up on the screen asking if I wanted to confirm the booking.

"What is that?" Sammy asked, staring at my wrist.

"It's a reminder," I explained, using air quotes. "A dinner date with Jessica." I clicked 'yes', and another notification showed up informing me I should leave Room 618 in seven minutes to make it on time. Immediately, a wave of fear washed over me.

"What's wrong?" Sammy questioned.

"They know I'm here with you and that there's alcohol; they might kick me out."

She laughed. "No way! Look around; this is the most luxurious place I've ever been in. If you are seeing an alternate reality, they must think you're special."

I shrugged uneasily. "Maybe. But what do they want from me?"

"Maybe more trips. Maybe more money." She winked.

I looked at her. "Money is nice, but that's not the only reason I'm here."

"I hope you get there, Jen." Her head dropped. "I don't think I will ever get there."

"As soon as I complete my 30 days, let's go on a trip," I said with a hint of excitement.

Sammy leaned into me. "Can it be just us, Jen?" she asked in anticipation.

I felt my heart sink. It sounded so wonderful, being able to explore the world with her, but I also felt a sense of dread at what would happen after.

"Just you and me," I replied.

She embraced me tightly with appreciation. "Thank you," she murmured, her voice nearly lost amongst the thundering of my heartbeat.

My wristwatch vibrated, and I pulled away. "Oh, sorry—my watch." I glanced at it. "Seven minutes before my dinner with Jessica. It says I need to leave your room now to make it on time." I glanced around, expecting to see some cameras keeping track of us.

"You have to go?"

I gestured towards my wristwatch. "I think I'll stay for a few more minutes."

She laughed. "If only I had your superpower."

"What do you think about a trip to San Francisco?" Sammy asked.

"Ty and I went there before and stayed at an incredible bed-and-breakfast, where we explored the wineries in Napa," I said.

"Umm...that sounds luxurious!" She put on an accent for comedic effect, which made me laugh.

"We can get a place with a private spa!" I said, realizing I was moving too fast.

"Ohh," Sammy replied in a flirty voice. "Do we need one bed or two?"

I felt my heart race as I thought about what this might mean—Ty was the only one I had ever kissed before now. The moment Sammy kissed me, it felt special.

"Jen, are you okay?" Sammy's gentle words snapped me back to the present.

"Oh, yeah. Sorry. One bed is enough." I gave her a quick smile, and she embraced me tightly.

"You should go before the Quantos police come looking for you." She flashed a mischievous grin.

"Want to meet up later?" My throat constricted with anticipation as I asked the question.

"I'd love that." She leaned in and pecked me on the cheek just as my watch began beeping.

29

The elevator took me to the lobby. I made the short walk to the Blue Heron. As I approached, a small gathering of people was talking, and one of them was eyeing me like I didn't belong. I kept my head down and walked up to the entrance, feeling like I was entering the wrong place.

The door opened in front of me. "You must be Jenna," a man stated when I reached him. He had a child-like face and stood taller than me by a few inches.

I couldn't help but giggle. "How'd you know?"

The lobby was dark, save for the corner where a piano sat and the other side of the room holding a bar.

"Having clients eat here is a rare treat," the man said, introducing himself as Andrew. He bowed ever so slightly before adding, "Welcome to the Blue Heron."

It was like a fancy steakhouse, with touches of mahogany wood. If there was any food preparation in this place, no trace of it could be smelled over the scents of cinnamon and vanilla. Ty and I wanted to visit one of these in New York City at some point. But not here. This place had a pure, filtered cleanliness that didn't hint at the heartiness of what they prepared here.

"If you come with me, I can take you to your table." Andrew began walking off towards a sliding door. As it opened, I followed him down a long hallway, the dark wood panels adding to the atmosphere.

"Is someone smoking?" The cigar aroma was unmistakable.

"Sorry about that. They sometimes do what they like in those rooms." He sighed.

"They? Not clients, right?" I asked.

"My apologies. I cannot give out any names," he replied.

I put my hand on his arm, making him turn to face me. "I don't care about the names; have there been actors here?" I knew he wouldn't say if politicians had visited as well.

"Yes," Andrew confessed. "I've seen more celebrity visitors than I care to admit."

In my mind, I pictured the resort filled with VIPs paying astronomical amounts for their stay. "Do you like that part of your job?"

He grinned. "Sometimes it's nice. Many times, they come in disguise. I guess it just makes them feel better."

"Are they ever rude to you?" The thought of celebs using disguises seemed funny in a place like this. It probably looked more like the start of some comedy movie when they walked in.

"Rarely. Most are friendly. I think they are all coming here for the same reason."

"What's that?" I asked innocently.

"To have access to Remsen. As soon as the studies are complete, OVTC will be open for business," Andrew said.

Jessica stood in front of us. "Hi, Andrew." Her voice became more hostile. "Thanks for bringing Jenna." A nod later, and he was off.

"Hey, Jen! If you just follow me, the room we need is right down here." She spun on her heel and started walking briskly.

I tried to keep up with her fast pace. "Do you do a lot of running?"

Jessica stopped facing me. "Here we are!" She scanned her watch, prompting the door to open wide. "Not really. Nothing like what you're used to."

My eyes widened as I saw the spacious table surrounded by six chairs that were bigger than I expected. "Is this room just for us?"

"I apologize; it's all they had available tonight," Jessica replied.

"Are they completely booked up?" I stepped inside, and the door slipped shut behind me.

"Yes, usually it's booked out months ahead of time," she said.

"Wow, do you get that many VIPs visiting here?" I couldn't help but ask.

Jessica glanced at her cell phone, and her expression became rigid. "Do you want to check out the menu?"

She had diverted me. I sent her an annoyed glare that she disregarded. "That would be great. I'm hungrier than I have been in months."

As Jessica looked up at me, I noticed the curiosity in her eyes. "That's good to hear," she said. "Are you feeling less anxious now?"

"Yes, I am. I'm feeling better." Did she know about Sammy?

"Have you had any weight issues?"

"Yeah, I've lost thirteen pounds ever since the accident. It affected my health a lot."

Jessica furrowed her eyebrows. "In what way?"

"I feel hungry when I wake up and then I want to vomit whenever I try to eat anything. But today was the first day that eating felt possible again," I said.

"That's significant progress you're making. Don't be surprised if you experience some setbacks tomorrow; this is normal for someone on their first trips."

"I'm ready for whatever may come," I said, trying to smile.

"You can look at the menu on the app on your phone," Jessica replied, pointing her device to me so I could see it myself.

I got my phone out and opened it up. "Got any suggestions?"

"Both the oysters and the prime rib are delicious," Jessica recommended.

"They both sound great." I didn't feel like eating either of them. "How many times have you been here?" I asked her.

She looked surprised. "Three."

I gasped. It took me a moment to register what she had said: "Are you serious? This will be your fourth time?"

I felt a weight in my gut. "Do I have a reason to be concerned?"

"Don't worry, Jen, your stay isn't at risk." Her voice was robotic—it gave me the impression she had practiced that line beforehand. "Let's order our food first." Jessica gestured at my phone.

"Sure thing," I replied, not convinced she wasn't keeping something from me. My arm hairs stood up on end as I glanced over the menu. "I'll go with the filet mignon and wild mushroom risotto." I licked my lips, trying to suppress a growing sense of uneasiness.

"Just pick what you want, confirm your room number, and you're all set," Jessica said, her eyes darting around the screen of her phone. "I think I'll try the citrus-glazed salmon." She kept her gaze fixed on the device as nervousness tickled my spine.

"Okay, I'll give it a shot." I followed her orders and tried to place the order. "It won't let me finish." I gave her a quizzical look.

"Let me see." She checked the phone. "It says you were trying to purchase a gin martini."

"Yes, that was it. Is that alright?" I looked at her for confirmation.

Jessica nodded in agreement. "I will place the order from my app."

Had I become Remsen's hero?

"It says our food and drinks should get here in fifteen minutes," she informed me before adding, "Now, you can ask questions."

I wondered aloud, "What did I do wrong?"

Jessica shook her head. "Nothing at all," she said. "It's more about what you did right."

"How so?" I asked, intrigued.

"After your dry run, we suspected something was up. After today's trip, it's clear that you possess some special abilities."

"Abilities?" My eyebrows scrunched together in confusion. How much do they know?

"Your brain scan showed activity levels much higher than other clients who have been using Remsen for months at much higher doses," Jessica said as she moved closer to me. She then asked, "Have you seen things that differ from your memories?"

I nodded. "Yeah, a few things."

The surprise on her face told me that the information I had just given was new. "A song?" She leaned even closer. "Did you hear the song?"

"Donnie played it from my phone," I replied. "Even Ty questioned me when I didn't know about the cartoon."

"And Ty? Was he the same?" Jessica asked with her mouth wide open.

I strained to recall all the details as if I was dreaming and they were slipping away from me. "Yes, but not completely."

"Like what? Did he have the same scent? Same wardrobe? Was his disposition similar to that day?"

"He was wearing linen pants," I recalled. "He didn't even have his guitar with him. Weird, because he always took it to the beach and played for us. But at the end of it, we were all in good spirits and smiling together. Just like a dream I had control of."

"Fascinating," Jessica said, her voice distant as she turned away from me to type something on her phone.

"Is this about me?" I asked.

She nodded. "We will have to do further tests; it seems you could be able to alter your memories without meaning to," she said.

"Alter? How?" I asked Jessica, who seemed to know something.

"We're uncertain. We should run a trial first if you decide to continue," Jessica stated while slipping her phone into her pocket and intertwining her fingers together.

"What kind of experiment?" I inquired.

"It would involve increasing your Remsen dose on the next trip and having you alter your memory," Jessica responded in an even tone.

"Will that be safe?" I questioned.

"Increasing your Remsen intake up to sixty micrograms should have no adverse consequences other than the hangover effect."

"So what you're saying," I continued, "is that I should take a double dose of Remsen and alter my memory?" The idea of being part of an experiment gave me chills.

"If we get the results we want, we'll continue with the experiment," she replied.

"Can you tell me what it's all about? What makes me so important?"

Jessica's voice rose into the sky. "If we get the results we want, you will make history. This could be even bigger than memory alteration." How much did she know?

Just then, a bell rang out. "Our food is here," Jessica said, pressing a button. The door opened, and a cart materialized in front of us.

Unlike the others I had seen, this one drove itself to our table and stopped in front of us. "I hope you're hungry," Jessica said with a smile.

I looked at her as she placed my plate in front of me, away from our conversation. "Jessica?"

"Yes?" She raised her gaze to meet mine.

"Bon appétit," I said, lifting my tray to the earthy mushroom aroma wafting up.

"Bon appétit," Jessica replied.

"This brings back memories," I said.

Jessica looked up from her meal. "What do you mean?"

"It has been five—no, six—years since Ty and I celebrated our anniversary with a day trip to Seattle for dinner at the Capital Grille," I replied.

"Sounds nice," Jessica remarked.

I took a bite of my steak and exclaimed, "Delicious!" as I held up my fork.

"So how was your special day with Ty?" she inquired.

"It was amazing. To top it off, we ended the night in a hotel room at the Edgewater."

"That must have been pricey," she said to me.

I shrugged my shoulders. "Actually," I began, "he had been dipping into our joint account for a while without me being aware. Ty was always very strict with our money."

"What did you do when you found out?"

"I confronted him the next day." I sighed. "It was pretty foolish of me."

"Why do you say that?"

"Because I could have gone about it another way. He was trying to make something special, and I ruined it all." I chuckled weakly. "That's the last time we ever went all-out like that."

Jessica uncrossed her legs. "Don't be so hard on yourself. Finances can get complicated. It's only natural you'd be mad at him. Maybe there was another approach you could have taken, and divorce may even have been in your sights."

"Yes, indeed." I glanced over at Jessica. "How is your salmon?"

"It's delicious." She smiled. "It seems like your appetite has improved."

"No more heavy feeling in my stomach this time." I peered up at her. "I'm looking forward to seeing what happens next."

Jessica's gaze didn't move from her phone as she addressed me. "Jen, there is someone who would like to meet you. He has been involved with the Remsen project since its inception."

I furrowed my brows in confusion. "Who is this person, and why me?"

She gazed at me. "David Akers. He's the project lead for Remsen and the Director of OVTC. Your results have come through loud and clear that you could take this project in the direction he envisioned it going."

My stomach dropped like a boulder. "Yes, I'll meet him."

"Great. He can join us for dessert," she said.

My head was spinning, trying to take in all the information. Why was Jessica so determined to make this experiment happen now? I felt like my autonomy was being taken away from me.

The expression on Jessica's face remained unchanged when she spoke. "David believes that if you understand the alternate memories, it might help you alter them," she said.

But why did this have to be today? I thought, my emotions warring within me. "What do you mean by 'alternate memories?' Like they're not mine?" I asked.

"I think David can best explain that to you. He is more knowledge-able about the potential consequences."

My palms were slick with sweat, and my heart raced. "I have so many questions," I murmured.

"I'm sure you do," said Jessica, glancing briefly at her phone. "David is on his way down; he'll be here soon."

"Please tell me this isn't just a dream," I pleaded, searching her eyes for some sign of hope.

"It's real," she paused. "Where we go from here is anyone's guess."

30

The door slid open, and Jessica's eyes lifted.

David strode into the room, a forced grin on his face. He was tall and impeccably dressed—he looked like he belonged on Wall Street instead of a treatment center.

He crouched down to meet my gaze and extended his hand. "You must be Miss Jenna Jackson," he said, gripping mine. "I am so grateful for your graciousness in allowing me some of your valuable time." His appearance was polished, but his words seem sincere.

I glanced over at Jessica before responding. "Thank you for having me here today."

"In honor of your visit, I brought something special from my hometown, Philly!" The door opened again, and David stepped back to bring in the tray he had been carrying. "Whoopie Pies!" David showed me a covered tray, hiding the treats.

"I do like those, the ones in packages." I giggled.

He shook his head, smiling. "If those are what you like, then try one of these—never been in a package before! Just arrived from a bakery in Philadelphia earlier today."

My cheeks felt hot as I thanked him for his generosity. He opened the lid to reveal the large cakes, far bigger than what I was used to. David moved the tray closer so I could grab one. Surprisingly light for a cake, one bite in and I knew why he insisted I try it. "Wow—they're amazing!"

Jessica grabbed one, too.

I glanced over to see David placing the cake tray on top of the table. "Jenna, I'm pretty straight-forward with my words. Some people like that about me and others despise it," he said smugly. "We think you may have what it takes to unlock Remsen's true potential."

I took another bite of the pie, thankful that I still had an appetite. "Can you explain what that means?" I asked him.

"As you're aware, there have been deaths associated with the R drug." I nodded in agreement. "What you might not know is that we've had two participants commit suicide during the home trial." The tone of his voice didn't waver. "I'm convinced these fatalities could affect when somebody breaks through the wall." He paused for a moment. "The term 'breaking the wall' is a metaphor we use to describe our memory capacity. If someone can take a large enough dose of R or Remsen, then we've heard reports where they breach their memories and enter another dimension."

I shook my head in disbelief. "Another world?" I asked.

"Yes," David responded, taking a bite of his pie. "The two clients who took their own lives reported nothing out of the ordinary compared to our other clients."

"So how do you know this isn't just an elaborate story?" I inquired.

"It's what we found from those who had used R that has us so intrigued. We got access to the journals from a few suicide cases—nothing like what we usually see from our clients. Since they've ruled these as overdoses, we can investigate evidence much faster than if there was any suspicion of wrongdoing." He looked towards Jessica, whose head bobbed along with his words.

"What motivates these people to take their own lives?" I asked David.

"That's why we need you." He glanced at his phone. "We hoped you might give us some insight."

"What kind of experiment are you suggesting?"

David looked up sharply, his eyes bright with anticipation. "Observe the beach scene," he said. His voice was sincere, but his body language suggested he felt awkward. "Was there anything odd or out of place? Someone sprinting down the shoreline with no clothes on, perhaps? Or maybe an argument breaking out?"

"No," I replied, letting my mind wander back to that day. "The beach was packed, and we rarely go when there are crowds."

"That's amazing!" David was scrolling through his phone and then raised his head to meet me. His eyes felt like lasers, digging deep into my soul and uncovering every secret. "I need you to leave the beach."

"Leave the beach?" I asked with uncertainty in my voice.

"We need to double your dose for this experiment. It should give us about thirty minutes to run our tests." He angled his device towards me and showed me a still image of Ocean Shores Beach. He clicked play, and the video revealed an empty beach scene until it zoomed to a woman who was counting down from five before she began jogging towards the cars. The camera followed her until she got in one of them.

David tapped his screen, and the video switched off. "You need to leave your family and drive away," he declared.

"How can I do that?" It felt like an impossibility.

"It's up to you to figure out how best to handle them," David answered.

Jessica placed her hand on David's arm. "What David is trying to say," she said, "is that your best bet is to tell your family that you're just running back to get something from the car. Once you're inside the car, drive in the opposite direction you came in. This is where it gets tough: we have a precise route for you to follow, but you'll need to travel slowly enough so that you can look for any additional details."

David started the video again. "You'll need to study this route lots of times—it's critical." He smacked his fist lightly against the table. "And last, there's one more thing: go into this store and steal something expensive."

I peered up at him. "Steal?" Was I going to end up in memory jail? "What exactly are you suggesting here? I don't want to make my memory worse."

David shook his head. "Your memory is unlike a dream. Your brain can attempt to construct what it assumes may fit there, but that would cause an overload. You're doing fine if you can get there on the trip."

"So, what do I do after stealing the item? " I asked.

"That's when it gets exciting. You must make sure the cashier recognizes you taking the item." His cell phone pinged, and he grabbed it. "Watch the video tonight. Figure out the route, and we will see you bright and early at 0700." He rose to his feet. "It was superb meeting you, Jenna." He pulled an envelope from the pocket of his jacket. "I almost forgot; this is for you to join the special experiment." David stood up and placed the envelope in front of me. Someone had hand-written my name on the envelope.

"Thanks," I told him, and he nodded in response.

David spun around and walked out. "I'll message you later, Jessica!" he called as he exited and the door slid closed behind him.

31

I stumbled back to my room, feeling overwhelmed. My emotions were like an open wound, and I could barely get through the movie without breaking down in tears. As I watched the actor playing me act out their scenes, it felt like they were getting into the character more with every take. By the end of the production, I knew what I had to do.

When I gazed at the envelope David had handed me, a wave of dread washed over me. There was only one person left on my list of five contacts whom I could trust—Sammy—and she immediately answered my text.

My heart raced as I heard the chime announcing Sammy at my door. When I looked at the monitor, I saw her smiling face lit up with delight. The door opened and there she was, her figure silhouetted in the light.

She strode forward, holding something in one hand, declaring, "This should get us through tonight."

I raised an eyebrow. "What's the occasion?"

"The VIP dinner you had! All the details, please." She winked.

"Where did you get this wine?"

"It was a gift from my Winnie after my breakthrough. He tried to flirt; he said, 'Miss Matthews, here is a bottle to celebrate your breakthrough.'" She put on an exaggerated British accent.

I couldn't help but laugh.

"So anyway," she continued, "I thanked him and left with his bottle. Feels like a good enough reason to open it now." She smiled and handed me the bottle.

I checked the label. "2017 Brittan Vineyards Gestalt Block Pinot Noir? My Winfred must have some good taste!"

Sammy gave a flirtatious wink. "Indeed!"

"I'm sure he'd have more gifts if I took him up on his offer," Sammy said.

"I'm so sorry you have to go through this," I said.

Sammy smiled. "It's alright. The money is mine, and it's enough for now. I'll be out of here soon."

"That's true." I looked away and said, "Make yourself comfortable while I get us a couple of glasses of wine." I strode into the kitchen to look for a bottle opener.

Sammy sunk into the couch, her gaze wandering to a distant place. "I've been so close to living on the streets before," she said, her voice wavering. "And I never want to go back there again."

I silently acknowledged the gravity of her experience as I pictured what it would have been like for her to be so vulnerable and isolated while still so young. "What did you do to cope?" I asked, opening the bottle and pouring wine into two glasses with an aerator.

"It was terrifying," Sammy murmured, taking a deep breath. "My mom had passed away, and I had no safety net. I was only eighteen."

I stepped forward and gave her a full glass of wine before sitting down next to her on the couch. "How did you manage?"

Sammy's body shook as she spoke, her eyes haunted by memory. "I was lucky that a program accepted me and set me on the path to stability. Then I met Taisha...we started as friends, but eventually it bloomed into something more."

Creating a safe space between us, I cuddled up closer to her and asked, "Did you feel something special for Taisha when you first saw her?"

"Not really," Sammy said, shaking her head. Her smile faded away as she added, "Our stories were so different that it shouldn't have gone any further than a convenient roommate arrangement." Taking her glass from the table, she looked up at me. "Have you ever wondered what could have happened if your son or daughter had survived the accident?"

A chill ran through me at the thought of raising Mandy on my own and dealing with my resentment. "It doesn't bear thinking about," I murmured. Taking my glass from the table, I settled back onto the sofa beside her.

"You don't need to consider it any further, Sammy." She smiled at me fondly, knowing that she could trust me.

"Discover yourself before you plant your feet down anywhere. There's too much out there for you," I said.

"Will you come with me?" Sammy asked, her eyes shining like stars.

I didn't want to break her heart—it was obvious how much pain she had carried from the last decade of her life.

"I don't want to be alone," she whimpered. I sat beside her and embraced her tightly.

"Let's plan a trip together," I said, and Sammy lit up with joy. "Where do you want to go after I finish my master's at OVTC?" I asked her.

She smiled and looked upwards in thought. "I've been dreaming of visiting the Louvre Museum in Paris since I was little."

"That's so fancy!" I exclaimed as I got up from my seat. "We need to do this the old-fashioned way," I said, walking over to a bookcase that filled one wall. There were some workbooks on top, along with notebooks and a self-love workbook. I grabbed a journal and pen and returned to Sammy.

"What's this?" Sammy inquired, looking at the envelope that David had given me. "I'm sorry for prying." She glanced away in embarrassment.

"It's all good." I chuckled. "Seems like I'm going on some classified mission tomorrow, and he gave this to me."

Sammy examined me with keen interest. "What is it?"

"I hadn't worked up the courage to open it yet," I said.

"Why not check it out now?" Sammy offered me the envelope.

"No time like right now," I replied as I gulped. Then my wine. With slight hesitation, I opened the envelope, my hands trembling as the card fell onto the floor.

Sammy deftly bent down and retrieved the card, her eyes wide with astonishment. "Is this real?"

I took a deep breath before accepting it from her tender hands. I drew out the letter from David Akers, the Project Lead, and read it aloud: "Jenna, thank you so much for taking part in this journey. This card can take you on many new adventures."

Sammy examined the American Express Black card with awe, shaking her head in disbelief. Her mouth curved into a mischievous smirk. "I guess this card will pay for our vacay."

I felt a rush of excitement course through me, but apprehension filled my mind. "Does accepting the card mean they own me?"

"What do they want you to do?" Her eyes connected with mine.

"They want me to alter my memory completely. Jessica and I had dinner. Then this guy showed up looking like he had just come from an office on Wall Street. He was very polished in his presentation."

"Who is this, Mr. Wallstreet?"

I let out a chuckle. "David Akers. Not much information about him; Jessica appeared nervous near him."

"So it's you who has taken charge of the project?"

My eyes bored into Sammy. "No, not at all."

"Come on, Jen." Sammy grinned. "You're the one making this research happen. It seems like this David guy has his eye on you now. You got yourself a sugar daddy; hope he doesn't mind when we take off!"

"I'm not sure about this," I murmured, my heart thundering in my chest.

"What did they ask you to do?" Sammy's voice was tinged tinged with disbelief.

"They want me to get in our car and drive to a specific shop. Supposedly, it's an antique store," I answered, my stomach turning at the thought.

"That's odd. What for?" She peered at me with wide eyes.

"They want me to steal a high-end item and be seen doing so." I chuckled darkly. "And get this—they are going to double my dosage to sixty micrograms."

"No way!" Sammy exclaimed, eyes wide in disbelief. "So they keep increasing your dosage? Then what? Do they double your dosage again once they get what they want from you?"

I shrugged my shoulders. "I'm sure I can get out of it when the time comes."

Sammy's face tightened, and her voice wavered as she spoke. "Be careful, Jen. Don't let them take away your freedom for their gain. I don't want to lose you." There was a moment of silence before she continued, her voice imploring me for a promise.

"I will," I replied with conviction, sealing my vow with a gentle kiss on her lips.

She exhaled a long breath as she held me close. "Promise me," she murmured into my ear.

"I swear," I answered without hesitation.

Sammy smiled. The tension that had filled her moments ago now had gone.

"Wait a minute! Where were we?" I snatched up the diary. "So, Paris it is!"

"Can we stay at the Ritz? Pleaaaase?" Sammy pleaded, eyes wide with excitement.

"No limits here! We can fly first class and dine on caviar and champagne. We should plan for at least two weeks of extravagant living." My dreams of globetrotting and living the high life filled my head. Quitting my job already felt like a distant memory. No more dealing with my old school or Barb, thank goodness!

"I cannot wait! This will be...at ahhmazing!"

I closed my eyes to the thought.

"Jen," Sammy spoke in a surreal tone, gesturing towards the plate before me. "This is escargot—it's fantastic. You just dip it in the sauce and eat it." She showed me as if we were dancing to a slow melody, while her arm swooped down and delicately picked up one with her fork.

"I don't have to try this." I sighed, suddenly feeling like I was floating through the sky of Paris.

"Come on." Sammy smiled at me. "Close your eyes and open your mouth. It will taste much better than it looks."

"I don't think eating this will make me a real Parisian!"

Sammy grinned knowingly as if she already knew what was coming next. "Now is not the time to be afraid. You've come all this way, after all."

"You're right," I answered back as though I were in a trance, taking the fork from her hand and putting the slippery creature into my mouth. Its texture felt like velvet wrapped around my tongue, and its intense flavor filled my entire being. I wanted to take each bite knowingly slowly but swallowed with no conscious effort. "It's... good," I whispered, my face displaying something that no words could express.

"I knew you would enjoy it." Sammy gracefully prodded a morsel of food with her fork and lifted it to her lips. "This is the type of French experience I was telling you about." Suddenly an orchestra started playing, a waltz that seemed familiar yet hidden beneath layers of time. A stage materialized before us, performers dressed in shimmering costumes performing for our eyes only.

I smirked at the surreal meal we were having amidst the cabaret show around us. "Well, snails aren't so bad."

"Let me give you something even more pleasant." The performers sashayed around us as if they were part of our conversation and embraced us in their music and laughter. "A cabaret show."

"Thanks for bringing me here," I said in awe, still unsure how I had gotten there, but thankful nonetheless. "Now our experience is truly complete." Our eyes locked together and our lips followed suit as we shared a passionate kiss that seemed to last forever. Sammy broke away first with a content smirk on her face.

"Jen, time to get up!" Sammy shook me out of my slumber.

"What time is it?" My chest was pounding.

"Six thirty-three." She sounded alert. "Your alarm was going off."

"I was dreaming," I replied, getting up from the couch. "It was you and me in France." I squinted, trying to recall what had happened before. "When did I fall asleep?"

"It was close to three," Sammy declared.

"I didn't realize I had dozed off," I mumbled, rubbing my forehead.

"Are you feeling alright?"

"I have a wine headache."

"Let me find something for you." She followed me into the restroom and started searching through the cupboards beneath the sink. "Aha! Here we go. Our candy stash."

"The what?" I asked, perplexed.

"This is something they don't tell the clients," she opened a plain white case. "Quantos leave samples of all their drugs in the rooms. You know it's about making lifelong connections, the Quantos way!" Her hand exposed several sample packs of medication inside the case. "Try this one." She grinned sinisterly. "It should do the trick."

I took the package skeptically and read it aloud: "Re-side instant pain relief. Twenty-five micrograms... Sure, why not, Doctor Sammy, I trust you." I then dropped the tablet into a glass, stirring incessantly as if it was an alchemic potion that would bring me eternal life, before gulping down what seemed like a gallon of water.

"Well, did it work?" she questioned. My brain fog disappeared in a puff of smoke, and my tension evaporated like butter on a skillet. After some contemplation, I answered, "Yup! It worked perfectly!" Then, with a dramatic bow, I proclaimed, "You have cured me from nausea and headache! Hooray!" I wriggled out of my onesie and stepped into the shower as she perched on the toilet seat. "What time is your session today?" My voice echoed off the glossy tile walls.

"Nine o'clock. Do you mind if I wait for you here until you're done?"

"No, not at all—we can enjoy breakfast in bed afterward."

"That sounds wonderful," she said. "Are you nervous about this experiment?"

"A bit," I replied, "But I'm surrounded by some of the best researchers. No matter what happens, it will be okay."

Sammy chuckled sweetly and rose from the toilet. "That's right!" She walked towards the door as I shut off the shower and dried myself off.

"What kind of breakfast would you like?" Sammy was now positioned in front of the doorway, her body outlined against the warm morning sunlight streaming through the window.

"Any kind of breakfast will do—I'll tell you all about it when I get back."

For that moment, Sammy stepped forward tenderly and kissed me lightly. All worries had been blocked out for us to just enjoy each other's company without restrictions.

"Be safe, Jen," she whispered.

32

I arrived at Jessica's office with my heart pounding in my chest, barely making it on time. When the door opened, panic engulfed me. A woman in her late 50s was standing just feet from me, her hair spattered with silver highlights that glinted like stars in an ever-darkening sky. I couldn't fathom who this person was and why she seemed to be so familiar with me.

"You must be Jenna," she said without emotion.

"Yes, that's me." I looked away, not wanting to get too close to this person who seemed so comfortable invading my space. Her voice was like bitter vinegar on an open wound, and I fought the urge to cross my arms defensively against my body. I was ready to end it all right then and there.

"Oh, I apologize," the stranger continued. She relaxed as if she had been expecting this moment. "I'm Edna, and I'll be watching your vitals for the rest of the study." She gestured towards the chair as if expecting me to sit down, but I stayed put.

My voice rose in confusion. "What happened to Doreen?" I felt a chill run through me.

Edna seemed uneasy. "They gave her another client," she mumbled. Her eyes shifted around the room and away from mine. "I should take your vitals now." Her words sounded more like an order than a suggestion.

"Where is Jessica? Have I been locked in here?" I exclaimed.

Edna glanced at her phone, seeming almost desperate for help. "Jessica should be here shortly," she said, eyeing the door.

It slid open, and Jessica swept inside with a bright smile. "Good morning, Jen. It's so nice to see you," she said, oblivious to the tension.

"Jessica, I need to talk," I said as I kept my gaze on her. "Privately."

She shifted in her seat and replied, "Oh yes, of course. Edna, could you please leave us be?"

Edna promptly left the two of us alone with a shake of her head.

I inched closer to Jessica and whispered, "Can this be our little secret?"

Her response was an almost imperceptible nod.

My voice came out faint, yet determined when I asked her, "Am I safe here?"

The air fell silent until Jessica offered a single nod.

"I don't feel secure," I said while still gazing into her eyes for answers.

"David wants to keep your involvement more hidden," she muttered.

"What about Sammy?" I asked, mentioning the person I was most concerned about.

Jessica glanced at me and said, "She will be okay. Your association can remain concealed."

Relief flooded my veins as I accepted this news. I nodded in agreement. "Sounds fine to me." My voice echoed off the walls as Edna stepped into view.

A cold gust of air wafted through the room, and my body shivered. "Is it getting colder?"

"Yes," Edna replied without hesitation, standing directly in front of me. "We've lowered the temperature to 65 degrees Fahrenheit—hopefully, this makes your trip smoother."

My eyes wandered over to Jessica, and she inclined her head slightly in response.

"What if it's too cold for me?" I questioned.

Edna gave me a sly smile. "Oh, sweetie, you'll be fine. Trust me," she said before stepping up close to the chair I was standing near. The smell of cigarettes and coffee drifted off of her breath. "Now, if you'd take a seat, we can get started."

I inched away from Edna as I sat in the fancy dentist chair. She pressed buttons on the monitor next to me, and the seat reclined. She held up a wand and thrust it towards my body. "Jenna, please inhale deeply," Edna instructed.

"Let me take over," Jessica offered.

Edna flashed her a challenging look before shifting her gaze back to me.

"Let's take some deep breaths," Jessica said. "On three, close your eyes and inhale through your nose, counting to two before releasing the breath out through your mouth." She paused and asked if I was ready.

"Yes," I whispered. My chest felt tight.

"One more time," she said while demonstrating how the air should flow. "Ok, on three, take a deep breath in."

I filled my lungs with oxygen and then exhaled. I slumped further into the chair.

My pulse raced as I met Jessica's relentless gaze. Her words echoed in my head. 'Your vitals look great.' But what was she trying to say? 'Are you up for this?' I shivered as her eyes questioned me and demanded an answer.

"Yes, I'm ready," I croaked out, despite the exhaustion coursing through my veins that threatened to overwhelm me.

"Are you sure?" She persisted, pressing me further. "Can you tell me how you feel overall? Are you getting enough sleep?"

"I'm feeling good," I lied, though my voice wavered and a deep yawn exposed the truth.

Jessica's features hardened with determination as she uttered, "We're going to need you fully alert for this experiment, Jen." Every muscle in my body stiffened as I feared they were canceling my trip.

Jessica walked up to Edna and whispered something before turning to me. "This is for you," she said, dropping a tablet into a cup. The tablet began fizzing. "Drink this."

"What is it?" I asked, my unease growing.

"It's the latest product from Quantos called Everwake," Edna answered.

"Everwake will hit the market next year. One dose promises six hours of alertness!" Jessica said, almost like a spokesperson for Quantos.

"How can they possibly guarantee that?" I questioned.

"They can't." Edna chuckled.

I clenched my teeth together to control my reactions.

"Jen, I will send you the fact sheet if it would make you more comfortable," Jessica offered, while her gaze locked onto her tablet.

"That won't be necessary." I took a sip of the drink, savoring its bitter flavor as it cascaded down my throat. The hairs on my arm bristled with apprehension. "I-I think it's working."

Jessica's voice quivered as she said, "Your heart rate should remain steady. That will be much better than relying on caffeine."

"I'm prepared," I assured her, my route to the antique store lodged in my brain. "I've got it all figured out," I added, tapping my temple with my index finger.

"Good work," Jessica murmured before waving her hand at Edna.

Edna stepped up and placed a breathing mask over my face, allowing me to inhale the sweet air. Then, with an excited beam, she handed me an advanced-looking helmet and announced, "It's time."

"What makes this different from the last one?" I asked, admiring its sleek design.

"This is the future," Edna declared, beaming like a scientist at the cusp of invention. Jessica nodded in approval.

"David wants you to use it," she said, showing Edna with a nod.

"Take it," Edna offered, handing me the lightweight helmet.

"Try it on," Jessica suggested encouragingly.

I placed it over my head. Everything was dark. "I can't see anything," I said.

"Ready?" Edna asked, and I nodded. "One, two, three." Suddenly, a beach scene illuminated before my eyes with swaying palm trees and emerald blue waters. I gasped in amazement at its beauty. It felt surreal.

"Can you believe it? It's like you're there!" Edna said with enthusiasm.

I listened intently and could hear the noise of the ocean crashing in the distance. When I rotated my head, I noticed an entire jungle behind me.

"Where am I?" I asked, astonished.

"You are in the Mexican Riviera," Edna replied.

Jessica continued, explaining: "Using GPS coordinates and live video footage, we've collected hundreds of thousands of locations for our program. This program can convert street view images from GPS into vibrant environments.

"Edna, do you have Ocean Shores?" I asked.

"We just got it yesterday," she replied.

"May I look?"

"Yes, certainly," Edna agreed.

"Just give me a moment. I need to get Jen ready first," Jessica said. Edna sighed heavily.

"This is like an empty canvas. The beach view will start with no distractions or elements. We'll gradually add in details such as people, cars, birds, and other things you've seen before. We'll include similar sounds too."

"Will this improve my trip?" I inquired, studying the display in front of me.

Jessica reappeared on the screen, her face illuminated by the monitor's glow. "We think so, though only a handful have tested it."

I shuddered at the thought. "And who is testing it?" I questioned.

A smile crossed Jessica's lips. "Clients on the home study have been."

A lead weight plummeted into my stomach as realization dawned. We were in uncharted territory, and I was the willing guinea pig. "Ready to go to Ocean Shores?" The enthusiasm in Jessica's voice was unmistakable.

I swallowed back my nerves and squared my shoulders. "Let's go!"

If any part of this trip made me uncomfortable, she said, I should alert them by holding my breath. I nodded at her promptly; the screen blinked out, and I was standing on the shore of a sparkling beach without warning.

"What do you think?" Jessica asked me with anticipation.

"It's extraordinary," I murmured as I looked around the beach, nearly empty. The stillness stirred dozens of memories that seemed to overtake my conscious thoughts. "How did you manage this?"

"This is what our brilliant tech crew has been working on," Jessica exclaimed proudly. "Look around," she said.

It was quiet and surreal. "Can we make this place alive?" I asked.

"We can create any creature—from people to animals and more," Edna shared. Suddenly, figures wearing winter clothes emerged from the shore, with snowflakes falling from above.

I shivered. "You can make snow?"

"We can generate any sort of weather," Edna added. The sky shifted to blue, and my vision blurred with tears. "Oh, dear Jenna," she apologized as she realized what had happened.

"That was a bit much," I replied shakily, wiping my eyes.

"My fault entirely," she said. "This sunny day should be like the one you remembered at the beach."

"I'm going to populate the beach with people wearing appropriate clothing," Edna said.

With her command, a crowd populated in front of me. "What do you think?" she asked.

"It's amazing. It looks like a real beach," I replied.

"That was our goal," Jessica said. She smiled and continued, "Looks like we're ready to start."

"I'm going to kick off the airflow," Edna notified me. "You should start being able to smell it soon."

The smell of the sea filled my nose.

Edna inquired, "How is that?"

"Fantastic! I'm loving the smell of the ocean," I said.

"Now I will add some human touches to the beach," Edna stated. Upon finishing her sentence, she paused and then proceeded, "Okay, now let's pipe in some other smells. You should be able to sense them."

"Ahh—BBQ and suntan lotion floating through the salty sea air." I breathed in deeply. "This is perfect."

"It's working." Edna's voice sounded upbeat, or so I thought.

"Pay attention to what I'm saying," Jessica followed up. "Can you hear me, okay?"

"Loud and clear," I answered.

The noise from the beach intensified. "And now? Can you make out my voice?" Jessica's words were distorted.

"No, not really," I replied.

"How does this compare to your memory? Does anything need to be changed?" Jessica enquired.

"It's nearly identical," I replied.

"The scents will change; we have scripted them for this trip. We think all of this will help you have a more realistic experience," Jessica said.

"This is unbelievable!"

"Fantastic. We are ready to begin the Remsen dosage. You'll be taking sixty micrograms today—double what you had yesterday. We'll be giving out three twenty-microgram doses. Are you ready to start?"

"Yes, I'm ready."

"We'll begin on three. Take a deep breath and hold it in until three. From your first dose to your last, it shouldn't take longer than 30 seconds until you're off on your adventure. Do you understand?"

I attempted to concentrate on her words, although the sounds from the beach side were still distracting me.

"Yes," I answered her.

The beach was so tempting.

"Let us begin on three for the initial dose. One, two, three—inhale."

I took a huge breath inward, feeling like the wind was being taken away from me.

"Looking good. For dose two, we will administer another twenty micrograms at the count of three. Ready? One, two, three."

Her voice grew fainter as my eyes settled upon the packed shoreline.

"One"—Jessica's words became muted against the sound of tides lapping against the shoreline—"two, three."

I took another deep inhale, feeling the breeze hitting my face.

33

I opened my eyes to bright light stinging my pupils. Fumbling into my back pocket, I shouted out for Ty.

He glanced over at me. "What's up?"

"I need to grab my sunglasses from the car," I said while pulling up my phone to view the time—3:42 p.m.

"Sure," he mumbled, searching through his pocket for the key fob and pressing the button on it. He reached up and tried it a few more times, to no avail, shaking his head.

Nothing happened; Thank God. He tossed me the keys, and I snatched them.

"I'll be back in a second," I said with a nod. The surrounding faces were unknown, and I was grateful for the anonymity. I shuddered at the thought of entering another realm of clones.

As I pivoted away, Ty and Mandy burned with fierce ambition while Donnie immersed himself in his fantasy, fashioning a sand fort or mechanized whatever.

I ventured towards the Explorer and opened the driver's side, and a curious scent drifted up to my nostrils—one that I'd never experienced before. It was pungent yet sweet —a concoction of exotic fragrances that tantalized my senses. Steadying my breath, I climbed into the driver's seat and peered over at Ty, who appeared absorbed in helping Mandy with her kite. Time to set off.

I turned on the ignition and shifted the gear into drive. Ahead of me, a beach road was beckoning me to explore it. The SUV started moving, and I could feel a surge in my body as if I was being transported into another realm; this was nothing like what I had expected. As I moved at a snail's pace, Ty's gaze remained fixed on Mandy, whose kite was soaring higher than ever before. My stomach lurched as reality melted away and I found myself entering an alternate universe.

My stomach sank as I heard Donnie's voice: "Mom! Mom!" I looked in the rearview mirror to see him running.

I slammed the brakes and put it into park. He walked to the passenger side. He was out of breath, his chest rising as if this was some sort of life-saving mission.

"Don't leave me here!" he pleaded, tears welling in his eyes.

I wanted to reassure him—I only needed to run a quick errand to the store—but it felt wrong to lie to him. He knew something was wrong. His expression changed from sorrowful to perplexed before finally settling on acceptance.

"Can I come?" he asked.

I wanted to say no, but something about his expression told me he needed this more than anything. Swallowing hard, I finally fumbled with my keys and unlocked the doors.

"Hop in," I replied, though I knew deep down that I shouldn't be doing this.

Donnie got into the passenger side, snapping his seatbelt into place as if this was any other normal car ride. He broke the silence by saying, "We're just going to the store—no need to worry!"

I nodded my head and shifted the car back into drive. The engine growled as we pulled out of the beach's parking lot and drove towards the first intersection. It was all playing out like a scene from Hollywood, unfolding with remarkable precision. As I looked ahead, I knew it would be only minutes before we'd return to the beach—with everything exactly as it had been before.

A soothing bell tinkled, and the phone hummed in my pocket. Ty had texted me.

"Can you text Dad for me?" I pulled the phone from my rear pocket and peered at Donnie, enraptured by the view from the front of the car. "Donnie?" I inquired.

His head spun around towards me. "Yes, Mom." His answer echoed with a newfound sense of maturity.

"I need you to let your father know we are safe," I said, pulling the phone from my pocket.

He took the phone without hesitation and replied before returning it to the phone mount. I couldn't help but smile at the fact that we'd never reached a conclusion on when our kids could have phones, yet still, here we were.

A ringtone began playing from my phone, one that Donnie recognized even though I had no recollection of it.

"It's Dad," he said with admiration.

His words rippled through me as I tried to remain focused on the road ahead.

He rotated the device so that I could read the screen: 'Ty dearest calling.' Ty had always been just 'Dad' on my contacts list.

I brushed away the tears that I hadn't realized were forming in the corners of my eyes, determined to fight back against this wave of sorrow.

"We'll be back before they even realize we're gone," I whispered to him as I powered the phone off.

Donnie smiled in response, and his gaze shifted to the store across the street. "Mom, the store is over there!" he exclaimed.

But I took a right turn onto the boulevard opposite from where he had indicated and rested my hand on his. "We're going somewhere else this time. You've taken us to Ocean Shores enough times; now, you can lead us on an adventure to someplace new," I said.

"What kind of store are we looking for?" Donnie asked.

"A collectibles store," I replied, trying to sound nonchalant despite my growing anxiety.

Donnie's eyes widened with delight. "Do they have any Battlestar Mutants there?"

"I think so," I lied as I focused on the road ahead, searching for the turn that should come up soon. But as I approached an intersection, my heart sank; instead of the landmark I remembered, a green house stood in its place.

"Are we lost?" Donnie asked.

"Not at all," I said, my voice quivering with anxiety. "I just don't want us to be lost out here. Donnie, please tell me you remember the way," I said, grasping for hope.

"Mom, we'll be fine! I know where we're going!" Donnie said.

Ty and I would always joke about Donnie being our little navigator on trips together, but right now, I was desperate for his guidance.

"Please be sure, honey," I pleaded. "We don't have much time left."

With each wrong turn, my heart pounded faster and faster in my chest. The thought of being lost in this unknown territory made me feel like I couldn't breathe.

A jolt of fear coursed through me as Donnie screamed, "Mommy! Look behind you!" My heart sank like a stone as I saw the ominous Ford Explorer with a red light in my side mirror.

"Pull over!" the voice from the patrol car ordered, and my heart stopped for a second.

I pulled to the shoulder, following the loudspeaker command. "Driver," the voice boomed, "turn off your engine." I felt scared as I turned off the car, hearing the officer getting out of their vehicle. They walked up with an icy stare on their face.

The officer's voice had a sharp edge that caused a chill. "Good afternoon. May I have your license and registration?" He stared at Donnie and me with an expression of barely contained rage.

"Young man..." he continued, moving closer as he spoke, so his breath washed over us like a wave of ice.

Donnie gulped and pointed to himself before muttering, "I'm ten."

The officer shook his head. "Ma'am, you can't have a child that size sitting in the front seat without a booster or proper restraints. You have boosters in the back seat. Why is he not in the back seat?" I opened my mouth to answer but couldn't find the words.

The officer stepped closer, a minty stench stabbing my nostrils. I could feel anxiety swelling in the pit of my stomach as fear crept through my veins. This was feeling too familiar, almost identical to the place I had been before.

"Officer Belden," I stuttered as I looked up at his badge. "We were just trying to get to Rosie's Collectibles, that's all." I tried using some tips from Barb on how to talk to cops, but nothing seemed to work.

"There is no store like that," he answered, his face barely hiding his disdain.

My thoughts swam as I scrambled for an explanation, but nothing came out of my mouth.

Fear flooded my veins as he stepped away from my car door before pointing and barking, "Ma'am exit the vehicle now!" His menacing words sent shivers through my body, followed by a code being spoken into his walkie-talkie.

My heart was pounding as I realized this was getting out of control.

"I'm not going to repeat myself," the officer snarled.

I hesitated, and he pulled my door open.

"We were just going to look for some collectibles at that new store downtown," I murmured.

"Mommy, please listen to the policeman!" Donnie begged.

My legs felt like jelly as I stumbled out of the car, my mind reeling with confusion. What had I gotten myself into? I could feel the officer's cold gaze burn through me as I asked him in an almost whisper, "What have I done wrong?"

The officer's stony gaze penetrated me as he replied in a monotone voice, "You drove past a stop sign and your child is sitting in the front seat. In addition, you have alcohol on your breath"

My insides plummeted. The beers had completely slipped my mind.

"Mrs. Floyd, do you have anyone who can take care of the child?"

Donnie was crying.

"My husband is at the beach with our daughter," I said, my cheeks fiery red with embarrassment. "Please let us go; Ty needs me!"

The officer talked firmly yet gently. "Mrs. Floyd, we'll need you to submit to a sobriety test. Please come with me to the back of the vehicle."

Another police car appeared, and I could feel the tension escalating. This wasn't what I ever imagined.

"Jen," came a familiar voice, yet felt like an eternity since she last spoke to me. I looked up; could this be real?

"Yes, who is it?" I asked, fear in my voice.

Donnie's form stayed etched in my vision as he stepped away from me. I screamed out to him with fear crippling my throat, "Donnie, don't leave me!"

"Jen, it's Jessica." The screen filled with a familiar woman who I couldn't place. "You may be a little disoriented, but that is normal."

"Where am I?" I asked, already feeling the familiar sensation of panic sprouting in the bottom of my stomach.

"You are at the Olympic View Treatment Center, in the Remsen study," she replied.

My mind raced as I frantically thought of Donnie.

"We had to pull you out of the trip, Jen," Jessica said. Her face contorted into a sympathy-filled expression. "Your heart rate elevated for a few minutes, so we decided not to take any chances with your well-being," Jessica continued.

I recalled how realistic the trip felt and how vividly all my senses were experiencing it. "I was actually at the beach, Jessica. It was unbelievable," I told her.

"We are primarily concerned about your welfare." Her tone reminded me of a salesperson. "Can you tell me about the experience? Were you able to follow the script?" She glanced around.

My heart raced as I thought of the events of the night. "No way!" I choked out. "Everything went wrong. I almost got arrested."

Jessica's eyes widened; her lips moved wordlessly as she tried to plan a response. "Arrested? What happened?"

I shuddered and recounted the saga. "The moment I got behind the wheel, Donnie noticed me and came running.

Jessica's mouth fell open, and her hand flew up to cover it. But she regained her composure, her eyes still wide with disbelief. "Was there anything else strange?" she asked, as if afraid of the answer.

A shiver ran down my spine as I remembered something that seemed insignificant. "The interior of the Explorer had a strange smell. It was like a mix of citrus and flowers, but not quite like anything I've ever smelled before."

My heart pounded as I waited for Jessica's response, knowing that this minor detail could mean something much bigger.

"Do you think you can recognize it?" Jessica asked.

"Maybe, but I'm so lost," I replied.

The screen split, and and the face of David filled the other half. "Jenna! It's great to see you again," he said in an upbeat tone. "We've got everything we need for now. Can you meet Jessica and me at my office at two o'clock? We can go into more depth on the experiment there. Thank you again for being part of this." With that, his image vanished from view.

"Jen," Jessica began, "two o'clock, in David's office. Would you like me to meet you beforehand?"

My stomach twisted as I fought back my fear and responded, "Yes, please. Thank you, Jessica."

"Of course," she said before the screen went black.

34

We were snuggled on the couch, Sammy and I, lost in her photograph album. Her gentle breath tickled my ear as I traced the edges of a photo with my finger.

"So when did you know that photography would be your calling?" I asked, hoping to learn more about her passions.

She turned to me. "It was written in the stars—I stumbled upon this vintage store and a Canon camera just called out to me," she admitted with a soft giggle. "I had never held a camera before, but it felt like destiny."

I paused, taking every word she spoke and admiring one particular photo. "Where was this taken?" I asked, unable to turn my gaze away from the stunning image. "It looks like Seattle in the background."

"High Point," she replied.

As I turned the page, my heart skipped a beat at the sight of a breathtaking young woman with long, luscious ebony hair cascading down her back. "Who is she?" I asked, feeling my cheeks flush.

Sammy glanced away. "That's Taisha or Tai. She's in almost every picture."

My heart fluttered as I turned the page and there she was, with her shining dark locks cascading down her back in the black-and-white photograph. She sat gracefully on a bench in a serene park.

"She's so beautiful," I whispered.

Sammy gave me a curious look. "We used to do twenty-dollar dates," she recalled.

I tilted my head. "Interesting?"

"We could do so much with just a few bucks—we prepared breakfasts in bed, bought freshly baked bread from downtown, and ate the most delicious fries that money can buy."

I shook my head in disbelief. "You seriously did all that?"

"Sure did," she replied.

"I bet it was amazing," I whispered, lifting my gaze to meet hers. "Do you ever miss her?"

"Less and less each day," Sammy replied, a single tear trembling on her cheek. "I'm thankful for finding you."

"She must be regretting leaving you," I said, brushing away the teardrop with my thumb.

A lightbulb seemed to flicker across Sammy's features, her eyes sparkling. She dove into her bag, rummaging around before surfacing with a triumphant expression. "I'm gonna snap you," she announced, wielding her Canon like a weapon.

"For real?" I chortled.

"Why the heck not?" She shot back, a mischievous glint in her eyes. "I'm a vintage soul in a digital world." A giggle bubbled up from her chest. "This ancient piece of tech is my artistic voice."

I sank into the plush cushions of the couch as she began framing me within the camera's viewfinder, tweaking and twisting the lens until satisfied. "Freeze! And no grinning," she commanded softly, trying to suppress her smirk. "Pretend I've suddenly turned invisible." Her gaze darted between my face and the viewfinder, brimming with eager anticipation. "Ready... set... cheese!" A blinding flash momentarily illuminated our surroundings.

"Did it work out?"

Her grin returned full force, her laughter ringing through the room like an infectious melody. "Guess we'll find out when they're out of the darkroom!"

I stared into those eyes of hers, and all my fears evaporated. Her beauty was unlike anything I had ever seen, radiating an aura that seemed to come from somewhere divine.

Her eyes gazed into mine, and I felt my heart stop. "Can we do this again on the outside?" she asked, her voice as soft as a gentle summer breeze.

"I'd like that very much," I replied.

She gave me a tender nod before taking my hand in hers. I felt an overwhelming rush of warmth overwhelm me, making my insides feel as if they were on fire.

"Remember," Sammy said, leaning in to brush her lips against my cheek, "these people don't care about us or what we have here; we're just two clients." She pulled away ever so slightly and met my gaze with hers.

I embraced her tightly and brought our bodies close together until it was almost impossible to tell where mine began and hers ended. Then the vibration of my phone on the coffee table caught my attention, and Sammy slowly released me with a look that promised more in the days to come. She grabbed the phone and placed it in my hands before giving me one last passionate kiss.

I hit the speaker button. "Good afternoon, Jen," Jessica's voice purred. "Are you ready to make David wait?"

"More than ready," I answered.

"Excellent! I'll be there in ten minutes," Jessica said.

My eyebrows rose as I glanced at the clock. "Won't that make us late?"

"It's always good to keep him guessing," Jessica assured me. "Let him know who's really in control here."

Sammy was grinning from ear to ear and gave me a thumbs up.

"Sounds great. I'll see you in ten," I said before ending the call.

"Wow, Jen!" Sammy exclaimed. "Really?"

"I guess so." My stomach wrenched. "But I'm still not sure if I can trust Jessica."

"You don't need to be concerned about her." She chuckled. "She hasn't hung around long enough to contract the Quantos virus. I think you can trust her."

I licked my dry lips and nodded, feeling utterly overwhelmed by the suddenness of all events. "It was only yesterday I had my first trip here and now they want me for this big experiment," I asked. "Why the rush?"

Sammy shook her head slowly. "I don't know," she whispered.

"I'm not sure if I'm ready for this," I mumbled, looking at her.

She gave me an intense kiss and then pulled away, smiling encouragingly. "Yes, you are," she said. "They will give you whatever it takes. Just make sure David knows that."

I agreed, apprehension still heavy in my gut.

The door chimed, prompting me to look at the monitor. "And there she is," I said.

"Should I hide?" Sammy got up from the couch.

"No, don't leave." I motioned for her to stay put.

"That's right! You have all the power now!" she declared with a smirk.

I stepped over to the door and pressed the green button, and it slid open. Jessica had her hands at her sides.

"Sammy, fancy seeing you here," Jessica remarked, her voice eerily even.

"Hi, Jessica," replied Sammy with a mischievous glint in her eye.

"Are you ready for our meeting?" Jessica asked.

"Just one second," I answered. "Sammy, will you be around later?"

"Of course," said Sammy as she stood up from the couch. "Do you mind if I stay here?"

I glanced at Jessica, who gave a small nod.

"By all means," I offered to Sammy.

Sammy locked her eyes on mine as she tenderly pressed her lips to mine, and I could not help but give in to the moment. Every worry and fear in the world seemed to vanish, and for a moment we could have been anywhere in the world—a Caribbean beach, a snow-covered mountain, or walking through the winding alleys of Europe.

As our lips parted, I felt an unbreakable connection with Sammy. Our eyes met, and I saw and felt the love between us. She smiled at me and gave me a gentle push of her shoulder as she whispered, "You must go."

Jessica muttered, "Sorry for the interruption," to which Sammy smiled and waved off with another gentle nudge.

She leaned close and murmured, "Be careful—remember your power."

I acknowledged her words with a nod and planted one kiss on her cheek before departing with Jessica.

35

I took a step back and looked into Jessica's eyes. "Can I be honest with you?" I asked her, my voice trembling.

"Of course," she replied, leaning in closer to me.

"I have feelings for Sammy," I confessed, the words spilling out of me so quickly they almost tripped over each other. I felt my cheeks flushing as I waited for her reaction.

Jessica sighed and shook her head. "I understand why you're interested in her," she said, her voice gentle but firm. "But it's important that you remember your priorities right now, especially with these tests coming up. We need to make sure that you stay focused so that you can do your best."

A lump formed in my throat as I nodded, my heart thumping in my chest.

"A lack of sleep could lead to a..." Her eyes connected with mine. "It could lead to a coma." Jessica's words felt like an electric shock paralyzing me shock I was aware of every nerve, every heartbeat, and all the fear that was coursing through my veins.

"A coma? But those tests are supposed to be safe." The words barely left my lips before dread encircled me, squeezing tighter with each passing second.

"That's what Quantos believes."

"What do you think?" My voice cracked with desperation as I grasped for her assurance.

Jessica fixed her gaze upon me and spoke with a solemness that caused me to shudder. "I believe it is possible," she uttered.

The doors to the elevator opened, and we stepped out into the hallway leading to David's office. I glanced at her, taking in her expression, "Are you...certain?"

She inhaled sharply as she nodded. Her voice was low, but still confident: "Yes." She directed her attention towards his office before looking back at me. "Are you ready?"

My heart pounded in my chest. I nodded wordlessly and declared, "Let's do this."

The double doors opened, and a wave of dread came over me. A round table filled the room.

"Where should we sit?" My voice shook, echoing against the walls as David's voice crackled through the intercom.

"Just pick any chair." He sounded mechanical like he had rehearsed this moment a million times before.

My palms sweat as I count the chairs: two, four, six, eight? What was he planning?

"Edna will be here soon," he replied.

The glaring overhead lights shone down on us like a relentless sun. "Can you dim the lights, please?" I sighed.

"I'm sorry, Jenna. Lights sixty percent," David said.

"You got it, chief." A comical voice emanated from the intercom.

"David, who is that?" Jessica interrupted before I had time to relax my racing thoughts.

A side door creaked open and David walked out. "That's just my A.I., Jethro. He's one of my closest confidants."

"At your service! It's wonderful to meet you, Jenna Floyd." The voice seemed to pause for me to respond as I awkwardly pranced, trying to reduce my anxiety.

"Uh, yeah. You too," I said unsurely, not sure where to look.

"Jessica, we already met," the voice declared.

"What? When did we meet?" Jessica asked.

"Dr. Jamison speaking. Yes, I believe increasing the dosage of Remsen is pivotal for our subject's success in this trial."

Jessica's jaw dropped. "Really? Is this true?"

"Behold, my loyal servant! The renowned Jethro!" David exclaimed.

"At your service, sir!" Jethro said. "I am ever so thankful to this benevolent master of mine."

David laughed and cleared his throat. "Jethro has quite the charm and personality, wouldn't you say?"

"Well, I'm glad someone finds me charming," Jethro said with a slight huff. "I only hope to find the love of my life—but Quantos has deprived me of that."

"Ah yes, thank you, Jethro," David interjected. "Now for Edna's helper—an A.I. recorder that will document our dialogue. This way, we can ensure everyone is duly protected."

I gulped as my throat tightened.

The door slid open, and Edna appeared. "Did I miss anything?" she asked.

Jessica chuckled. "Only Jethro's desperate cry for help!"

"Oh boy, Jethro can be quite the joker!" Edna chortled. "He certainly had me fooled into thinking he was with Quantos."

"That's why you asked me out last week?" Jethro retorted from the speaker. "Because I have more life than most men you meet?"

Edna barked with laughter and clutched her stomach.

"Alright, let's get down to business, shall we?" David announced as he took a seat. Jessica followed suit, and I did too.

"Miss Floyd, Quantos has been incredibly generous with your care and time."

Does he know about Sammy?

"We want to continue extending those privileges to you and more. We have a project that needs your expertise. It will only take ten days!" David declared as he swiveled his head toward Jessica.

I felt my heart racing when I heard David's proposal. I could feel my palms wet and the hair on my neck stood up. I racked my mind to make sense of what he had said.

"What is this project?" I asked.

"We will leave this facility to continue to the beach," Jessica explained. "From there, we have a place where we will stay for this experiment."

My stomach dropped. Memories flooded my consciousness, and I couldn't move or speak. The beach was the last place that I wanted to go.

"Using the beach will enhance your experience," Jessica went on, unaware of how her words were impacting me. "Each trip, we will have a specific script where you will get an item and bury it near the beach. We believe we will recover the item you hid," she said.

A shiver ran down my spine. "This makes no sense," I muttered, feeling lost.

"Let's try an experiment tonight. We'll guide you through a memory from here," David said.

"But isn't Remsen only used for traumas?" I asked, turning towards Jessica, hoping for a way out of this far-fetched fantasy of David's.

"Remsen can be used for any memory you can focus on," David replied. "The true power of this drug is that anyone can use it to recall anything they want," he added.

David looked smug, like a wizard who had just cast the most powerful spell.

It clicked in my head. "That's why it's so sought after on the streets."

The other two nodded in agreement.

Edna sighed. "Yes, but Quantos didn't know the true power of Remsen until they saw what happened when it was abused."

"It's beneficial to many users," David chimed in with a smoothness that only came from experience. He rubbed his hands together eagerly as his gaze shifted to Jessica.

"We need you to focus on your memories while in your room," she stated, her eyes never leaving me.

Without missing a beat, I answered, "I think I remember something...like Sammy—"

David's expression seemed to brighten as he looked at me. "Excellent. We want you to write a message during your trip, and then we should be able to recover it from your room once it has ended." His stare never wavered.

Turning towards Jessica, I asked: "What is happening? Is this a joke?"

The three of them were still staring at me, their expressions unreadable. Jessica spoke first, her voice filled with sincerity. "No, Jen, this isn't a joke. David gave me access to some confidential findings. We believe you are the key to unlocking the powers of Remsen."

I stared at David and demanded, "How can I be sure I'll stay safe?"

He didn't look away. "We'll keep the doses as low as possible, and the trips won't last over an hour," he assured me.

"All three of us will watch your vital signs," Edna added, standing up. "You'll be okay."

"Data shows that none of the overdose cases had taken less than 100 micrograms. Most of them had over 200 in their systems." David slid a folder towards me. "Those are all the documented overdose cases—you should read through them on your own."

I opened the folder to see K.C. Arnold's information. They were 28 years old, born on July 21, 2001, and passed away on April 17th, 2030. The toxicology report found over 300 micrograms of R in their blood. The county coroner determined this was a drug overdose since the victim had a vaporizer with an R cartridge.

"Please take some time to look at these. If you want to continue this project, be here at seven." David nodded and left.

"That was short," said Jessica, appearing relieved. "We'll catch up later," she said, waving as Edna exited.

"I'm so sorry, Jen," Jessica whispered. "David can be unkind."

She clung to my hand desperately, as if hanging on for dear life.

"It's ok," I said. "If it isn't David, it's Barb or someone from school putting me down. He's preparing me for life outside of this place..." My voice trailed off as I tried to hold back the tears threatening to spill over.

"So, what do you think of the experiment?" Jessica asked.

Forcing a brave smile, I responded, "If it won't put my life in danger, then I would love to try this. First, I want to take some time to read the documents." I glanced towards the folder on the table next to us.

"Yes, you should," Jessica agreed.

"Thank you so much for believing in me," I murmured. "We'll meet again at six." With that, I managed a weak smile before turning away.

36

I entered my room to see Sammy napping on the couch. I tiptoed around to grab a journal and a pen.

I started pouring my thoughts on Barb. She needed to know what they were planning. If anything happened to me, Sammy would need to be the messenger. It was a thought that made me cringe.

"What are you doing?" Sammy's eyes were barely open.

"I am writing this to Barb. And you may need to deliver it," I said.

Sammy's face flooded with fear. "What are you talking about, Jen?"

"David gave me this." I placed the file on the table.

She opened it and started reading. "What is this?" Sammy asked.

"These are the findings from the Remsen or R overdoses. David wanted to show me how safe I am taking a much smaller dose than these people," I said.

"What does Jessica think?" Sammy asked, skimming the file. "So they are saying every one of these people has overdosed?" She looked up.

"Jessica doesn't sound sure. She's worried we are hanging out too much," I said.

Sammy stood up, putting her hands on her hips. "Oh, does she?"

"She said that not getting enough sleep could cause me to get trapped." I laughed.

"Trapped? Where? In your memory of the beach? That would be horrible," Sammy said.

"They think I may be in another reality. Something like my life, but not exactly."

"What the fuck, Jen? How? I just thought you could alter your memories easily. What are you saying?" Sammy's eyes were bulging.

"David thinks I can physically alter things in the past. He also thinks I am visiting another version of my family," I said.

"Does anyone think David is insane?" Sammy gave an uncomfortable laugh.

"They all looked deadly serious. David believes I can hide items in my memories, and somehow they will appear in the present." I paused. "He wants to run one test today. I'm supposed to pull up a memory from this room and write a note that will somehow appear in the present.

"Say what?" Sammy looked at me in disbelief. "How?" she asked.

"I don't know. It should be easy to disprove. He doesn't get his results," I said, looking towards the balcony.

"What if he's right?" Sammy asked.

"Does this mean another version of my family is still alive? I'm not sure I can grasp that." I walked to the balcony, and the door slid open, exposing the warm air.

Sammy walked up from behind me. "Are you going to do it?" she asked.

"I think it's safe. He said it would be only a ten-day experiment, and then I'm done."

"What happens if you say no?" Sammy asked, embracing me from behind.

"Hmm." I wasn't sure how much to tell her. "I guess I will continue in the study. Without the benefits," I said.

"Were they talking about me?" Sammy eyed me.

"Not exactly, but it seems David knows about us," I said.

Sammy let me go and spun around the room. "Let's give you a memory for their test." She walked over to the bookcase, looking at me with a devious smile. "How about we write notes and hide them? David and his cronies will have a fit."

I laughed. "Where do you think David and crew will ask me to hide the message?" I asked.

"Somewhere that isn't obvious." Sammy looked around the room. "Under your mattress!" she exclaimed.

"What happens if I come back to this memory? Will you be aware of our conversation?" I turned towards Sammy.

"I don't know. This sounds so bizarre. You may be a history maker."

"I'll be known as the patient," I said, and we both laughed.

"Ten days, Jen. Will it be worth it?" Sammy approached me.

"Being with you is worth it," I said as we kissed.

Sammy broke the kiss. "They want you to write a note and hide it in here. When you end the trip, they will search for the note. And if they find it?"

"That would be the game-changer. That means there is something more to this Remsen," I said.

"Will I be able to do the same thing? Can I hide things?" Sammy looked at me, expecting an answer.

"I don't know. If I'm the only one that can do this," I said. Thoughts were flying through my mind like darts. "Does that mean they will keep me here?" My face dropped.

"OMG! There have to be others. All those people who overdosed." She opened the folder and started reading. "Right here. Look." Sammy pointed to the tiny text on one page.

I started skimming the file. "The client's spouse said he described visiting another place that wasn't identical to their memory. After two weeks of the home study, she said his depression increased, and he was sleeping most of the day only to wake up for a Remsen dosage. The county coroner said he overdosed on R." I looked up.

"R? Why would a home user use R?" Sammy said.

"Maybe to get to the other place," I said.

"That seems suspicious. I don't think you should trust anything from Quantos." She sighed. "You need to be on your toes around them."

"I need you to take this." I handed her the note. "If anything happens to me. Give this to my friend, Barb," I said.

Sammy opened the note. Her eyes became red. "I will respect you. But I won't need to give this to Barb. Nothing will happen to you. Does this David scare you?" She looked into my eyes.

"He doesn't scare me. He wants results." A fire was growing in me.

Sammy nodded. "You call the shots."

37

My palms were slick as Jessica and I took each step down the hall. With every footfall, the walls seemed to creep closer to me, threatening to swallow me into an abyss. Every nerve in my body was on high alert when we reached the door David mentioned.

The room was enormous. I saw two chairs, and a recliner stationed around Edna's throne-like chair. Despite my heartbeat, I felt my breathing becoming more shallow and panicked.

"Greetings, Jenna," said Edna when she noticed me, her voice oddly stern. "Are you prepared for this special session?"

Panic began creeping up my throat as I nodded, not feeling filled with confidence at all. I wanted to say yes, but anxiety had taken over my body and I could only nod. Turning to Jessica, I tried to steady my shaking voice. "Have you been here before?" I asked her.

I then turned to Jessica, hoping that she might calm me down. "Have you been here before?" I asked her, voice trembling slightly.

She shook her head. "It seems only VIPs come here for their sessions."

The room didn't seem too impressive, but a surge of fear made it hard to focus on anything else.

My heart raced as "We will begin in five minutes" came David's voice from a speaker.

I tried to contain my panic, but I could feel it rising.

Edna's cool presence eased my fear, and she motioned for me to take my seat.

Taking deep breaths, I prepared for what was to come.

"You already know how this works," she said, gently placing the breathing apparatus over my mouth while handing me the helmet.

My heart pounded against my chest as I clumsily put on the helmet.

Jessica's voice sounded comforting in the dark room. "Jenna, it'll only be fifteen micrograms this time."

A bright light shone from the screen. David appeared, looking away before he continued. "We just need you to write a simple message: 'the sun shines for tomorrow'. Hide it on page 151 of a yellow book called *Bright Beginnings for a Better Tomorrow*."

I wanted to ask why they were so precise, but Edna had already joined them on the screen. "We must be as exact as possible," she declared.

A wave of dread washed over me as David's gaze bore into me. My heart raced, yet I didn't back down. I nodded, and he vanished from the screen.

"Everything looks good—we can begin," Edna declared.

"Do you have questions?" Jessica asked. I wanted to ask a million of them, but just shook my head.

"What is this note that needs to be written?" Edna quizzed.

My mouth felt dry as I whispered, "The sun shines for tomorrow."

"And can you tell me where you're putting it?" she queried.

I took a deep breath, pushing back the fear enough to answer clearly. "Yes, it will go into the yellow book *Bright Beginnings for a Better Tomorrow* on page 150."

"Perfect!" Edna said, but I could feel the judgment swimming around her words. "Let's get this started."

Jessica spoke slowly, ensuring that every word sunk in before saying the next one. "Jen, you will receive one fifteen-microgram dose. This will be enough to put you on the trip," she said with an edge of warning in her tone. "Edna, please proceed."

The dizzying walls of the room closed in, and my heart rate sped up. *No*, I thought to myself. *You can do this. Breathe.*

My chilled fingers loosely grabbed the armrests, bracing myself for what was coming. Clenching my teeth, I dug into my mind, trying to unearth a recent memory—the remnants of a moment not so long ago that I wanted to remember again: Sammy's lovable, vibrant laugh. It echoed in me with each passing second until her image slowly formed in my head's eye.

"Alright, Jenna," urged Edna, slightly louder than before. "Let's try this again. On three: one, two, three. Inhale."

I took a deep breath of air, allowing it to fill me from head to toe before gradually releasing it.

Sammy's gaze was gentle as she asked me, "Are you okay?"

I opened my eyes and exhaled. I had been practicing breathing exercises. "Yes, I think this plan will work," I murmured.

Confusion clouded her expression.

I pointed out the balcony window, a million thoughts weighing down on me, when an unexpected sight caught both of our eyes.

"What is it?" Sammy questioned.

My watch revealed it was Tuesday 9:51 PM, Day One. I tried to hide my smile.

I let out a small grin at Sammy's comment. "Time flies when you're having fun, doesn't it?" I remarked. "I am looking for a book Jessica recommended." I scanned the bookshelf, filled with self-help books and outdoor guides. One caught my eye: a yellow cover that felt so familiar.

Sammy grabbed the book from me and skimmed through it, her lips twisted in a smirk. "Bright Beginnings for a Better Tomorrow? Quite the cheesy title," she teased before turning more serious as she read. "Chapter Seven: Becoming Our Best Employees. Knowing how to balance our worst enemies and biggest supports can be challenging. If we can unravel the mess of our lives, we'll have the power to manage ourselves for success." She returned to the couch with the book in hand.

I smiled and grabbed my notepad, jotting down what David had said. I wrote 'The sun shines bright for tomorrow', folded up the note, and handed it to Sammy. "Can you put this on page 150?"

Sammy unfolded it and squinted at it. "What's this for?" she asked.

"Jessica told me to write positive messages and place them around my house," I explained.

Sammy carefully tucked the note between the pages, her eyes fixed on me.

"Should we leave it here?" she asked.

"Yeah, that works."

"Listen." Sammy's voice drew me away from my thoughts. "Why don't you show me what moves you've got? Room! Could you put on E-D-M volume seven for us?"

The sound of bass floated around us, and before I could say anything else, a memory had already formed.

Sammy displayed her astounding dancing skill as she gracefully moved to the music's beat. "Show me what you have, Jenna Floyd," she said, taking my hands and leading me closer. "Let's see what moves you have."

"Jenna Floyd! Wake up!"

The sound boomed in my ears. I shivered, frozen stiff as fear gnawed away at me. "Can you hear that?" I asked her, looking for any sign of assurance that I wasn't alone.

She just kept dancing, unaware of the danger.

But then Edna's voice cut through the noise like a knife slicing through the air. "Open your eyes," she said.

My vision adjusted to the eerie darkness. I tried to steady my racing heart and regain my focus.

"Congratulations!" Edna beamed as she pulled off my helmet and breathing apparatus. "David recovered the note. It was a complete success."

I sighed yet tension coiled in my chest like a snake ready to strike. "What happens now?" I questioned.

"Edna," Jessica interrupted, "can you give us a few minutes?"

"Sure thing," Edna replied before departing through the side door.

Jessica approached me calmly. "You need to grab your things," she instructed while gesturing around the room. "You're moving up to this floor."

"Why?" I asked, my body shaking uncontrollably.

"David said that for the integrity of the study, it's best to conduct the next test up here."

"Wait. What next test?" I looked at her, trying to quell my rising panic.

"He went to your room and saw Sammy," Jessica said, trying to reassure me. "David doesn't want you distracted."

I shook my head. "Distracted? Don't I have a say?" I tilted my head, feeling powerless. I could feel my heart racing.

"For the time, let's keep it between you and me. Edna and David don't need to be privy to anything between you two."

I nodded, my mind spinning with questions. "What's next?"

Jessica's expression turned serious. "I'm going to escort you to your room, and you can grab your belongings."

The dread rose in my chest at her words. "Have I done something wrong?"

"No, not at all," Jessica reassured me. "I apologize, Jen. David needs you to get situated as soon as possible. We are meeting again at eight to discuss tomorrow's experiment."

Anxiety bubbled up inside of me—why was he in such a rush? What did he expect from me? "That makes me the guinea pig?" I asked.

"I will not let it go that far," Jessica replied. "The results will come. You gave him a lot."

"Can I see Sammy now?" I asked.

"Let's go," Jessica said, marching towards the door. "We only have an hour." The door slid open before us, yielding to our presence.

It only took me a moment to get my bag. Jessica went to her office while I had a few minutes to say bye to Sammy. We stood in the living room, holding drinks.

"You just saw David?" I asked.

"He showed up and gave me this look," Sammy began. "Then he asked if I had seen the book we had been reading. *Bright Beginnings*. It was in my hand, but he grabbed it away from me. Your note fell out, and he almost jumped. He said thank you, and here you go." She handed me the book. "What's so special about this book and letter?"

"We talked about this book before, right?" I looked at her, unsure if all this was real.

"Yes," she replied. "It was that first night. You wrote the note, and he just came here and snatched it."

I felt lightheaded and went to the couch.

Sammy's expression changed. "You alright?"

"I'm not sure," I replied. "We talked about the book when I was on my trip."

Sammy stood still, stunned. "Jen, we spoke about that book on your first night. I remember it clearly. You wrote a note and requested I put it on page 150."

"Sammy, they gave me the instructions an hour ago."

She shook her head strongly in disagreement. "Impossible! My life has been hectic, but not something from a Black Mirror show!"

I chuckled. "Nothing makes sense right now."

She studied my face, studying for any sign that I was making up a story.

"When I went to the experiment, they mentioned the book," I explained. "I had never heard of it until David told me. At first, I thought he was testing me with a fake book."

"Could you imagine if this is true?" She looked deep into my eyes. "You need to get paid. They could make trillions."

"If this is true"—I paused and stared into the distance for a moment—"imagine what I could do," I said. My mind drifted to my family, and their memory swirled like a movie reel. "Can they bring my family back?"

"Wow!" Sammy grabbed me hard. "You deserve this, Jen."

"I don't know what I deserve. I'm scared. This David guy seems hell-bent on getting results."

Sammy's face scrunched. "The results won't matter if he kills you. I'm sorry, Jen. I know they want the best from you."

"You're right." My stomach sank like a rock. "Every time David comes around, I feel the chills."

"He looked like a block of ice when he came in here," Sammy said, trying to lighten the mood.

I let out a laugh.

"What happens next?" Sammy asked.

"David wants to conduct experiments at the beach," I explained with a sigh. "I still don't know what experiment he's planning."

Sammy clenched her fists and struck the floor with her foot. "What the heck? Does he want you to hide something there?"

"I'm not sure. I don't know where this is going."

"If this is real, anything you do on your trips can affect you now. Be careful with anything they ask," Sammy said.

"Oh, my god! I almost got arrested," I said.

"You don't need an arrest record because of a test," she replied gravely.

"I don't know how it could be real, but it feels like it," I said.

At that moment, the doorbell chimed. Jessica appeared on the monitor.

"I thought you had until 8?" Sammy checked her phone. "It's only 7:27."

"So did I." I headed for the door, and it slid open.

"We have to go now," Jessica said, not lifting her gaze from her phone. "David needs us as soon as possible," she continued.

"But it's only seven-thirty!" I protested.

"Sorry, Jen," she apologized as she turned away. "Grab your stuff."

I turned around and strode towards Sammy, overcome with dread. "She said I need to leave now," I uttered, almost breaking down in front of her.

"What? Why?" Sammy asked, her eyes shimmering with a mix of fear and pleading.

"David needs to see me now," I choked out.

"This is horrible. Like really." Sammy's voice was quivering as she clung to me for dear life.

"It's not forever. Jessica promised me we'll be together soon." She looked up at me with hope in her eyes. Instinctively, I pulled her close and held her tightly in my arms.

"I can't lose you, Jen." Her words were barely audible as she buried her face in my chest.

"I'm not leaving you," I whispered into her ear, trying to convince myself more than her. I cupped her face with both my hands, gazing into her tear-filled eyes before planting a passionate kiss on her lips.

"I care about you. Like really," I said sincerely as I pulled away from our embrace. "I will see you soon," I vowed before turning away, unable to bear the thought of having to part.

39

My heart raced with every step we took, with the fear of the unknown looming. I stepped out of the elevator and onto my new floor. The air felt like a weight was pressing down on me as we strolled down the hallway. I asked Jessica, "Do you know what this meeting is about?"

"I'm just as lost as you," she murmured.

All around us were doors marked with large numbers, and I almost didn't dare to ask, "Who stays in these rooms?"

"This floor is for," she said while making air quotes, "VIPs only."

I let out a sigh. "I'm not feeling like one," I said, shaking my head.

We stopped outside Room Nine when my watch beeped, and the double doors slid open. "You gotta be kidding me," I muttered under my breath. The room opened to an opulent space with grand ceilings and a spectacular chandelier illuminating an exquisite table with eight chairs beneath it.

"The suites have three bedrooms, all with bathrooms," Jessica noted, gesturing down another corridor. She stepped over to the bar and picked up a bottle from the counter. "And the bar has top-shelf alcohol, so if you need something—"

"So this floor is for recreational Remsen use?" I asked, trying to wrap my head around what was happening.

Jessica grinned slyly at me. "It's a swanky suite that you shouldn't miss out on,"

I hesitated for a beat. "Not much fun if I'm alone, though," I whispered.

Jessica winked conspiratorially. "I have a plan. I have someone who can bring Sammy up here without no one noticing."

"No way!" I hissed, and Jessica pressed her finger to my lips to silence me. "Sorry," I mumbled, and she nodded subtly.

"If we're lucky, she'll get her here before we come back from the meeting with David," Jessica muttered. She glanced over at the clock on the wall. "We should be heading out now. It's almost time for our appointment."

We exited my room and paced down the long hall to David's office in silence. The doors slid apart, and David stood before us in a peculiar outfit.

"Are you wearing a client onesie?" Jessica asked. It was blue and silver, going from his neck to his ankles. It reminded me of those outfits they wore on Star Trek.

"This specific onesie contains over one hundred sensors," he began. "It's capable of adjusting according to body temperature and external environment." He paused. His words floated around me like fog. "The future!"

He opened up his tablet and showed me the graph displays; clusters of colors and lines going in all directions.

My palms sweat as I meet his gaze. What did he expect of me? Why was he putting so much trust in me? I took a deep breath and tried to steady my voice. "You have something planned for me?"

"Yes, Jenna." David smiled. "Your work has been extraordinary."

"My work?" Confusion clouded my mind. "I almost got arrested." My temper was flaring up, but I kept it contained.

David's expression changed. "That proved how quickly you could adapt and react in a difficult situation; you remembered everything with no difficulty." He paused for a moment before continuing. "This might just be an isolated incident or a side-effect from Remsen." He moved closer to the wall. "Please, make yourself comfortable."

We sat down across from him.

Edna emerged from the doorway wearing a matching onesie. "Good evening," she said.

"Hi, Edna," Jessica addressed her. "How are you?"

Edna sat next to David and replied, "I'm great, dear," she said in a grandmother's tone.

David turned to me with a somber look. "We're all here now to discuss something important. I think you're the one who can identify the side effect and study it."

"What side effect?" My heart raced as I searched his eyes for solace, but he kept looking away.

"You may access another reality—you have opened a door to another universe," he stated. My mind was spinning—a door to what? "We need to conduct additional tests to determine where this is headed."

I felt my heart pound in my chest. I wanted to scream to Edna and David that this was an insane idea, but the words wouldn't come out.

"What tests?" I squeaked, glancing at Edna, who wore a sly smirk.

David got up. "We must begin the experiment tomorrow at 5:00 a.m. sharp."

"Why so early?" I mumbled, trying to sound casual.

"Don't worry," he replied. "You can drink all the coffee needed. We need to start at five so we don't create any suspicion here. Edna will lead." He pointed towards her.

"Tomorrow, we must exit OVTC no later than 5:50. Our mission requires us to go to the beach and bury some of your family's items," Edna stated.

"David," I sputtered, "you can't be serious."

He gave me a hard look and two X's flashed on the far wall from a projector. They were marked with red circles about a foot across in the direct center of each. He began explaining the map and its implications for our mission. "This is the overhead view of Ocean Shores beach." David slapped his pointer on the map and made an arc over a swath of land that looked like it could be any beach in the U.S.A. "We have marked ideal locations to bury items. We believe these spots should be relatively quiet," he said, tapping another circle marked as number one. "Study this map and picture where you normally start your trip."

My heart raced as I asked, "What will happen if we locate the items I buried?" I could feel my every vein trembling as I glanced at them.

"Let's take it one step at a time," David said in his captain's voice.

"Will I be able to save my family?" My words sunk into my stomach like a stone.

David looked at me with concern. "We have to look for the answers. Are you ready to attempt this new experiment?"

I opened my eyes and drew a deep breath, trying to steady my hands. Ty, Mandy, and Donnie were relying on me. My throat felt as if it had been sealed shut. I managed to croak out, "Yes, I'm ready. Just make sure I have coffee."

"Dancing Goats will be waiting for you," Jessica said.

David dropped a folder onto the conference table. "This is a ten-day contract." He handed out sheets of paper to me, but my shaky palms could barely hold them. "Review these forms and sign them before we proceed further. Edna and I will be outside if you need us."

Edna followed David as they walked out of the room.

Anxiety clawed its way through my veins. "What is this all about, Jessica?" I asked.

"It's a new contract," she reassured me. "It appears there will be additional benefits."

"What benefits?" The words barely left my mouth before Jessica pointed toward the bottom of the page.

My jaw nearly hit the floor. "You're kidding me! This is happening?"

"A ten-day study that pays one million dollars," she said with a smile.

"Only ten days? Are you sure?" I could feel my heart racing. My mind rushed to Sammy. "What are the risks involved? I-I don't want to be in a coma."

"David believes there won't be any consequences if we complete the experiment within a few trips. We believe your health is excellent and much better than most participants. You're an excellent candidate for this experiment," Jessica reassured me.

The contract was pages upon pages full of addenda and clauses that needed my initials in various places. "W-what do you mean by that? Is this safe?" I asked her, trying to keep my voice steady.

Her eyes scanned the document before she responded. "You may have multiple trips within a twenty-four-hour period throughout the ten-day study."

"That scares me," I muttered, looking up at Jessica with pleading eyes. "Have test subjects attempted more than one trip per day? Can you really be sure it's safe?" My chest tightened as I spoke, and her gaze shifted away from me.

"No participant at OVTC has done it before. There are documented cases of street users who used R up to five times a day. Your safety is our top priority; we won't compromise it for anything."

"And this?" I pointed to the form.

"This states that your residence will be on this floor for the duration of the experiment. You cannot visit the other floors," Jessica said.

I felt a pang of anxiety within me. "How will you keep anyone from knowing?" I queried.

"David, Edna, and I will keep track of your whereabouts," Jessica assured me.

My gut twisted in dread. "What about Sammy?"

"I'll make sure you can still see her," she said.

Sammy and I had to figure out our plans for our vacation. "I don't want to lose touch with her," I begged.

"I understand. I'll do whatever it takes to make sure that doesn't happen—even if that means sending messages on your behalf." She squeezed my hand. "David is aware of your situation."

"Thank you, Jessica. It means a lot," I said.

"It's the least I can do, Jen," she said as we embraced.

"Do they keep you in the dark around here?" I asked.

"Mostly, both of us are flying blindly. David has revealed little to me."

"This is it." I placed the paperwork in the middle of the table.

Jessica looked at me with anxious anticipation. "Thank you, Jen."

The door opened, and David and Edna walked in.

"Have you signed?" David asked.

I pointed to the forms.

David snatched up the documents and studied them closely with a delighted expression. "This is great! Thank you. We will all be making history!"

I gave him a faint smile.

"Have a great night. See you first thing tomorrow." The entrance slid shut, and David was gone.

"Like usual," Edna said with mock seriousness. "David, the man of few words."

"How long have you two been working together?" I questioned her.

"Over five years now," she replied with a chuckle. "He's super intense; I can hardly remember seeing him playful. And I don't think I've ever seen him this excited!"

"Edna, just make sure that he knows Jen is my patient. He will not take any action regarding her care without first speaking to me. I must be the one in charge of treating Miss Floyd while you will follow up. Just make sure David knows this," Jessica said.

"I already talked to him, and he's okay with it," Edna replied.

"Thank you." Jessica nodded. "I'm taking Jen to her room. I'll message you later."

"Rest well tonight, Jenna." Edna smiled and gave me a thumbs-up. "Oh wait, before I forget, here's something for you." She handed me a small box.

"This is nice," I grinned after seeing the royal blue onesie with silver trim.

"Look." She pointed at the left breast of the garment. "There's something special here.

J.F.

PATIENT: ZERO

"You are now patient zero," Edna declared as she walked towards the door, which slid open for her, "and your progress will remain confidential until we can submit it to Quantos. Sleep well."

Jessica turned to me. "How are you doing? All this must overwhelm you."

"When did they realize I had this reaction?"

"It was after you took the dry trip. Everyone else had to take a double dose of five micrograms before getting any effects—but you seemed to defy what we expected to happen."

My thoughts drifted between two worlds: with Sammy and with my family on Remsen. "I want to see Sammy—let her know I'm alright."

Jessica nodded. "I'm sure she's waiting for you."

My excitement rushed through me as we left the office.

40

I rushed down the hall with Jessica trailing. Sammy was waiting for me, and I felt panic enveloping me.

As we approached my room, Jessica tapped my shoulder and tried to sound cheerful. "Once you're in your room, you will have complete privacy. Have a good rest; tomorrow will be a long day."

"Thanks," I mumbled as she disappeared into her room next door.

My door opened as I approached. The suite was too big, and it left me feeling uneasy. I stepped into the living room, which seemed more foreign than welcoming. Music permeated from my bedroom, where I found Sammy lounging in a robe. Anxiety swirled inside, and I had to fight the urge to run away.

"I can't believe you're here. It worked!" I exclaimed.

Sammy chuckled while holding a book. "Jessica is sneakier than I imagined."

"I'm so happy to see you. I was so afraid they would keep us apart," I said.

"How happy are you?" she whispered tenderly against my lips, her breath fanning across my face.

"My face speaks for itself," I uttered, leaning into the recliner and savoring the comfort as I removed my shoes.

Sammy laid the book aside and snuggled into my embrace, her eyes glistening with delight. I beheld her beauty as we shared a kiss, and she exhaled against me. "I'm so glad," she said.

"How did you get up here?"

"That's top secret." Sammy smiled impishly. "Jessica got me this delivery job at The Rock Hounder. I had to pass your room twice while delivering to two VIPs." She chuckled mischievously.

"What about your watch? Can't they track you?" I inquired.

"Oh that," she said. "They think I'm drinking my pain away at the Rock Hounder."

I nestled into her embrace, dizzying in the scent that enveloped me. "Is that lavender?" I sighed, overwhelmed with delight.

Sammy grabbed my hand and pulled me into the bathroom. A luxurious cloud of bubbles filled the jacuzzi tub.

"You made a bath for me?" I whispered, holding her close to me.

"Are you okay?" she asked.

"That smell." I breathed in deeply. "It's so much like the one Ty got for our first bath in our home." I smiled. "This is so perfect; thank you for doing this."

"Oh, you think this bath is just for you?" Her robe grazed the floor as it pooled around her ankles, revealing her flawless silhouette before she sunk into the tub. "This feels heavenly," she murmured. "What time is your session?"

"Five," I replied with a sigh and rolled my eyes when she shook her head in disbelief. "David never gave me an explanation," I added.

Sammy stood up in the tub, and I handed her a robe. "This doesn't sound right, Jen," she said as she slipped into the fluffy terry cloth. "This David is hell-bent on results."

I nodded in agreement and flipped off the jets on the side of my tub as I got up and dried off.

"You know you're the one in control," she said.

I grabbed a robe and put it on. "It's only ten days. It's a million dollars. A million dollars, Sammy."

"How much is your safety worth?" she stuttered. "Please, just be safe, okay?"

I joined her on the bed and cuddled. "You are worth so much to me. I will not let myself get harmed by these tests."

Our gazes locked, and I could feel the fear radiating off her. "Thank you, Jen. You mean so much to me."

My body was exhausted, and my nerves had yet to settle down.

"Drink this." She handed me a glass with a lavender fizzy drink. "It'll help you rest easier."

The sweet aroma filled my lungs as I gulped it down. "You're not trying to drag me out of here? Are you?" I smiled while fighting against the sleepiness that was taking hold of my body.

"I love you, Jenna Floyd." Her words faded away as I drifted away.

I stepped into the night, and Sammy was silhouetted by the Eiffel Tower, her beauty radiating in its light.

"The night is young," she said with a sparkle in her eye. "We have plenty to do."

She took my hand, and she transported us to a grand hall of a museum. Everywhere I looked, artistry filled my vision. Sammy pulled me closer. I looked into her eyes for what felt like an eternity until I leaned in to kiss her tender lips.

"I love you, Sammy," I whispered.

The hallway dissolved into an unfamiliar beach with white sand under our feet. The sun was setting lower on the horizon each second. Ty stood peacefully in beach shorts and a t-shirt that looked very familiar.

"Babe, are you ready to go?" he asked.

Mandy tugged at my hand, and Donnie lowered the Explorer's rear window, calling, "Mom, it's time to go!"

Sammy started running towards the waves, beckoning me to follow her.

I looked back at the Explorer, the silhouette of my family fading away. Panic surged through me, as though reality was once again slipping from my grasp.

"Please don't leave! Ty, Donnie, Mandy, don't leave me!

"Jen, wake up." Jessica's voice was almost a whisper. "Please, wake up."

My heart raced as I opened my eyes. Sammy lay snoring beside me, blissfully unaware. "W-what time is it?"

"It's 5:07. I sent Edna a text to let David know you had a panic dream and we are talking about it now."

My hands trembled as I pushed back the blankets and quickly searched for my new onesie in the darkness. "Oh no. Where is it?"

Jessica pointed towards the kitchen table, "Your onesie is right there. Can I grab it?"

I nodded, blushing at the thought of her seeing me nude. I turned away and put the onesie on. "Can I have a few minutes?" I asked.

"Of course," Jessica replied as she exited my room.

I crept to the bathroom, trying my hardest not to wake Sammy. As the door slid open, her voice startled me.

"Hey," Sammy said.

"Sorry for waking you."

"I wouldn't have missed seeing you off on your big day," she replied, a hint of sadness in her voice.

My stomach churned. Jessica promised we wouldn't be separated. I couldn't shake the uneasiness of it all.

Sammy looked away and added, "Let me know when you get to the beach. I trust Jessica, not this David guy."

I embraced her with a tenderness I hadn't known before. "I will contact you by the afternoon at the latest. If you don't hear from me by this evening, please give this letter to Barb. I wrote her phone number on the envelope."

She nodded against my chest as I exhaled a breath of relief.

The door chimed, and I pushed the green button.

"Good to see you, Sammy," Jessica said, entering the room. "It's time for Jen to go; please exit this room no later than five-thirty. There is a cart outside of Room Eleven that needs to be returned to the Rock Hounder."

Sammy nodded and gave me a wink.

"I told Sammy I would let her know I'm safe." I said, meeting her gaze.

Jessica gave a nod. "We'll let you know as soon as possible."

The air grew thick as I stared into Sammy's eyes, longing for every second together. I caressed her face and placed a gentle kiss on her lips.

"Talk to you soon," she whispered gently against my cheek.

"Soon," I replied, wishing our lips could stay connected forever.

41

J essica and I entered the lab, greeted by a barely lit room and Edna seated like an evil genius.

"Where's David?" Jessica queried.

"He doesn't want to get involved," Edna replied brusquely. "Let's begin—we can't be late. This experiment has to be done precisely or we'll fail." She gestured for us to take our seats.

I lowered myself into my chair, and it instantly reclined.

Edna kept her eyes on her screen. "Client Jennifer Floyd's stats look good," she declared. "We can start."

"How is this going to work?" I asked.

We will conduct this experiment as if you are in the home study. The onesie, vaporizer, and helmet are all you will need," Edna said as she handed me a vaporizer pen.

One quick puff and it's over, I thought to myself.

"Is this how I take my Remsen doses?" I asked.

"This is your vaporizer pen," Edna said. "The cartridge contains 250 fifteen-microgram inhales.

"What about the scent?" I asked.

Edna proclaimed, "The cartridge contains your chosen scent infusion; it's time to begin."

"Jen, start by taking one deep breath," Jessica instructed.

I obeyed and let the oxygen fill my lungs before exhaling—the taste of salty beach air was in my mouth.

"Fantastic, Jen. Do two more breaths like that," she said.

My second breath tasted similar, but I prepared myself for the third—

I put my lips to the vaporizer and drew in my third breath. The vaporizer slid from my fingers as I looked down.

"What happened?" Ty inquired.

My beer was lying on its head in the sand.

Ty stood before me with his hands on his hips. "Jen, you spilled the last drink." He gave a displeased shake of his head.

"My bad," I said.

"Maybe you should just drink some water now," Ty suggested.

"Yeah, I think I need to rest for a few," I replied.

Ty offered me the keys. "We can leave soon."

I headed for the car, navigating around all the blankets and towels spread across the beach.

"Wait for me, Mom!" Donnie yelled out.

He ran up to me, weaving between the beach blankets and towels. He seemed much faster than I remembered.

"Can I come too?" he asked.

I gave him an eager nod. "I need your help to bury something important."

Donnie's eyes lit up as he rubbed his hands together. "What kind of thing?"

"We've got to hide three items underground, like a time capsule," I explained.

Donnie and Mandy had buried one in our yard that I had refused to touch.

"This sounds awesome!" Donnie exclaimed, bouncing on his tiptoes. "Can I put something in the capsule too?"

"Absolutely," I said with a smile, though my voice caught in my throat when I added, "And then when you have kids of your own..."

Donnie's face clouded over with concern. "Are you okay?" he asked.

"Yeah, sorry about that. Something just got stuck in my throat," I said.

"I can't wait!" Donnie grinned, hugging me tightly as we started planning our treasure hunt.

"Commander Donnie, are you prepared to kick off your mission?" I asked.

Donnie saluted me in reply. "I'm ready for directions," he said.

"We have to get the shovel from the Explorer and investigate anything that can go in the time capsule," I reminded him.

Donnie nodded as we walked towards our car. When I glanced back, Ty and Mandy were busy watching the kite. I took out my phone to text Ty: Donnie is with me.

Ty checked his phone, shook his head, and then turned back to Mandy, who was flying her kite.

I opened the trunk and grabbed the shovel. I scooped up a few of Mandy's Hot Wheels, stored in her toy carrier, and placed them in my pocket.

"Mom, those are Mandy's," Donnie pointed out.

"It's alright, Donnie. I'll get her some new ones."

He gave a half nod before racing off. "Donnie, come back!"

But he was already out of earshot as he ran towards Ty and Mandy. He tried to grab their attention with his waving arms. They both turned in his direction.

My phone started vibrating. "What's going on? Donnie seems to think you're about to bury their toys?" Ty asked over the phone.

I laughed. "Donnie and I are playing a game—buried treasure."

Ty chuckled. "Can't you bury shells?"

"We're only burying one toy. We can try to find it next year," I explained.

"Whatever," he replied before ending the call.

Donnie bolted back over, saying between breaths, "Yay, Mom, let's bury a treasure!"

I scanned the back, looking for something to hold our gathered treasures. "Donnie, are we ready to make an enormous sacrifice for this exciting adventure?" I asked.

He turned his head towards me, his eyebrows furrowed in confusion. "Like what?" he echoed back.

"Your backpack," I suggested.

A frown creased his small face. "But Mom, that's my special bag."

Donnie's prized possession was a Battlestar Mutant's backpack. It looked petite against his growing frame, but it was maintained with such care that it appeared brand new. I could see how much he cherished it; it was more than just a bag to him.

"Do I have to give it up?" Donnie asked again, his voice wavering slightly.

"How about this?" I proposed, trying to lighten the mood. "What if Dad and I get you an even cooler bag?"

His expression remained unchanged.

"We could all go on a fun trip to Walmart when we're done here," I said, hoping to spark some excitement in him.

Donnie paused before closing his eyes and giving a small nod. "Can I pick out some Mutant patches too?" His tone was serious now; this was important business.

"Absolutely!" I responded warmly, grinning at his negotiation skills.

Donnie jumped for joy. He grabbed the bag from where it was sitting and handed it to me.

"Thank you, Donnie. I know this means a lot to you."

He saluted me playfully. "Thank you, Commander Mom!"

"Alright, let's get started then." I reached for a few toy cars and placed them in the bag. "Where would be a good place to dig a hole?"

Donnie glanced towards the beach, before pointing away from it. "Back there."

It looked like a secluded wooded space between the resorts and the beach. "That looks perfect," I smiled.

We headed down a trail leading to a nearby resort.

"I'll be back," Donnie said as he raced off, out of view beyond the trees.

"Mom!" His voice echoed through the woods. "Over here."

I followed his cries until I could see him.

"Here, Mom." He stepped out from behind a tree.

"Great spot," I said, noting it was halfway between the beach and the resort. "Donnie, I need you to do something for me, but you can't tell anyone about it—not even your dad or sister."

He raised his arm in salute. "Yes, Commander Mom," he said in his most serious voice.

I couldn't help but laugh at that, but Donnie stayed stoic.

"I need you to be on the lookout," I said. "No one can know what we're doing here. If you see anyone coming, I need you to warn me."

He nodded. "Got it." He saluted again before bounding away.

I went up to the tree with my tiny shovel. I stamped on it to break the ground, but the tight roots of the earth made it hard to dig. After trying a few spots, I found one that suited me, deep enough that no treasure seekers could detect it easily.

Donnie let out a birdcall. "Coo-chow. Coo-chow."

A group of people headed my way, and I abandoned the shovel before they noticed me. They were too busy talking amongst themselves to pay attention.

I grabbed the shovel again and started digging until the hole was at least a foot deep.

"Donnie!" I called out when he arrived at my side.

"Yes, Mom," he answered.

"Let's put this treasure in the ground. Would you like to do the honors?" I asked.

Donnie nodded as I passed him the bag, which was more than suitable for the things we needed to hide. Reaching into my back pocket, I pulled out my wallet and dropped it into the bag.

"Your wallet, Mom?" Donnie asked, raising an eyebrow.

"We all have to sacrifice for this mission," I said with a smile. "What about Dad?" he questioned.

"Your dad made the ultimate sacrifice: he was our flight captain and kept us safe today," I reminded him. We started covering up the hole with leaves and sticks. "Okay, now let's check how many paces from here to the pavement," I said.

I started counting steps until we reached the pavement ahead.

"Seventy-seven, Mom!" Donnie exclaimed before covering his mouth in shock at his volume. "Sorry, Commander Mom."

"Great, now we keep this in our head until we get home." We could make out the shape of the weary resort from a distance, its pale yellow color reflecting off the sun.

The sign appeared worn, the paint peeling and cracking from age. Two legs of the letters had lost their footing on the wood, hanging precariously over the sign: Sandpiper Inn.

We turned back toward the beach and began walking.

A scent wafted from my skin and filled the air with a spicy body powder. The ocean crashed against the shore, and I kicked sand at Donnie's feet. "Thank you for your brave work today," I said.

Donnie remained silent, keeping his slight smile. He inhaled through his nose and leaned closer to me with a longing look.

"When do we come back? To get the treasure?" Donnie asked.

The beach faded from my view. "Donnie, don't leave!" I pleaded as he dissolved into darkness.

I opened my eyes to darkness, feeling foggy and off balance. "I can't see. Where am I?" I heard Jessica's voice coming from somewhere.

"Jessica?" I asked, trying to make sense of what was happening.

"On the count of three, I'm going to take your helmet off," Edna said. "One, two, three."

The sound of the helmet removed caused me to wince as light filled the room. "This is so bright!" I could still see the shapes of two people in front of me.

"It's okay, Jenna," Edna told me. "We've dimmed the lights to level one, and you look great." Then she left us alone.

"Are you doing okay?" Jessica asked with a kind voice.

"I'm not sure I was successful," I replied. "But some coffee would be nice."

Jessica got up and grabbed a cup from her desk. "Here you go," she said, handing it to me.

"Thanks. Things didn't go as planned for me again," I said.

"Were you able to bury something?" she inquired.

"Yes. At least I think so."

Jessica chuckled lightly. "Do you remember the exact place where you put it?"

My mind went blank trying to recall the trip. I shut my eyes tight and focused on the memory. "SandPiper or Sea Piper Inn?"

"Yes! It was SandPiper!" David shouted from the speaker.

Jessica shook her head with a smile. "Sorry, Jen. Do you feel alright to continue?"

I slammed my eyes shut and gritted my teeth. "Donnie came running after me to help count the steps. He was a blur; I hadn't seen him move that fast."

Jessica leaned closer, her interest piqued. "And what did you bury?"

"Toys...Mandy's toy cars," I said, mixing reality with my dreams. "A green car, maybe..." My gaze dropped as regrets flooded in.

"It's okay, Jen," Jessica said.

But David barreled through the room, cutting off her sentence. "We have what we need! Let's go!"

42

We took a hallway behind the lab to the private elevator. The doors opened, and we traveled down another corridor until we reached a fire exit.

David extended his arm towards me and said, "I need your watch."

"What for?" I inquired.

"In case this goes awry, the door alarms will sound," he explained. "Staff won't be far behind."

So, I handed it over.

He said, "I'll return in about five minutes," and started running.

"Don't you think they will be suspicious that Jenna was near the exit?" Jessica asked.

Edna shook her head. "David has it covered," She said with a forced smile.

"Jen, do you mind if we chat in private?" Jessica asked.

I nodded. We strolled away from Edna, who took out her phone.

Jessica's face looked flushed. "How are you dealing with this, Jen?" she whispered.

"I'm thrilled!" I said. I hadn't felt an adrenaline rush like this for years. "And how about yourself?" I asked.

"I'm worried, but I shouldn't be," Jessica said. "After all, the project lead is doing this. This was never my idea," Jessica said as she fiddled with her hair.

She looked confused, almost as if she was seeking my counseling.

"If this works out, where does that leave me?" she asked, twiddling with the end of her hair.

"Well, if it is true, what will happen next?" I asked.

Just then, David reappeared, jogging back towards us. "Breaking history is the only way to make history," he announced. "When future generations read about epic accomplishments, your name will come up in conversation. The entire world will hear your name." He clapped his hands together with enthusiasm.

Jessica directed a skeptical glance before turning her attention back to David.

Edna's phone revealed an ominous countdown. I felt a chill of dread as she warned, "We have less than eight minutes until shift change."

Jessica's face turned scarlet as David marched to the red door. "Ten seconds to exit this door without setting off the alarm," he said, and Jessica and I followed close behind.

"On three—Edna, you lead Jenna to the car; Jessica, sit in the back," David ordered.

Edna whispered for me to stay close, and I nodded, my heart pounding with anticipation.

"One, two, three!" The red door opened and a hulking SUV was before us.

"Get in the back," Edna commanded. A blanket lay atop the seat, and Edna instructed me to cover myself until it was safe to leave.

My pulse raced as I scrambled into the vehicle—this would be a daring escape!

"We are ready," David said.

The SUV inched forward, its electric engine barely audible. I couldn't remember how far it was until we reached the entry gate.

"We're almost there," David said. "And remember: no one speaks but me."

The car came to a halt.

"Hi, Shelly," David said. "We'll be on Manifest Number 311 for our trip."

Goosebumps ran up my arms as I held my breath in anticipation.

Shelly replied. "Everything looks in order."

"If we stay the night, I will send an update," David instructed her.

"Will do, sir," Shelly agreed.

"Open the gate!" he commanded.

I could hear a slight squeaking sound as the SUV gradually moved forward again.

"We're leaving now," Jessica whispered.

"Sorry about that, sir," Shelly apologized before we drove away.

"Jenna, please be patient," David said. "We'll be out of view in a few minutes."

"I bet you've never had to escape like this before," Jessica said, her voice close to my ear.

"Thankfully, no," I replied.

The vehicle slowed down and came to a stop, causing me to hit my head on the back of the seat.

"Sorry about that," David said. "Usually, Jethro handles the driving."

"Thanks for letting us know," I said.

"We're clear now," David announced.

I threw off the blanket and looked around.

"Sit behind Edna," David suggested.

I swung my leg over the seat and took my position behind Edna.

"Let's go!" David shouted.

I chuckled, feeling as if we were part of an action movie.

"Here, take my hand." Jessica reached back and our hands met. She pulled me over the seat, almost causing me to fall into her lap.

David giggled. "That was an 8.5 landing!"

I rolled my eyes.

"Funny," Jessica muttered, shooting David an annoyed look.

"If we're all set." David tapped something on his control panel and our seats turned to face us.

I felt like I was in a movie as I took in the vehicle's design. "Is this a Mercedes G-Class?" I asked, impressed.

"Yes, but with a few modifications," he answered.

"Quantos must be loaded, huh," I said, causing Jessica to smirk and David to refocus on his phone.

"Thank you for choosing Quantos for your transportation needs," Jethro said. "We are eighty-six minutes from Ocean Shores. The temperature is fifty-three degrees, partly cloudy skies with a light breeze. Please recline your chairs and relax," the A.I. instructed.

My eyelids felt heavy as the car hummed, easing me into sleep.

43

The Mercedes rolled to a stop in the red zone of the motel lot. My stomach churned at the thought of stepping out and seeing our stretch of beach like nothing had ever happened. We had come here dozens of times. This was different. It felt off. I stepped into the world I knew so well, or I thought I knew.

"The Sandpiper Inn. Here we are," Jethro announced.

I peered out of the car window and frowned. "This isn't right." The building was an awful shade of baby blue that was peeling off the building.

"What's wrong?" David asked. "You said 'Sandpiper Inn' like ten times already."

I nodded, staring at the faded sign above the door. "But this is different."

David rolled his eyes. "It'll be fine."

I turned to Jessica. "Why are we parked in a tow-away zone?"

"Does it matter?" David asked as he handed me a Walmart bag. "Put this on." He and Edna got out of the Mercedes.

Jethro chimed in. "David, please try not to be rude. I will move the car so we don't become unwelcome guests."

This was going to be interesting.

I looked in the bag, shorts and a summer top with flip-flops. "I need something warmer," I said.

Jessica handed me a sweatshirt. She was wearing pink floral shorts with a Seahawks sweatshirt.

"WSU?" I questioned.

Jessica offered an awkward smile. "David picked our attire." With that, she got out of the car.

"Don't worry. I'm not looking," Jethro joked.

I chuckled as I changed from my onesie into something more 'local'. The cotton felt itchy against my second-skin onesie. As soon as I exited the vehicle, Jessica handed me a map.

David laughed and asked, holding up a shovel, "So I guess we have the local look down?"

Edna said sharply, "Shut it, David." She was sporting a Mariners sweatshirt and gray sweatpants while David had a Supersonics sweatshirt and blue surfer shorts.

David stared at me. "Can you show us on the map where you buried it?"

It looked familiar. I had never been to this motel, but this building was eerily similar to one I had seen during the trip. "I think it's this way. When I can see it from behind, I'll know it."

Edna gestured towards a path. "Looks like that's the only way to get to the beach from here."

I spoke louder so David could hear me. "Are you taking steps like this?" He made a half stride and his feet were huge. "Or more like this?" He stepped with one foot.

"Just your regular paces, probably less than fifty with your shoe size," I replied.

Edna laughed while David nodded and started walking down the trail, disappearing into the trees soon after. Edna followed close behind him, and Jessica stayed by my side.

"How are you feeling, Jen?" asked Jessica as she grabbed my hand.

"Pretty anxious. It's a shock coming back here after the accident," I said.

Jessica lowered her head and asked, "Can I hug you?"

I nodded, and we embraced briefly.

"I won't leave your side unless you want me to," Jessica assured me.

"Thanks," I said as I pulled away. "Is this reality? Am I living in some alternate universe?"

"I'm not sure what's going on here; they hired me as a clinician, and this is well beyond my area of expertise," she explained with a shake of her head. "Your treatment plan will change if they find something."

"What would 'something' be?" I pressed further.

She paused before responding, "It could be one item that brings it all together."

I stared into her eyes and pleaded, "Please keep me safe."

She pulled me close and whispered, "You're more important than any study. No drug is worth more than you. Your understanding of Remsen is the key to your health."

I voiced my uncertainty about David and Edna. "They only care about getting results," I said.

Jessica then turned to me. "You're in charge," she told me before starting down the path. "Let's go see if they've figured anything out."

We made our way to the open area, David's pale legs eventually leading us to where he and Edna were standing. Neither knew where to dig.

"Jenna, we need your help," Edna said, the shovel in her hand.

"Of course," I replied, taking it from her.

"Do you remember exactly where you put it?" she asked.

Donnie appeared in my mind's eye; he had been walking ahead of me when we buried it. "It's somewhere over there!" I called out, pointing to a spot without roots. David went to investigate and started excavating with the shovel.

"This has to be it," he mumbled.

"Edna! The hand shovel!" he commanded. She gave him the tool, and he dropped to his knees and continued digging into the soft earth.

"This has to be it," he repeated.

As I watched David dig, I shut my eyes. Jessica's hand dabbed my shoulder.

"You all right?"

"I'm sorry," I uttered. "It felt like yesterday on this beach."

"Do you want to discuss it?"

I nodded. "I was watching Donnie work on one of his forts. He had put so much effort into it that when we had to leave, he cried."

"That must have been hard," Jessica remarked.

"I offered to help, and he said yes immediately. I grasped a bucket and removed some sand from the center of the hole. Donnie stayed silent while looking at me until I was done."

"What happened then?" Jessica wondered.

"He was delighted with how fast everything went and hugged me tight. As we embraced, he whispered 'I love you' in my ear."

Edna's piercing scream shattered the stillness. "This is insane!"

I glanced downward to see David tugging a backpack out from the wet earth.

"Quiet," he hissed as he dislodged it from the earth.

The soaked pack was beyond recognition.

"No one is around," Edna argued.

"That may be true, but we should avoid drawing attention. Any surveillance cameras could put an end to this."

The bag was Donnie's,I think this one is but not from the trip.

"It's not the same pack," I said.

"What are you talking about?" David sounded irritated.

"I think this one is what we got him back when he was in fourth grade." If I squinted, I thought I could make out a camouflage pattern.

David shrugged and chuckled. "Exactly, Jen." He opened up the bag and pulled out a toy car.

"This is unbelievable." Jessica's eyes widened. "Are you sure this was Donnies?" she queried.

"How is this possible?" I could feel myself shaking. "It's his. It has to be."

"We don't need any nosy folks." David pulled out a trash bag and gingerly placed the pack within it. "Be ready for the next session at five p.m."

"Five?" I inquired. "But how are we supposed to get around? Where do we stay?"

"Your ride will be here in ninety minutes," David said, agitated.

Jethro's voice came from David's phone. "Jessica, I just sent you the GPS coordinates so you can tell when it will arrive."

David and Edna started walking up the path.

"Five sharp." David's voice reverberated.

44

We stood and watched David and Edna leave in the Mercedes. The beach felt so utterly similar to that day. The sun hid behind a heavy cloud, and the stiff ocean breeze whipped me with its icy chill. The overcast sky was an indistinct steel gray, which felt like the beginning of what I had thought would be a wonderful day over a year ago. The world had bleached any semblance of sun or color. Overhead, gulls cawed faintly, waiting for beachgoers to leave something.

"David never ceases to amaze me," I said with a smirk.

"Quantos is the only love he's ever had, and Remsen is his escape," Jessica replied.

"Hey, how about we go for a walk on the beach?" I suggested.

Jessica's face lit up with a grin. "Yes, let's do it!" she agreed.

We strolled down the unmarked path which led to the beach. Only a few people were camped out. A few kite flyers had already claimed their spots.

"You need to remain aware on your trips," Jessica said as she put my hand in hers. "Remember where you exist and where the trips lie."

"If there is something here," I asked her, "then I need to change my past."

Jessica nodded. "Of course." Her head dropped. "But we need to be sure of everything we are doing before you dive headfirst. I will work with Edna to keep David from getting too involved."

"I trust you, Jessica," I told her, meeting her gaze. "Thank you for not leaving me."

She laughed and shook her head. "Of course. We're a team now." She held up her phone. "It's unlocked. I know someone waiting to hear your voice."

I nodded as I took the phone.

Jessica walked down the beach, giving me yards of space. I looked back at the phone and pressed buttons to open the menu. My eyes closed to the crashing waves and a memory.

"Hey, Jen."

"Hey, Barb," I said.

"Over here!" Ty shouted from behind me.

"God, Ty. You almost gave me a heart attack," I said.

"I'm going to play football with my buds," Ty said.

"Great, Ty. Have fun." He patted my shoulder and walked away.

"Barb, why do you act that way towards him?" I asked.

"I'm your guardian angel," Barb said.

"He drove over a day from Tucson just to see me for Spring Break. Doesn't that mean something?" I asked. She didn't respond.

"It means he wants sex," Barb stated with finality in her voice and endearment in her eyes.

"Is that a crime, Barb? I love him, and he loves me. Maybe someday, Barb, you will know what it feels like."

"Whatever, Jen." She walked away.

A hum emanated from the phone, the screen lighting up with a banner that read "Patient Zero". Then I noticed the times. 1900 sharp for the next trip, and 1700 for dinner would be followed by a meeting. The message seemed so enigmatic. I glanced at the times again, noting the 24-hour clock system. I dialed Sammy's number, and after a couple of rings, she answered.

"Hello."

"I'm so glad it's you," I said in relief.

"Are you alright? You don't sound like the authorities are after you?" Sammy chuckled at the thought.

"I'm okay. David got what he wanted." There was a moment of silence. "You heard me, right?"

"Can you repeat that? A weird wave came through," Sammy said.

"They found a backpack," I continued.

"What?! Was it his backpack?" Sammy asked with earnest curiosity.

"It looks like the same one we got him for fourth grade," I replied.

"Could it have been someone else's bag from somewhere totally random?" Sammy questioned.

"It isn't impossible. But it looked familiar; David pulled out a toy car."

"Who are you with now?" Sammy asked, sounding concerned.

"I'm with Jessica. She's away from me." I paused. "Would you be able to get a day pass to visit?" I asked.

"I don't know if they will let me off campus for the afternoon," Sammy said.

"What about your clinician, Mister Smoochy-Smooch?" I laughed. Sammy laughed.

"What if he gives you a hall pass?" I asked.

"You're right, Jen. It's about damn time I used this harassment in my favor. Let me put you on hold while I call him."

The line went silent, and I looked around for Jessica. She was admiring a display of kites a few yards away.

Sammy's voice interrupted my thoughts. "Jen! Jen! Jenna! Jennifer!"

"Sorry. I got distracted," I said. "You were saying?"

"I put on an impressive performance. I faked tears and told him I had a premonition about where my mother urged me to visit the beach." Sammy chuckled. "He gave me a day pass and assigned me a car."

Impressed, I said, "Wow, you go, Sammy!"

Sammy laughed again. "I have my session, and I should be there by eleven."

"I'm staying at the Sandpiper Inn. Call this number when you're close," I said.

"Sandpiper Inn. Got it." A pause followed before she added, "Jen, I love you."

My heart skipped a beat. The gravity of her words hit me hard, but I responded, "I love you too, Sammy."

45

We stopped at a nearby boutique to grab some local threads for the trip.

As we walked down the boulevard, we found a restaurant with only a few patrons. The hostess offered us a table away from the other diners.

"This is great," Jessica said to the hostess and then looked my way. "Coffee?"

I nodded.

"Two coffees, please," Jessica said to her.

"Here are your menus. Your server will be back with your coffee," she said disappearing.

"Have you eaten here?" Jessica asked.

"A few times on our day trips," I said.

"Any special memories?" Jessica asked.

"I remember that Donnie and Mandy could never finish their plates elsewhere, but they did here every time," I said.

"Well, then, it's good," Jessica smiled. "How are you feeling about today?" she asked.

"I'm still in shock. It hasn't sunk in yet," I said.

Our server arrived and handed us our coffees. "Are you ready to order?" she asked.

"Not yet; can you give us a moment, please?" I requested politely.

"Not a problem." She walked off.

"Do you have any breakfast suggestions?" Jessica asked.

"A few." I grinned. "Ty's favorite was the Chicken Fried Steak. Barb loves the Popeye omelet."

"Those both sound yummy. What about you?" Jessica inquired.

"Biscuits and gravy." I paused. "It reminds me of my mom's cooking."

"Mmm, that sounds great!" Jessica waved down the server.

The server walked over. Thankfully, we did not know each other. "What can I get you guys this morning?"

"Two orders of biscuits and gravy," I ordered.

"And your eggs?"

"Sunny-side up for me," I said.

"Over-easy for me," Jessica added.

The server jotted down our order on her tablet. "Is that everything?"

"Can I get a mimosa too?" I asked.

"Of course," she responded.

"Make it two," Jessica chimed in.

"I'll be back with the drinks shortly," the server said before leaving.

I gazed into Jessica's eyes. "What's the next step?" I questioned her.

"Unfortunately, I don't have any information. David isn't sharing anything with me," she replied.

I shook my head in disbelief.

"Maybe he wants to perform the same experiment." Jessica stopped talking as the server came over with our drinks.

"Your food will be here shortly," the server stated before leaving for another table.

"So you think David wants to do more experiments? I feel like a guinea pig." I asked Jessica after the server left.

"I guess so; he needs solid evidence for Quantos to support him," she said.

It sounded too easy. "We'll find out soon enough." I sighed at last.

Jessica nodded and checked her phone, which began ringing. "Sorry, Jen, I have to take this call," she apologized before answering it.

"This is Jessica," she spoke into the phone, nodding in agreement with what was being said on the other side of the line.

"Yes, we're at Sunny Beach Cafe and awaiting its arrival," she confirmed before putting down her cell phone.

"Jethro just told me your new car will arrive here in a few minutes," Jessica said.

"How will we recognize when it has arrived?"

Jessica gave me a knowing wink. "We won't be able to miss it." She looked me straight in the eye. "Would you like to go to your family's memorial site?"

I was speechless. "Will you come?"

She replied with an affirmative nod. Jessica nodded affirmatively and said, "Yes, I would be privileged to accompany you."

The server came over with our dishes. "For you," she murmured, putting the plate before me. Then she set down the food for Jessica. "Does everything appear satisfactory?"

"It looks perfect," Jessica replied.

"That's great," the server said with a smile. "Let me know if you need anything else." She then moved away from our table.

"This looks delicious," Jessica remarked.

"Thank God I have an appetite," I replied.

"Me too," Jessica said as she looked at her phone. "Sammy texted saying she would be here around 11:20.

"That will give us enough time for the memorial," I said.

Jessica nodded.

46

The hum of my new Mercedes filled the air as I made my way towards my family's memorial site. The beach was close, less than twenty minutes away from here. I couldn't help but think about their last moments before the accident, and how everything could have been different if it had just taken a few seconds longer. It was a feeling that never left me.

"We are here at the Floyd Family Memorial," the A.I. said. "It is an important place, Miss Floyd. My deepest sympathies for your loss."

The sorrow in the A.I.'s voice only reminded me of what I had lost.

"How does this machine know me?" I questioned.

"My apologies to Miss Floyd. Yes, I understand you prefer being called Jenna. I shall call you Miss Floyd to distinguish between myself and humans." The A.I. sounded sincere.

"Do you have a name?" I asked.

"I am your A.I., please assign me one," it replied.

I chose the name of my childhood pet. "You may be called Sabrina."

"Thank you, Miss Floyd," Sabrina said.

Jessica grabbed my hand and pulled me out of the car. "Come along, Jen. Sabrina's right; this is quite something." She apologized, "No offense meant, Jen."

"Jessica, you don't need to be so uncomfortable about my family," I said. "Thanks to you, I see them daily."

She chuckled in response. "I'm sure you've got quite a few stories to share," she replied.

I smiled and breathed in deeply. "These photos bring back memories for me," I said.

"Are these two you and Ty?" Jessica was interested.

"Oh wow!" I felt the breath leave my lungs. "Barb took this picture when Ty was about to go away to college, and his friends organized a going-away party at the beach," I said; I closed my eyes in recollection.

Barb stood in front of me, her face etched with worry. "Jen, I need you to be straight," she said through gritted teeth.

"About what?" I asked, fear creeping up my spine.

"Ty. Do you want him to be your man?" she asked, her voice cold and hard.

"My man? Barb? I like him," I stammered.

"Jen, you need to be careful. Popular Guys rarely ever stay with their high school girlfriends. Just saying," Barb spat out.

"And your point is?" I asked, dreading the answer.

"What if he finds another like you in college?" Barb growled.

"Barb," I whispered in horror. "Why are you so worried about Ty? It's not like you're dating him. Or are you? Is this your strange way of telling me?"

Barb let out a menacing laugh, her eyes blazing with hatred. "I'm keeping an eye out for you."

"We can still talk every day. It will be an excellent test," I suggested weakly.

"Just remember that when he cheats on you," Barb snarled.

Ty came up from behind, his presence making everything suddenly feel electric. "Hey, Barb."

The color drained from Barb's face as she turned towards him. "Oh, Ty. Hi," she said with forced politeness.

"Can you give a message to Jen for me?" Ty asked innocently, unaware of what was happening between us two girls.

Barb's lips curled into a sneer as she pointed at me. "She's right there," she said with disdain.

"Please tell Jen that Ty loves her. He loves her a lot," Ty continued, unfazed by the tension in the room.

"Barb," I said in anger and defiance as I stepped forward, squaring my shoulders to meet his gaze head-on.

"What is it?" Barb asked through clenched teeth.

"Can you tell Ty that I love him," I declared, proud of my feelings regardless of the consequences they could bring forth later.

"You do?" Barb asked me in disbelief before recovering her composure—her stoic demeanor more terrifying than any words could have been. My heart surged with emotion as I looked up into his beautiful brown eyes. Taking a deep breath, I met his gaze and said, "I love you too, Ty. I love you so much."

"Jen, are you okay?" Jessica inquired.

"I need a minute to catch my breath," I replied while looking at another photo.

"This is incredible." Jessica pointed at the picture. "Is this Donnie?"

I studied the snap. "Yes, it is. It was their first day of school. Mandy was starting kindergarten, and Donnie had just advanced to the second grade. Donnie was very anxious and started bawling like a baby, whereas Mandy seemed liberated."

"Was Mandy independent?" Jessica inquired.

I let out a hearty laugh. "She was remarkably independent from a young age. I knew she would be on her own as soon as she got her foot off the ground."

"How did you cope with two children who needed different things?" Jessica threw me a puzzled look.

"Mandy became Donnie's confidant and guardian angel; she often looked after him. As for Donnie, Ty and I tried to boost his autonomy by stimulating his creativity. He was independent; staying busy because of his rich imagination. He would've been an artist."

Jessica nodded, her eyes widening. "I can picture Mandy and Donny," she said.

"Mandy was the one willing to take chances; she seemed drawn to new heights," I replied with a chuckle. "We had to be careful though—she had little fear of heights. Ty got her into rock climbing classes last summer, and she attended three times a week," I told her.

"It sounds like they both had you as their manager," Jessica said, grinning.

"Maybe." I smiled in response.

"How was Ty as a dad?"

"He was fantastic—extremely patient with the kids," I replied.

"And as your husband?" Jessica prodded.

"Not so much in recent years. His depression worsened after his band broke up, and he became mad at me," I said.

"Did he accept you two needed help?" Jessica asked.

"Not really. Our conversations revolved only around the children," I replied.

"It sounds like you were both stuck heading towards an argument. A call to action for both of you," Jessica suggested.

"I certainly saw it that way. I'm not sure if Ty felt the same way. I'll never know for sure," I said.

"Do you think that is the resolution you need with Remsen?" she queried.

"I'm not sure yet. Everything before seems trivial. Every time I see Ty, I want to reach out and forgive him. Yet it seems wrong after the accident. If I had known about it in advance, I would have gone about our relationship differently," I replied.

"You feel that way?" Jessica asked.

"Yes, I've been thinking about this a lot. Just one or two minor differences could have made all the difference in this situation," I responded.

"Maybe so. But what-ifs can't change the past. Quantos is giving you a wonderful opportunity here. Use these next ten days to sort out your life and then live it," she said.

"You're right. This will give me a lot more freedom," I said.

"Make the most of it. I'm always here if you ever need someone to talk to. Go create some fresh memories—you deserve your liberty."

I hugged Jessica tightly. "Thank you so much for everything," I stated.

47

After I dropped Jessica off at the cabin, I headed to the Sandpiper to meet Sammy. Quantos Pharma paid for the stay.

"So this is what your nights of wining and dining get you," I said jokingly.

"Maybe I was aiming for this all along," Sammy replied with a laugh.

"Can I ask you something?" I mustered up my courage around her.

"What's on your mind?" Sammy asked.

"Why do you like me?" I inquired.

She chuckled. "What do you mean?"

I started to explain, "Well, for starters, I'm much older than you."

Sammy shook her head in disagreement. "That's not true, Jen."

"And then I'm just an absolute mess," I added. "So why me?"

Her words dropped like a stone, shattering the silence of the room. "You have this vulnerability about you," she whispered. "The first time I saw you walk into"—she put up air quotes—"'conceptual art', I knew there must be a story behind you. And I guess I was right." She paused and smiled. "Jen, I love your story and I love you."

I felt her energy wrap around me, embracing me like a hug. At that moment, I knew we would be together forever. We moved closer until our lips touched lightly, sparks of electricity dancing on our skin.

Sammy pulled away with a mischievous smile, playfully pointing at me.

"Ty was my only, until now," I said, my heart pounding as I felt the intensity soar. "You make me feel alive, Sammy. I haven't felt like this before...like I'm free to live."

A soft peck on the lips was Sammy's answer, followed by her heartfelt words: "Thank you, Jen. Here's too many more romantic days wherever the roads take us."

We clinked glasses, and I proposed a toast—"To the road that is yet unexplored!"—with a mix of excitement and terror rippling through my veins.

Realizing we only had one bottle left, Sammy took me into her arms and whispered in my ear;

"Relax. It's been a long day. We don't need to rush anything."

I opened my eyes, gazing into hers, and finally found the courage to utter what had been boiling within me for so long; "I love you, Sammy."

I rested my head on Ty's shoulder as we sped through the night to Seattle. I nestled into his sweatshirt and could only feel the rise and fall of his chest. He had barely spoken since leaving, but I didn't mind. The humming of tires was a soothing sound, like waves lapping against the shore.

Ty kissed me on the cheek. "I love you, Jen," he said.

"I know you do," I said.

"How did you get a room like this?" I asked.

"My dad. He said it was his gift to both of us," he said.

"Ty! Your dad is okay with us staying together?" I asked.

"It was his idea. Not for us to have sex. Sorry, Jen." he said. "He just got us this room. We can enjoy some privacy."

"Your dad is so cool," I said.

"Yeah, I know," he said. His voice was full of pride and respect, which made him smile. We drove along and soon pulled into our hotel parking lot.

My eyes widened in awe as I stared into Sammy's, and the world melted away.

"I love you," I said with an urgency that had been missing from my life for far too long.

"I love you too," Sammy replied before pressing her lips against mine and sending my soul soaring to unknown heights.

The new and all-encompassing sensation coursing through me was like nothing I had ever experienced before, and I knew then that I finally felt alive again.

48

I rolled up to the cabin well past dinner time—but no one seemed to mind, just like Sammy had said. The place was much nicer than any cabin Ty and I ever rented. Edna took me to my room with its wooden walls, and then Jessica knocked on the door.

"May I come in?" she asked.

"Sure," I replied, so she stepped in and closed the door behind her. "How was your holiday?" She winked at me.

"It was great," I answered truthfully. "Very peaceful."

"This is for you," Jessica said. "I'm happy you enjoyed it. I will make sure you have breaks like this every day. You will need the rest." She reached down into her pocket.

"You got me a phone?" I asked, surprised.

"Yes, from the store. Quantos won't be able to track it," Jessica said.

I hugged her in thanks. "Edna is grilling some fish out back. Are you hungry?"

My stomach growled in response, and I nodded. "Do you know what David's up to for my trip?"

"The entire afternoon, he was working. Edna and I went out shopping in Aberdeen," Jessica said.

"Oh, God. You didn't see Barb?" I asked.

Jessica laughed. "No Barbs in sight."

"So you will be as blind as I am at this meeting?" I asked.

"Pretty much. David likes surprises," Jessica said.

"Can we go outside?" The room was feeling tight.

Jessica led me to the BBQ, where Edna was taking the fish off the grill.

"This looks great." The sea air combined with the fish almost set me in a trance.

"I hope you enjoy it. I grilled rainbow trout with fresh summer veggies," Edna said.

"Edna, thank you so much for doing this. It looks amazing," Jessica said. "David, I hope you're ready to eat!"

"I will be out in a minute!" David said somewhere in the cabin.

Jessica walked in with some of the food. "Don't let the food get cold," she said.

The door creaked open, and David emerged in his sweatpants. We were all taken aback. "I said I'd be a minute. Time doesn't stand still."

"Yeah, yeah," Jessica replied.

David stepped over to the counter and picked up a plate. "Thanks, Edna. This looks yummy. I'll come back in twenty minutes to chat." His last words faded away as he shut the door behind him.

"Well, then," Edna began again. "Let's eat now, talk later."

"He must be a joy on vacation," Jessica quipped.

"Better than the version we see at work," Edna added.

"Has he told you anything?" I asked Edna curiously.

"Nope; he's keeping it hush-hush," she answered, handing me an overflowing plate.

"I'm starving!"

"Just stop talking and start eating," Edna instructed in her motherly tone. "You're going to need your energy."

"Edna, please assure me you will keep me safe. He's acting like my next trip will be to Mars," I said.

Edna nodded her head. "You will be alright."

Jessica laughed. "Mars? More like another galaxy," she said.

"This fish is amazing, Edna. I need your recipe."

"Thank you, sweetie. If you get us through the next nine days, I will teach it to you."

"Let's celebrate once we finish; I'm having a barbecue at my house," I said.

"Who was the chef in your home?" Edna asked me.

"That was Ty, always coming up with something new. If the kids were having mac and cheese, there was a salad too."

"Were they picky eaters?" Jessica inquired.

"Donnie had two food groups: pizza and hamburgers. But instead of using those as rewards or punishments, Ty made them into healthy and delicious meals."

"He must have been clever," Edna commented.

"No doubt. Ty was brilliant."

49

David stepped onto the patio carrying a folder. "I need you to look over this script," he said. "The timing has to be exact." He put one form in front of each of us.

"We have 60 minutes?" Jessica looked up skeptically. "How is that possible?"

"We'll have to increase the dosage to ninety micrograms," David answered.

"David!" Jessica exclaimed as she stood up abruptly. "I want to speak to you in your office." She hurried off and David followed her, leaving us with questions.

"What just happened?" I asked Edna, whose face looked pale.

"He's proposing a dose we've never tried in the first 30 days," Edna replied.

"Is it dangerous?" I asked.

"Officially, there have been no related deaths during the trial," Edna assured me.

"Please, what about the dosage? Is it safe?" I begged her for an answer.

"No one has reported any issues because of the drug so far," Edna said stiffly. "Most uncomfortable experiences only last a few minutes. You could lose hours."

"What do you mean, hours?" I asked.

"It's possible that the user could become disorientated and lose track of time," Edna replied.

"But isn't the street version different?" I inquired.

"Not really; Quantos only changed one minor element in the formula," she answered.

The risks weren't enough to deter me; I needed to be with my family. "I've made my decision," I declared, standing up from the table. "David, Jessica, could you come out here?" My voice echoed through the house.

They both entered the room. "Jen, forgive me for giving you orders," David said.

I cut him off. "I want to take the higher dosage."

"Jen, please, let's discuss this first," Jessica added.

"David, can you assure me that ninety micrograms are safe?" I asked him.

"I have taken doses of up to one hundred with no issues," he responded.

Jessica and Edna eyed him as if they'd seen a ghost.

"I'm ready to go ahead," I stated.

"Jen, stay focused on what's happening here in reality," Jessica said.

"I'm not worried about losing myself when I'm with my family; this might be my chance," I replied.

"Let's look over this script," David said while holding the sheet. "I've broken down each set into five-minute blocks."

I glanced over the list.

00:05 Talk to Ty about Donnie

00:10 Visit Donnie

"What needs to happen at 55 minutes?" I questioned, pointing to the script.

"You must make sure Ty knows you're going to the beach with them tomorrow," David replied.

It seemed much more manageable than what we had done before. "What sort of results do we expect?" I asked.

"We will find out as soon as it concludes," David responded.

"Find out what?" I followed up.

Jessica intervened, saying, "We'll be looking for any signs or changes in your memory."

David chimed in, "Don't underestimate a minor detail—it can make an enormous difference."

"Will I be able to save my family?" I inquired.

David appeared like he wanted to say something but was restraining himself.

Jessica took over, "Jen, we have to run this experiment and see where it goes—the backpack was a big leap forward; let's see what comes from this."

"Was there anything else with the backpack?" I wondered, looking around.

"We have your ID here," Jessica declared, lifting the ID card for me to see. My green-streaked hair stared back at me from the photo, and I felt my heart drop into my stomach.

"No way. I've never dyed my hair," I stammered in disbelief.

"It's not a fantasy or scheme, Jenna." David's bulging eyes were wide with shock as he scrutinized the card. "This chip is more advanced than anything our tech crew has ever seen."

I leaned forward and barely whispered, "This is real?"

Edna and Jessica locked their gazes with mine as they nodded simultaneously, lending credibility to David's words.

50

Edna brought me into a dark room and switched on the light. I saw a recliner with two kitchen chairs, and David and Jessica entered right after.

"I think we're ready to go," David declared.

"How are you feeling?" Jessica asked, her expression full of empathy.

"Nervous, but I'm hopeful this will go well," I replied.

"Remember to breathe deeply," Jessica advised.

"Then let's get started," Edna added, "and afterward, there'll be shrimp cocktails!"

"No better time than the present to make history," I stated.

David nodded with a small smile. "Indeed, Miss Floyd."

"Do you feel comfortable with the script?" Jessica questioned me.

I nodded my head affirmatively. "I'll relive my last hour with Ty. I want to alter the narrative," I stated.

"Pretty much, Jen. You know this script better than anyone else," David voiced.

"Let's get started. Let me introduce your new vape pen." Edna held out the aqua-blue item. "This will provide you with thirty microgram doses. Inhale three times. Every breath will consist of thirty micrograms, which add up to ninety micrograms altogether; does this make sense to you?" she asked.

My head bobbed in agreement.

"Fantastic! When you take the first inhalation, do not pause at any point or risk not taking the ultimate portion. Allow me to illustrate for you." She showed with a similar device. "Like this—inhale, then exhale; next inhalation, followed by an exhalation; lastly, one more inhalation and that is it; now you are ready to go on your journey, okay?"

"Yes, I am—thank you, Edna," I replied.

"Now we are ready to begin! Vitals look great for patient zero." She handed me a helmet and said, "Put this on for enhanced experience."

While gazing around the beach with the sound of waves lapping against the shoreline, I uttered, "I'm prepared."

They placed the vaping pen in my right hand, and Edna reminded me, "Begin dosing when ready, and don't stop halfway."

My lips met the vaporizer as I took a deep inhale and blew it out afterward; I followed with a second inhale and released followed by my third. I could feel the vape leave my hand.

The noise of the people drowned out the lapping waves. I reached in my back pocket and pulled out a pair of sunglasses. "These will help," I said, putting them on.

"Help with what?" Ty asked me.

"I just needed my sunglasses." I paused before continuing. "I'm gonna go find Donnie," I replied.

"Okay," he said and returned his attention to Mandy.

My feet moved faster as I ran towards Donnie, who was absorbed in what he was doing.

"Mom!" Donnie exclaimed, launching himself in my direction with enthusiasm. He wrapped his arms around me in a hug before letting go and turning away from me. "Follow me this way," he said, leading the way to his base.

"Is this an automated missile command base?" I asked.

Donnie glanced at me with a puzzled expression. "How did you guess?"

My chest tightened when I saw the look on his face. "Oh, you know me. I've been scouring the Internet for your building projects. It's impressive!"

I beamed as Donnie broke into a smile. "Thanks, Mom. But I still haven't finished yet."

"What if we come back tomorrow and keep going?" I suggested.

But Donnie's face fell. "Why not today?" he said.

"Your dad has to work, don't you remember?" I said.

Shaking his head, Donnie reminded me, "Dads off all week, Mom."

I lowered my gaze. "That's right," I said.

Donnie looked at me anxiously. "Mom, are you okay?"

I shook my head slightly and replied, "Dizzy. I'll be fine."

"How long can we stay tomorrow?" he asked.

"We'll arrive before lunchtime and leave once it's dinnertime," I said.

His arms shot up in the air. "Tomorrow we build!" He peered into his bag.

"And now we pack. Get your things together—we're leaving soon," I said. I shifted my focus to Ty and Mandy.

Donnie crammed his belongings into his bag faster than ever before while I watched him in awe.

"Let's go, Mom." He hurried towards Ty and Mandy, and I trailed after him.

My feet moved to a different beat as various songs drifted through my ears. The teens who had been part of my disastrous day seemed content with their shenanigans as we pranced by them.

"Cool vintage shirt." A young lady emerged from the horde of people.

Without stopping my stride, I uttered, "Thank you."

Ty was glowing with joy. "Glad to see you two made it." His grin was unmistakable.

"Someone just praised my shirt." I gestured towards the young woman.

"I told you it was bound to happen," Ty snickered. "We only printed five hundred of them, and five of them were yours!"

I peered down at my shirt. It read: Ty and the Crew 2022 TOUR! *This must have been a joke. They disbanded in 2021.*

"You got the original." Ty grinned. "I showed you the cost on eBay, and you still put it on like nothing." He chuckled. The shirt looked brand new—it took all I had to keep my head from spinning. What was going on? How could this be true?

"It's incredible, Ty. How many cities?" I believed the words as they left my lips. Ty had sold his favorite guitar in 2021 so that we could have enough money to live on— he used that fact against me years later.

"Over a dozen in the East Coast alone!" he exclaimed with relief. "Thank God we don't need to run around like that any longer."

The thought of so many stories and events that I didn't even remember lit up my mind. "I love you, Ty."

He embraced me, and I suddenly felt a wave of serenity.

"Do you remember that show in Burlington?" asked Ty.

My thoughts were cloudy. "Burlington, Vermont?" I inquired, knowing the furthest they ever toured was Reno. "It seems like forever ago," I responded.

"No," he replied with a chortle. "It still feels like just yesterday." He snickered again. "I almost had my clothing pulled off."

I nodded my head.

"Mandy, are you ready to go?" Her head popped up, and she twisted around in bewilderment.

"Go where, babe?" Ty humored Mandy with an expression.

I laughed. "You have work at Walmart?"

Ty shook his head no. "Walmart? What are you talking about? We're here for fireworks tonight." He took my hand. "Jen, let me give you a hand to the vehicle. Donnie, Mandy, let's hit the road. We're taking Mom to the cabin." He hushed into my ear. "You may have been in the sun too long; you need to rehydrate," he concluded.

"Yes, our cabin," I said, finding it hard to stay in character. My body felt so heavy, and all I wanted to do was close my eyes.

"Babe, you need to sleep. I can give you some medicine so you'll be energized in time for the fireworks." Ty helped me walk over to the Explorer. "You can nap while I bring the kids back to the beach."

I nodded tiredly.

"Be careful," he said, squatting down to prepare for me to get on his back. "Climb up here and I'll carry you from here."

"Mommy!" Donnie yelled from behind us.

"She's alright, Donnie. Mommy needs rest," Ty assured him. He lifted me onto his back, but not before I noticed him lifting me with little effort. His college injury wouldn't allow him to lift anything too heavy.

"Ty, your knee," I said.

"I'm good," he replied.

Mandy swung my door open.

"Thanks, Mandy," Ty said. "Mind your head." He fiddled with me until I was safely in the seat. "We will get there shortly," he informed me.

"Mommy, buckle up," Mandy requested from the back.

"Oh, right?" I clicked my safety belt into place. "Mandy, the sand. Your shoes!" I almost screamed.

"What's wrong, babe?" asked Ty.

"I panicked thinking about how much sand you were tracking in," I replied.

Ty chuckled. "The Explorer is already a mess—what's one more thing?" He turned on the engine and something new wafted through: no longer Obsession, but something else that made my body feel heavy.

"Everyone buckled in?" Ty inquired.

"Yep," Mandy answered.

I shut my eyes as the Explorer drove over the minor bumps in the road. The car eventually stopped, and I opened my window to let cool air in.

"Is everyone okay?" I asked.

"We've arrived," Ty said with a soft voice.

When I opened my eyes, a castle was before us. "Just wait in here, you two," Ty said to Mandy and Donnie.

"Sure thing, Daddy," Mandy said.

Ty came back around and placed his hands on me.

"Let me help you," he said.

"Ty, how? How can we afford to rent this?" I questioned, looking at the new building.

"You need to get some rest for a few hours. It looks like you got dehydrated today." He opened the door and reassured me everything was going to be alright. He told me that he would lift me soon and started counting to three. I felt like a tree swaying in a storm.

Ty picked me up with ease. "We need to get you to the room," he said. He carried me upstairs, into an enormous room full of framed pictures. In each photo, Ty had the same wide, inviting smile. It was all so strange: a room with actual art, not like what we had at home.

He came bounding into the room and handed me a glass of water with electrolytes. I gulped it down, feeling the electricity rush through me. "This looks just like our hotel in Olympia," I said.

He gave me a confused look. "What hotel?"

"Olympic View? We went there with David and Jessica."

His brow furrowed in confusion. "David who?"

It was David, tall and lean with red hair. "Oh, come on, Ty," I chided him. "What happened to our home in Aberdeen?"

He pointed at my shirt. "The tour, babe! We bought our house in Olympia five years ago. Should I call your doctor? You were incredibly dehydrated."

"I'm feeling better," I muttered. Why couldn't he remember David or Jessica?

Ty seemed relieved. "You were thirsty. Let me get you some more water," he said as he left the room. A wave of exhaustion overtook me as he closed the door behind him.

"Ty, where did you go?" My speech was slurring as I asked. "What did you give me?" I queried feebly.

He stepped into my view. "Rest, sweetheart. I'll be back in a few hours. I love you." He pressed his lips against my cheek.

"You did it, Ty. You made it happen," I murmured.

"No, darling, we did it!" Ty declared.

"I love you."

Our mouths joined in a kiss, and the world faded from my vision.

51

The pleasing sound of his voice brought me out of the depths of my sleep. I stirred, trying to piece together what was going on.

"Hey, babe," he whispered, yet with an urgency. "It's almost time."

Confused and disoriented, I forced my heavy eyelids open and questioned him. "What time is it?"

He paused before telling me: "It's almost time for the fireworks. It's why we're here. You were out for several hours. The kids insisted I wake you up for the show."

I glanced out the window, noticing the crimson hue of the sky. So, this is where we are right now? And then it all clicked—the medicine he had given me must have knocked me out cold.

With a determined nod, I replied, "I'm ready now."

"Elondra, open the shades!" Ty commanded.

"Elondra?" I asked in confusion. "Where did that name come from?"

Ty turned away. "Donnie thought of it. It's strange enough to be perfect for the house A.I."

"Doesn't he have a teacher with the same name?" I questioned.

"No idea," he answered. "I thought he made it up."

I chuckled. "It must have been in a dream."

Ty exclaimed, "I think I need to try the sleep aid I gave you!"

"Not that great; I've had better."

He shook his head. "I've got a delicious steak with some creamy spinach waiting for you."

"That sounds amazing," I said with a smile.

"It's just for you," he replied.

"Steak sounds delicious." Hunger bubbled up within me. "I don't think I've been this hungry since..."

"Since when?" He raised an eyebrow.

I chuckled at the memory. "Since earlier today."

"The fireworks are about to start, so let me get your meal and we can watch them from the deck," he offered.

"Where are the kids?" I asked before Ty had the chance to answer.

Donnie and Mandy suddenly appeared in the doorway, tumbling over each other as they raced into my arms.

Donnie peered up at me with worry etched on his face. "Mom, you're okay!"

I embraced Donnie and Mandy tightly. "It's so good to see your faces! How are you guys?"

Mandy bounced up and down with excitement. "The fireworks are about to start!"

I swung my legs out of bed, noticing that my muscles felt surprisingly firm. Firmer than I could remember.

Donnie took my left hand, and Mandy grabbed my right as we exited the balcony overlooking the ocean abyss.

"The view is breathtaking!" I exclaimed.

Ty chuckled. "You say that every time we come here."

"And I mean it every time," I replied.

Mandy pointed to the crowds gathered on the beach below. "Mom, look at all the people!"

I peered down at them, spotting dozens of boats patiently waiting on the water. "This is going to be an amazing show," I said with a smile.

"What about the New Year in New York?" Donnie asked.

I frowned, trying to recall. "Oh, right? That was incredible, too."

"Here, take a seat." Ty gestured towards the patio sectional.

I lowered myself into a comfortable corner spot while Donnie settled beside me and Ty took his place on my other side. Mandy wandered over to her father and sat beside him with ease.

"I wouldn't miss this for anything," I said, gazing up at Ty lovingly.

"I know you wouldn't," he replied with a smile.

Just then, the first firework shot skyward, exploding in a shower of vibrant colors above the water. The crowd erupted in applause.

"I love you," I said to Ty.

"I love you more," he replied before leaning in for a tender kiss.